A Stone of the
Heart

Also by Eugene McEldowney

A Kind of Homecoming

Eugene McEldowney

A Stone of the Heart

HEINEMANN : LONDON

First published in Great Britain 1995
by William Heinemann Ltd
an imprint of Reed Consumer Books Ltd
Michelin House, 81 Fulham Road, London SW3 6RB
and Auckland, Melbourne, Singapore and Toronto

A CIP catalogue record for this title
is available from the British Library
ISBN 0 434 00010 8

Typeset by Deltatype Ltd, Ellesmere Port, Wirral
Printed and bound in Great Britain by
Mackays of Chatham PLC, Chatham, Kent.

For Caroline

Too long a sacrifice
Can make a stone of the heart

W B Yeats, Easter 1916

1

That morning, Morgan woke tired and irritable. He had spent the night tossing and turning in the narrow little bed, and then, just as the first traces of dawn smeared the window pane, he had fallen into a fitful sleep and dreamed that he was going to die.

He'd had this dream before. When he thought about it, tried to place its beginning, he realised that it had started weeks earlier, about the first time that Mr Cronin had come into the bar to talk to him. He could remember Mr Cronin's face as it had appeared then, thin like a priest's in the shadow of the confessional, his voice low and urgent, the nervous eyes for ever darting around the room, alert for eavesdroppers.

He had spoken slowly at first, a few generalisations to break the ice and put Morgan at ease. 'That's a cold one, Sean.' Mr Cronin nodded towards the street and rubbed his hands in an exaggerated show of energy. 'Not a lot of heat about.'

He lifted the foaming glass of beer and took a deep drink, wrinkling his face at the bitter taste, while Morgan patiently waited for him to come to the point.

'It's not too bad, Mr Cronin. It's warm enough in here.'

'That's because you're running around. You're busy. You're kept on the go. But outside …' He shivered and made a joke of disappearing deeper into the folds of his Crombie overcoat. 'It'd skin you alive. Know what I mean?'

Morgan waited. He had known Mr Cronin since he was a child, watched his steady progress through the ranks of their tight little community. Now he stood in a position of some authority, owner of several shops that opened day and night and sold everything from milk to firelighters. In the depressed economy of the ghetto, Mr Cronin was a wealthy man.

'Tell me something, Sean,' he said. 'Do you work nights all the time?'

'Not all the time, it's flexible.'

'So you could get a day shift if you wanted?'

'Sure.'

Mr Cronin sat back and studied him, his free hand playing absently with the rim of the glass.

'I'm told you're good with cars,' he said at last.

Morgan felt the colour rise in his face.

'Don't be modest, Sean. If there's something you're good at, you should flaunt it. You'll get few enough chances in this town, believe you me.'

'Who told you this?'

'A wee bird. Several wee birds. I hear you're the best driver in the business.'

'It's a hobby,' Morgan said dismissively.

'I've a wee job for you.'

Mr Cronin bent his head and leaned forward in a conspiratorial way so that Morgan could see the thick black hairs sprouting like wire from the crevices of his ears.

'What sort of job?'

'An important job.' He tapped his finger gently on the rim of his glass. 'For the organisation.'

Morgan felt a worm of fear.

'I'm not sure ...'

'There's no risk,' Mr Cronin said quickly. 'I wouldn't expect you to do anything like that. It's just ... well a few of us were discussing this job and your name came up. The people I was talking with spoke very highly of you. They said you were the best. And I thought, what with your father and everything ...'

2

'My father?'

'After what happened to your father, Sean, I thought ...'

Morgan felt his face flush again. 'My father's dead.'

'But he was a good man, Sean. A brave man. And you're his son. You must never forget that. That's something to be proud of.'

Morgan felt confused. 'Look,' he said, 'I don't even know what you want.'

'Of course, of course. I'll explain it to you. It's a small thing, but important in the overall context. Know what I mean?' Mr Cronin leaned forward again and whispered, 'We need a car.'

'A car?'

'Yes. We thought you could find a car for us. There'd need to be certain specifications, of course.' Mr Cronin was suddenly the successful businessman. 'I don't expect an immediate answer. We can talk again. But Sean ...' He reached out and touched Morgan's sleeve and there was a note of caution in his voice. 'Not a word of this to anyone. It's just between you and me, you understand. Strictly confidential. Know what I mean?'

He raised a finger to his lips and tipped Morgan a broad wink, then smiled to show that there was nothing to worry about.

The door flew open and a crowd of students came in, shouting and clapping one another on the back and making a big deal about blowing into their hands to keep warm.

Mr Cronin sat back and gave Morgan a playful shove. 'Go on. You have your work to do.'

Morgan got up quickly and left him, glad to get away. Glad of the excuse. He felt confused, drawn in conflicting directions. He busied himself pulling pints for the gang at the bar and, when he looked again, Mr Cronin was gone and his half-finished glass sat in the middle of the empty table.

Soon after that, the dreams had begun.

In this dream, he was being pursued by black police cars with sirens wailing and lights flashing.

He was outstripping them, leaving them farther and farther behind. The car he was driving was new and the engine had been fixed so that the faintest touch on the accelerator made the car leap forward.

Morgan felt superior – the car gave him a sense of power, a feeling of energy and strength.

He looked into the mirror and saw the police cars falling away. All around him traffic was hurtling past in a blur of colours. He began to laugh: at his own power, at the futility of the police, at the uselessness of the chase. He was escaping. They couldn't catch him. He turned into a side-street and the feeling drained away.

The road was blocked by a delivery truck. He saw a couple of men in overalls rush to get clear. He slammed on the brakes and the car filled with the smell of burning rubber. He heard the noise, saw the wide-eyed horror on the faces of the men. He tried the brakes again but nothing happened. The truck loomed above him like a great white wave, the name of the delivery company painted in bold letters. He closed his eyes tight and heard his mother calling from the kitchen.

He came awake with a start and lay in the tangled sheets listening to his heartbeat. The familiar landmarks of the room began to reassure him: the wardrobe, the chair with his trousers draped on top, the picture of Jesus above the door with his sad eyes imploring repentence. He heard his mother call again, nearer this time. She was in the hall and shouting up the stairs. 'Do you want this food or not? It's getting cold. Nine o'clock, you said.'

'I'm coming.' Morgan put his feet on the cold lino. A radio was turned on and a polite voice begin to read the news. Out on the landing, he caught the warm smell of bacon and eggs.

The bathroom door was locked. He heard water splashing and his sister's voice telling him to wait. Washing her bloody hair again. He trudged back into the bedroom and opened the window. The street was deserted. A thin mist was rising above the black outline of Divis mountain and behind it a feeble sun struggled to get through. He pulled on his trousers and got a clean shirt from a drawer. When he tried the door again, the bathroom was free.

His mother was sitting at the kitchen table with a morning

4

paper. She put it down and peered under the edge of her glasses but didn't speak until he was seated.

'You don't look well,' she said. She stood up, walked to the cooker and came back with a teapot in a knitted cosy.

Morgan grunted and sawed an egg in two.

'You look pale.'

'I didn't sleep very well.'

'Well, who's fault is that?'

She was staring at him. Her glasses pressed hard against her nose, one arm stuck with sellotape.

Morgan felt his temper flare. Why did she have to badger him before he was half awake?

'Fault? What do you mean fault? Some nights I don't sleep so good. It could be something I had to eat.'

'Maybe,' his mother said and folded the paper on her lap, watching him while he ate. 'Why didn't you lie on? It's your day off.'

'Because I've got business.'

'What business?'

'Just something I have to do down the town.'

'Anything important?'

'Jesus,' Morgan said, 'what *is* this? An interrogation or something?'

'I was only asking.' His mother looked offended, opened the paper and pretended to read.

Morgan looked at her, the grey head bent over the page, the light from the window reflecting off her glasses. He put down his knife and fork and reached for her hand.

'I'm sorry,' he said, 'I didn't mean that. I don't like you worrying over me.'

'It's because I'm concerned about you, Sean. A boy your age needs a father's hand.'

'I'm not a boy, Mother. I'm twenty-six years old.'

She sniffed. 'Why did you change your shift?'

'I told you. I prefer working days.'

'Is that the truth?'

'Of course it is.'

He wiped his hands on a towel, stood up and kissed her

cheek. 'I have to go now. I'll be back in time for dinner. You have something nice, okay?'

She followed him down the hall and watched while he opened the front door. In the scrawny front garden, the hulk of a Morris Minor stood on a platform of breeze blocks.

'When are you going to get rid of that thing?' his mother asked. 'It's a show-box. You're making a laugh of the place.'

'Relax,' Morgan said from the gate. 'Don't worry.'

'I can't help worrying,' his mother said and waited until he had passed from view at the top of the road before closing the door.

Morgan walked up the sloping valley of the estate, past the locked gates of the Community Centre, its walls scarred with graffiti and stained with paint. The place was still except for the occasional yelping of a dog, an anguished cry as if the animal were wounded or in pain. He passed a waste ground where a group of kids was building a bonfire. They stopped to watch him, and from the corner of his eye he could see them getting up the courage to make some remark. But they could think of nothing to say, so they changed their minds and went back to their job.

When he came to the shops he hesitated. A couple of men were lounging in the doorway outside the shuttered off-licence, their dirty anoraks pulled tight against the cold. As he approached one of them stepped forward and held out his hand. 'Could you help us out?'

'What?' Morgan said, taken by surprise.

'A few pence for a cup of tea.'

The man was staring into Morgan's face. His eyes were red, his breath foul with the smell of stale wine. He swayed unsteadily on his feet, rocking back and forth in an effort not to fall.

'I've no change,' Morgan said and tried to push past, but the man reached out and caught Morgan's sleeve. 'How about a couple of cigarettes?'

Something clicked in Morgan's head. 'Just a minute,' he said.

6

He looked at the face, the bloodshot eyes, the unshaven chin. 'Don't I know you?'

'Know me?'

'You're Anto Quinn. You went to school with me. We used to sit together at the same desk. Don't you recognise me?'

The man tried to pull away, but Morgan held his arm. 'Sean Morgan. We went to St Mary's together. You were in my class.'

'Sean Morgan?' the man said, and lowered his eyes. 'Sean Morgan?'

'You sat beside me, Anto. What are you doing here? Where's your wife?'

Through the fog of alcohol, Morgan had touched something. The man turned his face away. He rubbed a dirty hand across the black stubble on his chin.

'She threw me out.'

'For drinking?'

'We didn't get on.'

'So where do you sleep?'

'Round the back of the shops. We've a place there. It's dry and we can light a fire to keep warm.'

'Look,' Morgan said, 'why don't you go home to your children? This is no life. It'll kill you – sleeping rough, drinking your head off. Jesus Christ, it's only ten in the morning and you're drunk already.'

The man hung his head as if uncomprehending. Morgan felt a flash of anger. Anto was a young guy. This was such a waste. He took him by the lapels and shook him roughly.

'Stop this, do you hear? Go home. Pull yourself together, Anto.'

'Sure, I will.'

Morgan searched his pockets and found some coins. 'Here,' he said, 'get something to eat.'

He turned quickly and walked away. He felt the anger like a pain in his chest. It was only when he got to the taxi rank that he realised he'd forgotten what he had wanted to buy.

The black taxi came farting and panting up the hill, belching fumes in the cold morning air. It turned at the church, paused to allow a mail van to pass, turned again and lumbered across to where Morgan was waiting.

The driver got out. He was a short fat man with a jolly face. He puffed up his cheeks to show how cold it was, then bent and opened the door. A couple of elderly housewives climbed out, shopping bags clasped tight in their gloved hands.

'Castle Street,' Morgan said and paid his fare. There was another passenger in the car, a surly-looking man with a narrow face. He stared at Morgan for a moment and then shifted along to let him sit down.

'Bitter, bitter,' the driver said as he got back behind the wheel and started up the engine. 'This bloody weather. It would get you down. When's it going to end, that's what I want to know?'

'At least it's dry,' Morgan said, 'that's something.'

'Yes,' said the driver, 'at least it's dry.'

The taxi rattled past the estate, the houses like little boxes, their black roofs shining in the sun. Outside the petrol station it stopped again and more people got in. Morgan sat in his warm perch on the back seat and felt his anger subside.

He watched the traffic pass, the lorries and buses and the occasional jeep, grey and menacing in the morning light. In particular, he watched the cars, the Audis and Fords and a brand new Mazda 626. He remembered what Mr Cronin had said. Something roomy and fast, but not conspicuous something big enough to hold four or five people.

They passed the landmarks on the way into the city. St Paul's church, the hospital, Dunville Park where a crowd of young-sters was already kicking ball, St Mary's school, the iron railings wet with dew and the black gates austere and forbidding as a prison.

The sight of the school made him think again of Anto, drunk at ten in the morning, sleeping rough behind the shops. Some morning they would find him dead, stiff with frost, discarded like a piece of cardboard. He remembered a bright-faced boy, quick and eager to learn; the teachers had said he would go far. He was intelligent, brains to burn. In those days they thought they could do anything they wanted. They hadn't learned how the system would grind them down, the young promise ending as dust.

It would have to change. Morgan had known that for a long time now, even before Mr Cronin had entered his life. He could see it all around him; the injustice, the inequality, the discrimination, and he had drawn the lessons from his own experience. They would have to destroy the system, pull down the whole rotten structure and build a new one. Something that was fair, that gave opportunity to people, that treated them with respect.

He waited till the taxi had passed down Castle Street and he could see the traffic moving along Royal Avenue, and then leaned forward and touched the driver's shoulder. 'You can drop me here,' he said.

The car shuddered to a halt and the driver started to get out. 'Are you all right?' he said. 'Can I help you?'

Morgan stared until the driver looked confused. 'No,' he said, 'I don't need help.'

He climbed out of the cab and slammed the door shut. He saw the driver's round face staring sadly from his seat.

'There is *one* thing,' Morgan added gently. 'Where would I get a bus for the Cavehill Road?'

The driver perked up. 'That's easy,' he said, 'back of the City Hall. You can't miss it.'

Cavehill Road was dozing in the morning sun, row after row of neat detached villas, white paint, big picture windows, hedges newly clipped. It was a world completely different from the one he had left.

In the fields above Carr's Glen, Morgan could see cows grazing and threads of smoke curling near the turrets of the castle below Napoleon's Nose. Just beyond the bend of the trees, his eye caught the bright flash of sunlight on water; a reservoir or mill pond.

He started along the first road. It was deserted save for an elderly man with a miserable-looking dog on a lead. The man nodded a greeting, but Morgan turned his head away until the man had passed. The place was quiet as the grave. Probably they were all at work or indoors sipping coffee. That's what they did up here in the mornings: drink coffee while they planned the next church bazaar, daintily-painted women chattering over their currant scones. A bare mile away across the city, his mother and her neighbours were scrubbing floors and washing clothes and changing nappies. Anto was drunk behind the shops with a bottle of cheap wine.

He checked the houses as he went by. Most had names chiselled on little wooden boards fixed to the pillars of the gates. Hy-Brasil, Mount Vernon, McArt's Fort. The gardens were newly manicured, hardly a blade of grass out of place. Some had beds of late-flowering roses, pink and yellow blooms, and trees with russet leaves like gold in the sun.

He paid particular attention to the cars. Nearly every driveway had one, many parked carelessly inside the gates as if abandoned. Some had two. One large house at the corner of the street had four, and more parked in the road outside; a plaque on the wall beside the front door told him it was a doctor's surgery.

Morgan came to the top of the road and stopped. Another road, much the same, twisted away at right angles, ending in a jumble of rooftops at the foot of the mountain. He hadn't much time. If he hung about too long, someone was bound to notice him. Some nosy bitch, distracted from her coffee cup, would ring the police.

He started back the way he had come, checking the cars even more carefully, searching for something that would suit. Roomy, fast, not so flashy that it would draw attention. He stopped outside the doctor's surgery and studied the cars again.

One caught his eye. A blue Toyota Sprinter, recent registration, a bit mud-spattered as if the owner had been driving across fields. But nothing a good wash wouldn't fix. As he approached, he examined the bodywork, searching for dents or scars, any blemish that would act as a telltale sign. He stopped and looked up and down the street; no one was in sight. He bent quickly to peer in the window; a lady's spectacle case was on the dashboard, a magazine on the back seat, a chocolate wrapper on the floor where some child had dropped it.

He studied the car closely now: new tyres, power-steering, no alarm that he could see. The back would take three easily, and another apart from the driver in front if necessary. He felt in the pocket of his coat and found the key he had been given. He thrust it into the lock, pressed down gently and heard a dull thud as the lock slipped. He carelessly pulled the door open and sat in the driving seat.

For a moment, he did nothing. Just sat there examining the controls. There was a half-full tank of petrol, more than he would need. He opened the glove compartment and poked among the papers and documents. He put the spectacle case away. He took off his cap and smoothed his hair. Then he inserted the key into the ignition and turned. The engine fired. He released the handbrake, slipped into first gear and slid the car silently away from the kerb.

There was a lot of traffic on the main road – cars and lorries and the occasional bus struggling up the hill. He tried to appear nonchalant; the worst part was over now. It had gone smoothly. The owner would discover that her car had been taken and report it to the police, but it would be too late. By the time they had finished with it, the car would be unrecognisable.

At the Waterworks, he turned right and started for Ardoyne. All at once, he saw the check-point, blocking the road ahead. He saw the khaki uniforms, the dark metal of the rifles, the cars slowing to a halt while they waited to be examined. His first instinct was to turn back, try another route, then he realised that he was already in the slipstream of traffic. In the rear mirror, he saw a van fall in behind him. To try to turn now would draw attention surer than anything. He slowed down and in his mind ran through what Mr Cronin had told him to do if he was stopped.

The car went over the first ramp with a sharp bump. In the middle of the road a sergeant in fatigues was waving vehicles into a lay-by for checking. His face was blackened and a pencil was stuck between his teeth. Morgan could see more squaddies lying along the ditch, hands clutching their rifles, white eyes shining in their darkened faces.

He took the second ramp and watched the sergeant walk out

in front of the car and hold up his hand for him to stop. Without thinking, he switched on the radio and dance music flooded the car. He saw another soldier check the registration number and write it in a notebook. He wound down the window and the sergeant poked his head in.

'Where you goin'?'

'Cliftonville Road,' Morgan said in his best voice. He felt his heart begin to thump. He reached over and turned the radio down.

'Where you comin' from?'

The sergeant spoke in short bursts in a strange English accent.

'Cavehill …'

'Uh-huh.'

The soldier glanced quickly around the interior of the car, then his eyes came to rest on Morgan's face.

'Any particular business?'

'Just out for a drive,' Morgan said. He tried to remain calm.

'Uh-huh.'

The sergeant hesitated and then straightened up. He looked at the tax and insurance discs and back again at Morgan.

'All right,' he said. He raised his arm and waved Morgan through.

Morgan felt relief wash through him. He drove along Westland Road, resisting the temptation to speed away, until he saw the smooth green turf of the golf club. It looked calm and peaceful in the morning sun.

At Cliftonville Circus, he turned right, away from the mean streets of Ardoyne and up into a quiet avenue and more big houses. He slowed down and began to count the gateposts, watching for the signs that Mr Cronin had mentioned. Detached house, white gates, men in painters' overalls.

It stood back from the road, a squat fortress with numerous chimneys and a wooden garage at the end of a pitted drive. The garden looked rough and untended and he saw the rusting remains of a child's swing. As he approached, a man looked up from a wall and wiped his hands on a rag. He put down a pot of paint and walked towards the car.

'Sean?' he asked cautiously.

'That's right.'

'We were expecting you.'

The man looked around nervously, then bent again to the window. 'Take her up the drive to the garage. I'll go ahead and open it.'

Morgan turned the car and the man pulled the gates wide, then walked up the path and opened the garage doors. As soon as the car was through, the doors slammed shut and a light went on. Another man came forward with a bundle of newspapers in his hand.

Morgan blinked in the unusual light. Against the walls were a number of benches with tools and engine parts. In a corner he saw a heap of tyres beside a new set of number plates, loosely tied with twine. The second man had put down the newspapers and was taking off his gloves. Morgan disengaged the seat belt and stepped from the car.

Immediately he saw the shock on the man's face as he glanced at Morgan's legs and then looked quickly away.

The man tried to cover his confusion by reaching out to take Morgan's hand.

'You did a good job,' he said. He stood back again and admired the car. 'Sprinter's good. Fast engine. Smooth to drive.'

Morgan felt a ripple of pride.

The man who had opened the gates came from the back of the garage and ran his hand along the bodywork.

'Last year's model. You did well.' He peered at the clock, 'Six thousand miles. Sure, she's hardly been driven at all.'

'You know about cars?' the first man said.

'A bit,' said Morgan. 'It's a hobby. I like messing with them.'

'Well, you sure picked a beauty. Any problems?'

Morgan shook his head. 'I was stopped by the Brits at the Waterworks, but they let me through.'

'Did they question you?'

'Just asked where I was going. But they have the number.'

'That won't matter. We've new plates and we'll give her a spray job. When we've finished the owner won't recognise her.'

The men laughed and Morgan found himself joining in.

'There's a few things in the glove compartment,' he said. 'Papers and things. You'd better destroy them.'

'We'll look after all of that,' the first man said. 'Don't you worry.'

He pulled out a packet of cigarettes. 'So that's you finished then. You won't be calling back?'

'No.'

'Okay then,' the man said. He held out his hand once more and Morgan took it. He walked to the front of the garage and opened the doors and the sunlight came flooding in. The other man joined him.

'How're you getting back?'

'I'll get a bus.'

'You sure? We could give you a lift.'

'No,' Morgan said, 'I'll be all right.'

'Well, good luck then.'

Morgan stepped into the sunshine and started down the drive. He walked awkwardly, like a crab, his large trunk too heavy for his spindly little legs. At the gate he turned and looked back; the men were talking. He knew what they were saying.

They were saying: Why did they pick a guy like that for an important job like this?

2

Chief Superintendent Drysdale turned away from the drinks cabinet and held up a decanter.

'What'll it be, Cecil?' he asked Megarry.

'Have you forgotten what I drink?'

'No. I haven't. Bushmills and water. I just thought maybe ...'

'Bushmills will be fine,' Megarry said. He sat up and watched Drysdale fuss with the glasses. The uniform fitted him like a glove. If any man becomes a uniform, it's Drysdale, he thought. I can't imagine him without it.

Drysdale brought the glasses and sat down. He pushed one across the table and raised his own, 'Good luck.'

'Good luck,' Megarry said.

'How's the family?'

'They're fine.'

'You're back with Kathleen?' He approached the subject gingerly, uncertain of Megarry's reaction.

'Yes. I thought you knew.'

'I'd heard something, but I wasn't sure. And your girl Jennifer? How's she?'

'Jennifer's fine. She's back at work. She's got a young man now so we don't see much of her. But she's better, thank you.'

'Good,' said Drysdale and took another sip. 'You've lost a bit of weight. You're looking fit.'

'Have I?' Megarry said, surprised, 'I haven't been doing much. Sitting about the house, mostly. Going for walks. Nothing madly exciting.'

'But you're being looked after, that's the difference. Regular meals, decent sleep. You should have given up that bloody flat a long time ago. And you're probably drinking less.'

Megarry saw him lower his eyes as he said it.

'Why did you want to see me, Jack?'

'Well, now,' Drysdale toyed with the glass for a while, then set it down in the middle of the table. 'I'll come straight to the point. They want you back.'

'They being *who*?'

'The Security Committee. We had a meeting yesterday. They've completed their inquiry into Prescott's death. You're in the clear. They've decided it was an accident.'

'Well, that's nice to know,' Megarry said sarcastically, 'that I'm in the clear, I mean. But it was no accident. It was self-defence.'

Drysdale sighed. 'It was an accident, Cecil. Why argue?'

'He attacked me. What was I supposed to do? Let him shoot me? I explained all this in my submission.'

'I've read it.'

'Well then ...'

'You were defending yourself and the gun went off. By accident.'

'And what about the murders? He killed at least three people.'

'Those cases are now officially closed.'

'Jeee-sus,' Megarry banged the table and the glasses shook. 'Does nothing ever change around here? I was going to charge him. The man was a murderer.'

'That was never proved.'

'He was a psychopath, Jack.'

Drysdale eyed him from across the table, his face flushed. 'He was a senior intelligence officer. Killed accidentally in the course of duty. The murders are unsolved and the cases are closed. That's official.'

He got up and walked to the window and stood with his back

to the room. His heavy desk squatted in the corner with a battery of phones and the framed photographs of his family. Megarry could hear, in the next room, the soft tapping of a keyboard as Drysdale's secretary started work. The trappings of power. The rewards of a good and faithful policeman.

'Is my report going to be published?'

'There's no need for that.'

'So it's going to be a cover-up?'

Drysdale turned from the window and breathed deeply. He wiped his brow.

'Cecil, Cecil. How long have I known you? Thirty years? Thirty-five years? We were cadets together at Enniskillen, for god's sake. Have I ever given you bad advice?'

Megarry said nothing.

'Look, this whole business is a big embarrassment for them, you must see that. A senior guy like Prescott gets killed by the Superintendent of Special Branch. Do you know what a meal the press would make of that?'

'That's not the point, Jack.'

'It *is* the bloody point. The service must go on. The war against the terrorists must continue. This could do enormous damage if it got out. And what would be gained? Prescott's dead. He can't be punished now.'

'It could serve as a warning to others. And what about the destruction he left behind? What about the widows?'

'They'll be compensated. It's already in train.'

'So, I'm to go back and just pick up the pieces as if nothing has happened?'

'You're to go back, Cecil. Your old job's waiting for you.'

Megarry shook his head and left his glass down. 'I can't do it.'

'You *have* to do it. You're part of the problem. We can't have you kicking your heels around the place. They'd start asking questions … I've already had some jackal from the BBC on to me …'

'No,' Megarry said firmly, and stood up.

Drysdale put an arm across his shoulders. Megarry could smell the sharp scent of his aftershave.

'Look Cecil, I realise you're unhappy. I don't like it myself.

But nothing's perfect in this world. This is the best we can do in the circumstances. You have to come back.'

'I'm taking early retirement.'

'Cecil. Don't be silly. You're a relatively young man. What age are you, fifty-two, fifty-three? You've nine or ten years to go. Sit down, let me talk to you.'

He took Megarry's glass and recharged it.

'You know how they calculate your pension? You know what you'd get if you left now?' He waved his hands dismissively. 'You wouldn't get enough to keep yourself in cigarettes. You'd have to sell your house. You couldn't even afford to run a car, for god's sake. And there'd be all that bad blood. Because you defied them.'

Megarry said nothing.

'Cecil. This is not wise. Believe me, I know what I'm talking about. This does not make sense.' He took out a handkerchief and mopped his brow again. 'Look, I've been authorised to tell you. You come back, they're going to bump up your salary – a good hike. A consideration for what you've been through. That all goes to build your pension. In due course you can go out with a decent screw. You'll be able to live comfortably. You owe it to yourself, for god's sake. You and Kathleen. Give the woman a break.' He sat back. 'Think about it. Don't do anything hasty.'

'You don't understand, Jack.'

'I do. Believe me, I do. You've got principles, you can see all the things that are wrong. But we're only human – poor fallible, human beings. We're not bad people.' He pursed his lips and blew softly through his joined hands.

'It's all the lying,' Megarry said. 'All the deceit, all the bribery, the blackmail.'

'This is police work. For Christ's sake, we're not the Band of Hope.'

'All the interference ...'

'That'll stop.'

'When?'

'I've a guarantee. From now on, you run your own show.

You're accountable only to me. From now on, nobody inter-feres in your work.'

He raised his glass and waited for Megarry's response.

'I need to think about it.'

'You've little option, Cecil, this is the best thing for all concerned. And you'll get brownie points, they'll owe you for it. You're doing them a favour, remember that.' He took a mouthful from the glass and set it carefully in the middle of the table. He lowered his eyes. 'Anyway, you've no time to think. They've got work for you. A case they want you to take.'

'Now just a minute,' Megarry said angrily, 'I haven't agreed to anything. What is this?'

'Just a bank robbery. But they want *you*, Cecil.' He pointed his finger at Megarry's chest.

'Who does?'

'The Security Committee. They were unanimous, yesterday.

'Why me?'

'Because you're the best we've got.' Drysdale tried to smile. He finished his drink. 'Wait here.'

He went into the next room and came back with a blue folder. From where he was sitting, Megarry was able to see a blond woman in a white blouse, typing at a desk. She was young, about twenty-three. She smiled when she saw him looking at her. He seemed to recall that Drysdale favoured young secretaries, although he had never taken him for a philanderer.

'Tuesday afternoon, last. Great Northern Bank, Chichester Street. You know it?' Drysdale sat down and opened the folder.

'Vaguely. What was taken?'

'Cash. Papers. Here, read it for yourself.' He tossed the report to Megarry.

'This is a sop,' Megarry said. 'It's a sop to lure me back in.'

'No, Cecil, believe me, it isn't. This is a serious case.'

'But I don't normally handle bank robberies. Any decent detective could do this job. Harvey could do it. Nelson could do it.'

Drysdale's face had gone grave. 'They asked for you specially. I get the impression somebody's pushing this one.'

'Have you anyone in mind?'

Drysdale stroked his chin. 'I don't know. Honest. Just a feeling I've got. Maybe a politician. Somebody with leverage leaning on the Committee. You know the way you sense something sometimes?'

Megarry turned a few pages. Drysdale watched him for a moment, then casually changed the conversation.

'You and Kathleen ever go out these days?'

'Sometimes. Why do you ask?' Megarry lowered the file on to his lap.

He felt his anger ebbing away. There was no point in fighting with Drysdale; he was only doing what they told him to do.

'Just an idea … why don't you come across for dinner some evening? I'll ask Margaret to arrange it.'

Megarry didn't reply. Drysdale reached over and took his empty glass. 'One for the road?'

He came back with two tumblers filled with whiskey.

'Good luck,' he said and raised his glass.

'Good luck.'

'Why don't you just take the case, Cecil? Get back into the rhythm of things. You'll enjoy it. We can talk about all that other stuff later.'

Harvey's office was at the end of a lengthy corridor, squeezed between the canteen and the lift. It was meant to be the control centre, with all calls, reports and queries routed through it. When Megarry had been suspended after the Prescott affair, his partner John Nelson had been transferred to work with Harvey.

Megarry went in and found the pair of them huddled at a desk crammed with files and folders, newspaper clippings, an ancient Remington typewriter and three ashtrays, each one overflowing with butts.

The office looked even smaller than he remembered, the two of them squeezed in so tightly there was barely room to move. And the smell was still there, the odour of cabbage and onions wafting from the canteen and lodging in every crack and crevice of the room.

Megarry coughed gently and Harvey looked up to see his

bald head framed in the doorway. There was a momentary pause and then Harvey struggled out of his chair and leant across the desk with his hand outstretched.

'Well, by the hokey. Look what the cat dragged in.' He beamed at Nelson. 'Your old boss. Soooperintendent Megarry. Have you come to pay us a visit or what? Here, sit down.'

Harvey extricated a chair and cleared a space on the desk. 'Cigarette?' He pushed across an open packet. 'I'm sorry I can't offer you a drink, Cecil, but they've taken away my cocktail cabinet.' He laughed at his feeble joke and fumbled with a cigarette lighter. 'We were talking about you only the other day.'

'Who's we?' Megarry asked, settling into the chair.

'Some of the lads. Gilchrist over in the Traffic section was getting married. We had a bit of a stag. We booked the lounge in the Montrose. Everybody got pissed. You'd have enjoyed it.' He smiled at Megarry. 'Just like the old days.'

'Saying good things about me, of course?'

'Of course, of course.'

Harvey puffed on his cigarette and examined Megarry. 'You're looking fit, Cecil. Relaxed, nice colour. This break is doing you good. Still overweight, mind you.' He pointed to the policeman's midriff, tumbling from the white folds of his shirt.

'That's not what Drysdale told me.'

'Drysdale? Were you talking to him? What does he know about anything? Drysdale just tells you what he thinks you want to hear. Anyway, it's good see you again.'

'You too,' Megarry said. 'What's been happening?'

'Everything. After you left, the place just fell apart. Honest to God, Cecil. Nobody's taking decisions any more. I think they're all shit scared, to tell you the truth. All these uniforms just pushing stuff down the line. And you know where it all ends up?'

Harvey bared his teeth and raised a palm before Megarry could reply. 'It ends up here. Look at this.' He indicated the desk, crammed with files and boxes. 'How am I supposed to manage? This place is just a shit-heap.'

Megarry nodded sympathetically. He had come here to take

back Nelson; it was going to add to Harvey's sense of grievance. 'You get so much work to do because they trust you. They know you'll do a good job.'

'Trust me? Don't make me laugh. This is insurance. This is covering your ass. Number One rule of police work. Blame somebody else. You know what they're doing?'

He leaned across the desk and gazed into Megarry's face. 'I'll tell you. They're forcing me to make the decisions. That way, if it goes right, Drysdale and company get the credit. And if it goes wrong, I get my butt in a sling. I tell you, Cecil, this is no way to run an army.'

'I know,' Megarry said, 'sometimes you can be too good at your job.'

Harvey observed him quizzically, not sure if he was being facetious. 'But they're not paying me, Cecil. If they want to promote me, well and good. We can discuss that. But this isn't what I signed up for.'

'You've had Nelson to assist you since I left.' He nodded towards the young detective in the chair beside him. He'd used the past tense but Harvey failed to pick it up.

'Yes, of course. I've got Detective Nelson.' Harvey grabbed Nelson's head in an armlock and wrestled him to the desk, then let him go and ruffled his hair. 'He's not bad, but he's still got a lot to learn. He'll be all right when I've finished with him.'

'Has he been treating you okay?' Megarry asked Nelson.

'Don't answer that,' Harvey said. 'There's so much to do, Cecil, you've no idea. This is the control centre. These phones never stop ringing. Every lunatic that's got a problem gets put through to me. They think I know everything. The whole bloody operation hinges on this one tiny office – and look at the place. Christ Almighty, you couldn't swing a cat in here.'

He blew out smoke and tapped the end of his cigarette.

'You know what it is? I should have had an assistant a long time ago. All these years working here on my own. I must have been crazy.'

'I have to take him back,' Megarry said quietly.

'What did you just say?'

'I've got to take him. I'm sorry.'

22

'You can't just walk in here and take my assistant. Goddamit, I've just been telling you what absolute bedlam this place is. Who's going to answer the phones? You can't do this, Cecil. I've got *some* rights.'

Megarry pushed Nelson out into the hall and quickly closed the door.

He heard a crash and breaking glass as something shattered against the wall: 'Dogs, dirty dogs,' Harvey shouted.

'What's all this about?' Nelson asked as they settled into Megarry's car. 'Where are we going?'

Megarry pursed his lips. 'Something's come up. We've got to talk to some people.'

'What sort of people?'

'Bank people. Their place has been hit.'

Nelson turned in his seat. 'A bank robbery? You mean …?'

'Yes.'

'Well, it *must* be important.'

'It's so important, they reckon only you and I can handle it.'

'You're kidding.'

They drove north, along roads that wound through dull suburbia, past abandoned cinemas and sprawling supermarkets and here and there a church with locked gates and overgrown lawns. It had been raining earlier, but now a weak sun was struggling through a sky of dirty cloud. As they neared the city centre, the car was forced to crawl behind a grey army personnel carrier, nervous squaddies peering from its gloomy depths.

'You don't normally handle this sort of thing,' Nelson said after a while. 'Is there some security angle?'

'I don't think so. I've only read the preliminary report.'

'Anybody get killed?'

Megarry shook his head.

'So what did they get?'

'Money, papers.'

'How much?'

'A few grand.'

'Seems odd to ask you to take on this kind of job. But at least you're back. You know, I had my doubts. During the last few months, I wondered if you'd ever return. You were supposed to ring, remember? You said we'd go for a beer.'

'No,' Megarry said, 'you were supposed to ring me.'

'Was I?' Nelson turned his head slightly. 'Anyway what's it matter? You're back on the job again.'

'Don't go too fast, John.'

'What do you mean?'

'I told Drysdale I'd look at this case. I didn't give him any commitments. I didn't agree to take it. I just said I'd look at it.'

'Okay,' Nelson conceded. 'You're back on the job for the time being.'

'Yes,' Megarry said. But he spoke without enthusiasm.

The Great Northern Bank was an imposing edifice of glass and steel which dominated Chichester Street and dwarfed the surrounding buildings for several blocks. It looked strangely out of place among the subdued Victorian shopfronts and offices, gloomy headquarters of solicitors' firms and sedate auctioneering companies. It struck Megarry that it resembled a massive goldfish bowl and would be a most difficult place to rob.

The manager, Mr Glendinning, met them in the foyer. He was a tall man in a pin-striped suit with an awkward habit of staring over the shoulder of the person he was speaking to. He introduced them to Mr Clinch, an energetic young man in a white shirt and fashionably baggy suit, the teller who had encountered the robbers.

'Maybe we should go up to my office?' Mr Glendinning said, looking past Megarry's head and straight into Nelson's face.

'Why not,' said Megarry, and they trooped off past a security guard, and down an oak-panelled corridor until they came to a lift. When the doors opened, they were met by a thin woman in a business suit who immediately drew Mr Glendinning aside and whispered something.

The manager listened, then stood back and began waving his hands dismissively. 'Not now,' Megarry heard him say, 'tell him I've got people with me. Later, later.' Glendinning made a sort of shooing noise and drove her before him like a sheep.

'I can see you're a busy man,' Megarry said as Glendinning pushed open a door and ushered them into an office. It looked like a small conference room, with a large mahogany table dominating the centre of the floor.

'People are so inconsiderate,' the manager said. 'They don't think. They expect me to be available at all hours of the night and day.'

He pulled out some chairs. 'Can I get you something to drink?' He looked from Nelson to Megarry and back again. 'Is that allowed? Drink, I mean. Alcohol? It's not against the rules?'

Megarry was shaking his head. 'Not while we're on duty. But coffee would be nice. They don't mind us drinking coffee.'

Mr Glendinning smiled and clapped his hands, 'Coffee it shall be.'

There was a percolator on a table and a tray with cups. Glendinning looked sternly at Clinch; the young man got up, came back with the tray and began pouring for each of them.

'Where do you want to begin?' the manager asked.

'At the beginning.' Megarry tapped a spoon on the side of his saucer and looked into Glendinning's face. 'Just take us through the events of the day from the time you first realised that the bank was being robbed until the raiders had gone. We may ask you questions from time to time, but feel relaxed. Just tell us what happened.'

'Well, in that case maybe Clinch should begin.' Glendinning pointed across the table to the teller, who had loosened his tie and was sitting anxiously on the edge of his seat. 'They went to him first.'

'That's fine.' Megarry turned to observe the young man. Twenty-five, twenty-six, he thought. Eager beaver, by the looks of him. And he certainly is deferential, which never did anyone any harm. He noticed the beads of sweat on Clinch's forehead.

'Are you comfortable?' Megarry asked. 'It's quite warm in here. Maybe you'd like to remove your jacket?'

The teller glanced quickly across the table, where Glendinning was already signalling that this was in order.

'I've made a statement about this already.'

'I've read it,' Megarry said, 'I just want to hear firsthand what happened.'

The young man cleared his throat.

'Well, it was raining. Quite heavy rain. It was bouncing off the roof of the atrium, making a noise like someone practising on a drum. It was five minutes to four and we were coming up to closing time and it was getting dark. There was only a handful of customers and I remember thinking that the rain would slow things down and we might get an early night. I turned to my screen and began to prepare for close-down.'

He looked at Glendinning. 'We have quite a bit of work to do after the bank has closed. Some people don't realise this.'

'I know,' said Megarry. 'What happened then?'

'Well, when I turned back again, I was looking down the barrel of a gun. Quite literally staring into this big black revolver. There was a guy on the other side of the counter with a stocking over his face and this thing pointing right at my head. My first reaction was to set off the alarm. We have panic buttons on the floor. You know about that. It's in the statement.'

'Yes,' Megarry said.

'He seemed to know about it too. He ordered me to stand up and place my hands flat on the counter and not move.'

'And you did as you were told?'

'Of course.'

'I would too,' Megarry said with a smile. 'What did he do next?'

'My work station is right beside the staff entrance. It separates the public banking hall from the bit only bank staff are meant to be in. Which, on reflection, probably explains why he came to me. There's a combination switch on the door and he ordered me to open it for him.'

'And you did that too?'

'Yes. I'd no option.'

'What was happening in the rest of the hall while this was

going on?' Nelson was speaking for the first time and Clinch switched his attention.

'Until this, I'd only been concerned with my own situation. I was frightened as hell. I'd never been involved in anything like this before and I'd no way of knowing whether this guy was nervous or whether he might let loose with his weapon.'

'Was he?' Nelson said. 'Nervous, I mean?'

Clinch shook his head. 'I don't think so. It's hard to know because I couldn't see his face on account of the stocking. But he seemed calm … as if he knew exactly what he was doing.'

'What about the rest of the hall?' Megarry reminded him.

'Well, I suddenly realised that there were two more raiders, a man and a woman. These two were wearing those false faces, you know, Halloween masks, Frankenstein or Dracula or something like that. One of them had locked the main door and was pulling the blinds across the windows, so that people outside couldn't see in. The other one had rounded up the customers, there were only about half a dozen. And the security guard. They'd taken his walkie-talkie, so he was immobilised.'

'Both armed?' Nelson asked.

'Yes. They both had heavy hand guns, the same as my guy.'

'Did no one set off the alarm?' Megarry asked. 'During all this time, did no one get a chance to activate the alarm?'

'The wire was cut.' It was Glendinning. He leaned across the table and stared past Megarry's shoulder. It seemed to the police chief that his face was flushed. 'We discovered this later when they'd gone. One of them must have cut the wire, so the alarm was no damned use.'

'No one tried to use the phone?'

'It all happened so quickly,' Glendinning said, glancing nervously at Clinch for confirmation.

'That's right,' the teller said,' it was all over in a few minutes. I certainly had no chance to phone.'

'All right,' Megarry said, 'let's start again. They've locked the doors and pulled the blinds. What happened next?'

Clinch cleared his throat again. 'The guy who was facing me ordered me to open the door. I'd no choice. The other two came through, security guard and all. Everyone was told to sit on the floor. One of them pulled out a sack and began clearing out the tills. They took cheques, cash, everything. When they'd done that, the first guy put the gun to my head and ordered me to take him to Mr Glendinning's office.'

'Did he ask for him by name?'

Clinch hesitated for a second. 'I don't think so. I think he just said, "The manager's office".'

'And you obeyed?'

Clinch nodded. 'I certainly did. He had this thing pressed right under my ear.' He indicated with his finger. 'I could feel his breath on the back of my neck.'

'And you knew nothing about any of this, Mr Glendinning? You were here, in your eyrie, blissfully unaware that the bank was being robbed?' Megarry smiled at the manager. If there was irony in the remark, it was lost on Glendinning.

'Well, that's true. How could I? The alarm had been cut and Clinch has explained how no one could use the phones.'

'The phones weren't cut?' Nelson interjected.

'No, just the alarm. The first I knew that anything was amiss was when Clinch came through there with Janet.' He pointed to the door. 'Janet's my secretary, the lady you met a few minutes ago. And this man holding a gun to Clinch's head.'

'Were you frightened?'

'Absolutely. We've never been robbed before. We do have a drill for this sort of thing … bit like fire drill. But nothing can prepare you for the terror of the real thing.'

'What did he want with you?'

'The keys to the vaults.'

'The vaults?'

'It's where we keep the valuables. People leave things with us for safekeeping – silver, jewellery, paintings sometimes. People deposit things, maybe when they're going on holiday. It's a service we provide for customers.'

'I never knew you could do that,' Megarry said.

'Oh yes. We've always done it. But it's become more popular in recent years with the increase in burglaries and thefts.'

'And he wanted the keys.'

'He wanted me to open the vaults. Thank God there was very

28

little there. I took him down with Clinch and Janet and he had a rummage about for a few minutes, took some things and then brought us back to the main hall.'

'What did he take?'

'Documents. Personal papers.'

'What else was in the vaults?' Megarry asked.

'A couple of silver dinner sets, some glass, jewellery.'

'And he didn't bother with them?'

Glendinning shook his head. 'No, just the documents.'

'Don't you think that's odd?'

'Well, maybe the other stuff was too bulky. I don't know what was going through his mind. But it was to our advantage. I mean things are bad enough without even more being taken.'

'What about the jewellery? That wouldn't be too bulky, would it?'

'I suppose not.'

'But he left it alone and just took the documents?'

'That's right.'

'What sort of documents are we talking about?' Nelson asked, putting his coffee cup down carefully on the table.

'Wills, passports, birth certificates, title deeds. People lodge all sorts of papers. Mainly they're important documents that they don't want mislaid.'

'Would you have a list of what was taken and the owners?'

'Normally not. But,' Glendinning held up a bony finger, 'about two years ago, we changed the system. We had an unfortunate incident and some material was lost. Now we ask the client to supply us with an inventory. It's a kind of insurance for the bank.'

'So you can tell us what was taken?'

Megarry thought he saw a shadow cross the bank manager's face.

'Do you intend to interview the owners? They've already been informed.'

'We might want to conduct some inquiries.'

'Well now.' The manager looked agitated. 'This has been very distressing for us, you understand. The bank would naturally be concerned to minimise the inconvenience to our customers. I'm not sure that having the police ...'

Megarry's voice took on a hard edge. 'Let us be the judge of that, Mr Glendinning. If you will let us have a list of what was taken and the owners, I'd be most grateful.'

'Of course. There's no question. It's just that ...' Glendinning reached for the phone and spoke to his secretary in the other room. He turned back to Megarry. 'You'll have that information right away.'

'Now,' Megarry said. He sat up quickly and bounced a teaspoon off the edge of a saucer. 'How did these people get away? Who'd like to tell us about that?'

Clinch and Glendinning exchanged glances, and the manager waved a hand for the teller to continue.

'They locked us in the lavatories.'

'The whole staff?'

'And the customers.'

'How many people?'

Clinch did a quick count on his fingers.

'Eighteen?'

'Hmmph,' Megarry said. 'That couldn't have been comfortable. How long were you in there?'

'Forty minutes.'

'And who released you in the end?'

'The cleaners.'

Megarry looked at Glendinning, but the manager had lowered his eyes.

'That must have been very embarassing for you all. And when you were released, the raiders had gone?'

'That's right.'

'No information about means of escape, getaway car, anything like that?' Megarry addressed himself to Glendinning.

'No,' the manager said. 'Afraid not.'

'Anything left behind by these people that might help us?'

Glendinning shook his head. 'Your forensic people came over right away and carried out tests. They must have made out a report.'

'What about descriptions? Anybody get a good look at them?'

'They were of average height,' Clinch said. 'Faces covered at all time, gloves I think. Two men and a woman. The man who approached me, the one with the stocking, he seemed to do most of the talking. Run-of-the-mill Belfast accent. Not that he said very much, and his voice was distorted because of the stocking.'

Megarry sighed and looked at Nelson. He gathered his notebook and the handful of notes he had written. As he made to stand up, the door opened and the thin woman in the business suit was back. She had a file in her hand which she gave to Mr Glendinning, then bent and whispered animatedly into his ear. Megarry watched as the manager's face grew dark. He took the file without saying a word and dismissed the woman with a peremptory wave of his hand. He turned to Megarry and forced himself to smile. 'Here's the information you were seeking, Superintendent.'

Megarry took the folder, opened it and let his eye run along the neat lines of typing. After a minute he closed it with a flourish and stood up. 'Nine thousand, three hundred and sixty-five pounds.'

He glanced at the file again. 'And sixty pence.'

He puffed out his cheeks. 'Plus a number of documents. Hardly worth the time and effort, if you ask me.'

3

Megarry looked up from a letter he was reading and cursed under his breath.

'Did you say something, Cecil?'

His wife observed him from across the breakfast table, coffee cup an inch from her mouth.

'I said goddammit. That's what I said. Goddammit. GOD-DAMMIT.' He crunched the letter into a ball and hurled it with some force towards the waste-bin. It missed, skidded across the floor and came to rest underneath the sink.

Kathleen looked shocked. She put down her cup and examined him. 'What's the matter with you, Cecil?'

'McDonald is the matter with me. You know McDonald? That weasel who runs ...'

'Your bank manager?'

'Yes, my bloody bank manager. He has just sent me a goddammed threatening letter demanding that I drop every-thing I'm doing and trot off down there to see him. Jeeesus H Christ. The cheek of these people.'

'Please Cecil!'

'You don't understand,' he began. 'You always take their side.'

'It's not a matter of taking sides. Are you overdrawn?'

'What's that got to do with anything?'

'If you're overdrawn, then naturally Mr McDonald is going to be concerned. How much do you owe them?'

'A couple of hundred quid.'

'Why don't you just give him a ring and make an appointment to see him? It'll be all right.'

'You don't understand,' Megarry said again. 'The money isn't the point.'

'But of course it is. He's probably got somebody breathing down his neck. He's got his instructions. It's not personal.'

'But he knows me, for god's sake. He knows where I live. He knows what I do to earn a crust. He knows I'm not going to run away. Isn't banking supposed to be all about lending money to people? Isn't that the whole idea?'

'It's just his job.'

'It's his attitude,' Megarry said with emphasis. 'They're all the same. They think because they run a goddammed bank that the rest of us should go in awe of them.'

'Have some more coffee,' Kathleen said sweetly.

But Megarry wasn't to be diverted.

'I was talking with one of them only yesterday. A long drink of water in a pin-striped suit called Glendinning.' His face had grown flushed with excitement. 'When I think of all the favours I've done these guys over the years, locking up crooks and gangsters, you'd think they'd give me free bloody banking as an expression of gratitude. Instead of which they're ...' He searched for an expression with the right degree of venom, '... persecuting me.'

The phone rang, rattling down the hallway and into the kitchen. Megarry paused.

'Are you here?'

'Depends who it is.'

She shot him an exasperated glance. 'What use is that, Cecil? I can't read your mind.' She wiped her mouth with a napkin and went out into the hall. Megarry pushed his plate away and reached for the morning paper. When he lifted his head again, she was standing in the doorway with a bemused look on her face.

'You'll never guess who that was.'

33

'Are you giving any clues?'

'It was Margaret Drysdale. I haven't spoken to her for months. Not since before your ... suspension.' She spoke the word with distaste. 'She wants us to go over there for dinner some evening. What do you make of that?'

Megarry took a deep breath. He folded the paper carefully and put it down. 'I'm sorry,' he said, 'I meant to tell you. It was Drysdale's idea. It just slipped my mind.'

'But what does it mean, Cecil? We haven't bothered with the Drysdales for ages.'

Megarry puffed out his cheeks and looked uncomfortable. 'It's part of the rehabilitation process, I suppose.'

'Rehabilitation?'

'Yes. They want me back.'

'Who does?'

'The Security Committee. That's what Drysdale wanted to talk to me about. They've discussed the whole Prescott business and they've come to the conclusion that the best thing is for me to go back to work as if nothing had happened.'

'You told them "No", of course?'

'I told him I'd need to think about it.'

'*Cecil!*' She came and sat down beside him and took his hand. 'After all we've been through. After all the agonising, all the discussions. I thought we'd dealt with this. I thought we'd agreed that you'd take early retirement. God almighty, Cecil, can't you just tell them where to get off? Just for once? Can't you just turn your back on the damned place and walk away?'

He looked at her and saw the disappointment in her face. This was what he'd feared and what he'd put off, hoping to avoid a confrontation. But now there was no escaping it. He prayed that it wouldn't blow up into a full-scale row.

'It's not that simple,' he began. 'There are aspects of this thing that I wasn't aware of ... pension rights and so on. And there's my reputation. I don't want to leave under a cloud. You know what sort of a rumour factory it is. You know what they'd say.'

'Who cares what they say? What about your health? What about our marriage? After that business with Prescott, you swore you'd never go back again.' She was furious with him.

'But you can't resist it, can you Cecil? You really believe that place would grind to a halt without you.'

'No, Kathleen, you've got it wrong. I don't want them whispering in the corners of pubs. Looking at me with pity in their eyes. Talking about me behind my back. When I leave, I'll leave with my head high. On my own terms. With no cloud or hint of scandal.'

'Who are you kidding?' She sat back from the table and her lips parted in a bitter smile. 'I've heard all this before. There's nothing new. We've been down this road a dozen times and we always come back to the same damn thing. Cecil Megarry's pride.'

'*Stop!*'

The word was shouted. Immediately he regretted it. 'I'm sorry,' he said, 'I didn't mean that.'

He heaved a sigh. 'Look, I haven't agreed to anything. They want me back so that they can put a brave face on things. They're worried about perceptions. What the papers will say. What people will think. I can see the way their minds are working. I'm not stupid, Kathleen. But it might suit me too.'

For a while they sat in silence. At last Megarry stood up. 'They're going to bump up my salary. They're going to give me carte blanche. No interference. I haven't had that sort of regime since these troubles started. It'll make a big difference.'

Kathleen shook her head. 'You're going back, I can tell.'

'I'll play it to suit myself,' Megarry said. 'There'll be none of that nonsense I used to get when I looked around the Security Committee and saw all those neat suits and uniforms with their heads stuffed with rubbish and their fingers itching to interfere. This time things will be different.'

As he said it, he realised how hollow it sounded.

'Drysdale has asked me to look into something for him.'

'What is it?'

'That man Glendinning I mentioned. It's a bank robbery, a small case. It shouldn't take long. I've already started some inquiries.'

He stood in the kitchen doorway and watched her face to see how she would react.

'That's just to lure you in,' she said.

'I know,' Megarry said as he closed the door.

He collected the keys from the security desk and began the slow climb up the long flight of stairs to his old office. He had decided to do this rather than take the lift because he wanted to be seen about the place. He wanted his return to be noticed and commented on, he wanted people to stop each other in the canteen and in the corridors and say; 'Hey, guess who I ran into this morning?' But as it happened, he tramped up the long staircase, halting on each landing to catch his breath, and didn't meet a soul.

There was a fusty smell in the room, a fug of cigarette smoke and stale air as if no one had been in since he had left, all that time ago. The blinds had been drawn and the place was in shadow, but he saw at once that the room had been cleaned. Everything had been stacked neatly away, the coffee percolator had been emptied and scrubbed. Someone had even collected the paper clips on his desk and put them tidily into a plastic cup.

He walked quickly to the window and pulled the blinds. A shaft of sunlight burst into the room and glinted off a little metal calendar holder on his desk. He lifted it and read the date: 10 July. It was the night they had arrested Blair. The following morning he had driven out to the Castle grounds and confronted Prescott.

That was three months ago. Afterwards he had been visited by Drysdale and told not to report for work. Later there were teams of detectives, men he had trained himself. He could see how uncomfortable they were as they sat with him in the quiet of the front parlour and awkwardly took down statements, half expecting him to launch into a tirade, berate them, send them scurrying off into the night, chastised, tails between their legs.

Three months, while he had rested at home and the inquiry team had racked its brains for an acceptable explanation as to how a military adviser to the Commander Land Forces gets shot dead by the Superintendent of Special Branch. In the end

36

they had decided that it was an accident, an act of God, like choking on a chicken bone.

Megarry shook his head and a smile puckered the edges of his mouth. Some good had come of it in the end. It had forced a crisis that had been slowly building; it had made him examine his career, his marriage, his life; forced him to take a hard look at his options. He remembered Kathleen's words, 'You're not a young man any more. They're only using you. What do *they* care if you live or die?'

'What do *they* care?' She'd got it wrong. She hadn't taken account of his own inclinations, the ties that bound him to the job – the camaraderie of the office, the comfort of the routine, the security of the daily grind, the challenge he couldn't relinquish.

He went to his desk and for a while just sat there and allowed the atmosphere to wash over him. Then he pulled open a drawer and rummaged among the notebooks and files until his fingers found the neck of a bottle.

He drew out a half-filled flask of whiskey and a stained coffee mug. A memory came filtering back – nights reeling home from the Montrose Hotel to his lonely room, the peeling wallpaper and the unmade bed. Mornings when the sunlight split his head and his hands shook so badly he could scarcely shave.

Kathleen had taken him back and calmed him down, restored order with clean sheets and regular meals. Now she wanted to stop him returning to this life altogether.

He unscrewed the cap of the bottle and watched as the whiskey tumbled into the mug. When he looked up, Nelson was standing in the doorway.

Megarry raised the bottle and gestured towards a chair. 'You're just in time to join me.'

The younger man shook his head. 'Too early.'

'Too early? Don't talk nonsense. Sit down and do as you're told.'

Megarry poured another measure and pushed the drink across the desk. He raised the mug. 'Hump the begrudgers.'

Nelson reluctantly raised his glass.

'How did you know I was here?' Megarry asked as he wiped his chin.

'I rang your house. Kathleen told me.'

'How did she sound?'

'Cross.'

'She *is* cross. She doesn't want me to get involved again. She says they're only using me. She wants me to get the hell out of here. Take early retirement.'

'And what do you think?'

Megarry didn't reply. Instead he waved his arm around the room. 'This place looks sad. There's something about it, something melancholy. Too many memories. How long did we work here, John?'

'Six years.'

'That long?' He shook his head. 'It seems like yesterday that you came through that door. A callow youth, just promoted. Sent to me to knock the rough edges off. I suppose I didn't do a bad job in the end, you turned out fine, John. I made a detective out of you.'

Nelson looked embarrassed. 'What about this case?' he asked.

'What about it?'

'Are you going to take it?'

Megarry swilled the whiskey in the mug.

'Let me ask you something. Our interview yesterday with Glendinning. Anything strike you as odd?'

Nelson slowly shook his head.

'What do you think they were after?'

'Money. What are people usually after when they rob a bank?'

'Nine thousand pounds?' Megarry raised an eyebrow. 'And all that organisation. All that planning, alarm wires cut. They went through that place like a knife through butter. And all for a miserable nine thousand pounds?'

'Nine thousand pounds isn't that miserable.'

'It is when you consider what they could have got and all the trouble they took. They didn't even bother with the jewellery or the stuff in the vaults. Just the tills and a bunch of documents.'

'Maybe they were rushed, maybe they didn't have time.'

'No,' Megarry said.

He took a paper from his coat and gave it to Nelson.

'That's the list I got from Glendinning. People whose documents were taken. Look at the names.'

Nelson let his eye run down the page. The names were in orderly columns: Duffy, Duggan, Dukes, Dunne. Egan, Ellwood, Enright. It was like leafing through a telephone directory. He looked up.

'They all begin with D, E, F or G.'

'That's right. As if they were deliberately selected.'

Nelson studied the list again. 'But it's as Glendinning said – wills, leases, birth certificates. What use are they?'

'What use indeed?' Megarry took the paper and folded it. 'But they took them, nevertheless. They took them in preference to the jewellery.'

He drummed his fingers on the polished surface of the desk. 'What if the nine thousand pounds was only incidental? A sort of bonus. What if they left the jewellery because it was too difficult to offload, or fence or whatever the hell you do with stolen jewellery these days. What if it was the documents they were really after?'

'Well ...' Nelson said.

'Well nothing, John. This thing has a smell about it.'

He finished the whiskey and stood up. He walked to the window and gazed out over the city.

'I think I'd like to talk again to Messrs Glendinning and Clinch. Only separately this time.'

There was an excitement in his voice, a tension Nelson remembered from the past.

'Sometimes people talk better when they're isolated. Don't you find that, John?'

He picked a crowded restaurant in the centre of the city, bustling with afternoon trade, women with bags of shopping and students in from the cold with their books spread on the tables, preparing to linger over a single cup of tea.

He felt the heat the moment he opened the door. In the

window behind the tea urns, tiny balls of condensation were forming on the glass beside the cakes and fancy pastries. Megarry chose a table near the back, half-hidden by a pillar, but commanding a view of the whole floor. He waited for the waitress to take his order.

He sometimes did this, picked a rendezvous in a crowded place. An old Branch hand had taught him years ago that there was safety in numbers, at football matches, race-tracks, cinemas. Megarry had met his informants at all of these. Nevertheless, as he settled back into the soft cushions of the seat, he pressed his elbow against his side to feel the reassuring bulk of his revolver.

He ordered coffee and opened an evening paper, every now and then letting his eyes wander across the room towards the door. At the next table a couple of long-haired youths were playing chess on a pocket set. Megarry watched as one of them took out a tin of tobacco and began to roll a cigarette with one hand while his eyes concentrated on the game. It was the sort of small, insignificant thing that impressed Megarry, a useless skill like taking the caps off bottles with your teeth. He had known someone once who could do that, biting the metal caps like carrot tops and spitting them from the side of his mouth.

He saw Clinch's tall frame bustle in from the street and stand baffled for a moment beside the bread counter, his eyes gazing from under a peaked cap, blinking at the rows of faces in the crowded room. He was ambitious, Megarry had noticed that at their first encounter, and bright, a lethal combination. Megarry raised his newspaper and waved. Clinch began to push past the tables to join him.

'Am I late?' he said and started to take off his overcoat. 'Couldn't get away. Last minute rush. Pile of orders came in for payrolls and we weren't expecting them until tomorrow.'

'You're not late,' Megarry said, 'I've only just got here myself. What would you like to drink?'

'Coffee, I think.'

'Something to eat? Cake, pastry?'

Clinch waved a hand. 'I'll be eating dinner soon. Coffee will be fine.'

Megarry raised the paper again to catch a waitress's attention.

'Why did you want to see me?' Clinch asked when the coffee had arrived.

Megarry pretended not to hear. Instead he said, 'Do you like your work?'

The directness of the question made the young man flush. 'That's a very interesting question. I've never asked myself before. I suppose I do like it, all things considered.'

'But you don't want to do it all your life, do you? You'd like to move on eventually, do other things.'

'Naturally. Everyone would, I suppose.'

'Would you like to have Mr Glendinning's job for instance? Would you like to be a manager?'

Clinch burst out laughing. Megarry sat back and observed him. It was obvious that the idea was not entirely displeasing.

'It's never crossed my mind,' Clinch lied.

'Why not? He's bound to move on at some stage. Retire, get promoted. You're young. You seem to be bright, keen, energetic. Highly motivated. You're the type of person they promote.'

'But there are other people ahead of me, people who are more senior.'

'It doesn't necessarily work like that. Buggins's turn – that's old fashioned. Nowadays they promote on ability, energy, skill, vision. You've got all those.'

'No,' Clinch said, and shook his head, 'I'm afraid you don't know how that place works. Anyway. You didn't bring me here to discuss my career prospects.'

'Well, not entirely,' Megarry said and sipped his coffee. 'I wanted to ask you a few more questions about the robbery. It strikes me, going over my notes, that there are some things that don't quite add up.'

'Like what?'

'Well, it looks to me like a very professional job. Well planned, well executed, right down to cutting the alarm wires. And yet they behave like a bunch of amateurs. All they manage to steal is nine thousand pounds and some documents. I wondered if the same thought had crossed your mind.'

Clinch sat forward and looked into Megarry's face. 'Of course it did – and they could have got so much more.'

'They could?'

'Yes. Didn't Mr Glendinning tell you?'

'Tell me what?'

'That was a Thursday night, wasn't it? I remembered because Mr Glendinning plays cards on a Thursday night and likes to get away early, and we thought because of the rain, and everything, we were going to have an early night. But Thursdays, we also get a big lodgement from Collins', the supermarket. Thursday is their special offers day and the takings are always up. They like to lodge the bulk of it before three thirty and put the rest into the night safe.'

'How much are we talking about?'

'Fifty, sixty thousand pounds.'

'That much?'

'Sure, maybe more. Depends on the volumes they've put through.'

'And how come the robbers missed it?'

'Because they didn't look for it. They cleaned out the tills, but that was only a trifling sum – small deposits, that sort of thing. And then they made Mr Glendinning take them to the vaults. If they'd done their homework properly, they'd have known about the Collins' lodgement. It's a regular.'

'And where was it?'

'In the manager's office. Right under their noses. But they were so damned eager to get down to the vaults that they missed it.'

Clinch suddenly looked alarmed. 'I shouldn't be telling you this. I feel like I'm betraying Mr Glendinning.'

'Nonsense,' Megarry said with emphasis. 'You're being a good citizen, assisting the police. That's what the bank would want you to do, isn't it? We want to catch these guys.'

'There's been hell to pay,' Clinch said. 'God knows what would have happened if they'd got that lodgement. Things are bad enough as it is. We've had the area manager almost every day since the robbery, *and* the chief accountant, *and* a bunch of people from the security section. It's not as if it was Mr Glendinning's fault. It could have happened to anyone.'

'Indeed,' Megarry said. 'It was his misfortune that they picked on your branch … Unless, of course, they were after something else.'

The young man stared. 'I'm not sure I follow your drift,' he said.

The policeman leaned forward and drew him into a confidential huddle. 'Let me ask you something. You were down in the vaults weren't you? With Mr Glendinning and the raider? How come the personal files he took all begin D, E, F and G?'

'Because that's all he could carry.'

'What do you mean?'

'He asked for all the files at first, and then when he saw how many there were, he changed his mind and said 'D, E, F and G.' Mr Glendinning gave them to him. And I can't say I blame him. You've got to remember that this guy had a gun and looked as if he might use it.'

'Of course. Did he say anything else?'

Clinch shook his head. 'No. Just waved the gun around and acted menacing. Didn't even have to act. He scared the life out of me without even trying.'

'Well,' Megarry said and looked out across the restaurant floor. The crowds were starting to thin out and the waitresses were clearing tables and cleaning up. 'You were very good to meet me. I'm extremely grateful.' He held out his hand and the young man grasped it.

'Do you think you'll get them?'

It was a question they always asked, as if being interrogated by the police made them part of the inquiry team. Megarry had a stock response. 'I expect so. In time.'

'And do you know what it was all about?'

'No,' Megarry said, 'not yet, but I will.'

'I hope I was able to help you.'

'You were indeed.'

'And you'll keep it confidential? No one else will know? I

don't want Mr Glendinning getting the impression that I was going behind his back.'

'No one else will know.'

Together they walked through the restaurant. 'Do you play chess?' Megarry asked as they passed the students.

Clinch shook his head.

'You should,' Megarry said, 'it's a fascinating game. Sharpens the mental processes. Trains you to think logically. I think you'd be good at it.'

Outside, a wind was whipping up off the river and Megarry pulled his collar close against the cold. They stood in the doorway watching the people hurrying home in the evening gloom.

Megarry looked at Clinch.

'Something you said. Mr Glendinning plays cards on a Thursday night?'

'And Saturday and Sunday. It's a big thing with him.'

'Really. What's he play?'

'Stud poker, mainly.'

4

After he had stolen the car and delivered it to the garage on the Cliftonville Road, Morgan knew that it would only be a matter of time before Mr Cronin came to see him again.

Meanwhile he went about his business as if nothing had happened. He told no one, but privately he drew a warm pride from the knowledge that they had trusted him and that he had carried out his task well. He recalled the words of the man in the garage, 'You certainly picked a beauty.' Of course he had picked a beauty. He knew about cars, probably more than they did. They looked at his withered legs and their instinct was to write him off. He remembered their shock when he stepped out of the car – as if they couldn't believe someone like him could pull off a job like that. That's the way it had been all his life. He was used to being written off. It made the satisfaction much greater when he achieved something.

After delivering the car, he had gone to the cinema and then to a club in the neighbourhood where he hung around for a couple of hours playing snooker and drinking with people he knew. Normally he didn't drink much, but on this occasion he had several pints and then a couple of whiskies. He was on a high. He could still feel the adrenalin buzz when he had stolen the car.

At six o'clock, he went home for dinner and then watched

television with his mother. The drink had made him drowsy, but he fought it off for her sake. She liked him to sit with her, liked to fuss over him, as if she felt a need to protect him. But he often found himself resenting it; there were times when he felt that she was smothering him, boxing him in with her love.

When the news came on, Morgan leaned forward and turned the sound up, half-expecting to hear some announcement about the car theft.

His mother watched him from the depths of the settee. 'What are you doing?' she asked. She liked stability, routine, order. Any deviation from the habitual, any disruption, was seen as a threat. Even a simple thing like switching channels could upset her.

'Something I'm interested in.'

'What is it, Sean?'

'Nothing, Ma. Just the news.'

'When did you get interested in the news?'

'I've always been interested.'

'You could have fooled me.'

She got up and went into the kitchen: 'I'll get you fresh tea,' she said, pulling the door closed behind her.

He knew it was silly. Dozens of cars went missing every day. Nevertheless, when nothing was mentioned, he felt a vague disappointment. He watched a couple of soaps and a comedy show and, when he could decently get away, he went to bed and began to relive the excitement of the day. He closed his eyes and felt again the tremor along the dashboard as the engine exploded into life, saw the outstretched hand of the army sergeant at the roadblock and the look of admiration on the faces of the men at the garage when they saw the beautiful car he had stolen. Finally he fell into a deep sleep and dreamt that he was being chased by the police.

Mr Cronin called to see him a few days later. He slipped in by the side door and stood near the snug until he caught Morgan's attention. Then he ordered a bottle of stout and invited Morgan to join him.

'You did great work, Sean, just what we wanted. I told them you wouldn't let us down.' He punched Morgan's shoulder

46

playfully and Morgan felt his heart warm. 'That's a great car. We couldn't have done better if we'd ordered it straight from the showroom. Know what I mean?'

The corners of his eyes twinkled. He looked around the deserted bar. 'Are you busy?' He rubbed his hands in an exaggerated way, then before Morgan could reply, he answered the question himself: 'Looks quiet enough.'

'We're stock-taking. We do that in the morning.'

'When do you get your break?'

'One o'clock.'

'Not until one o'clock?' Mr Cronin checked his watch and saw that it was half-eleven. 'I need to talk to you, Sean, but not in here. Somewhere more private, somewhere we won't be disturbed.' He drummed his fingers on the black table-top. 'I'll tell you what. You know the Bernardo Grill in Castle Street? Up near the lights?'

Morgan nodded.

'I'll see you there. I'll buy you lunch.'

He rapped the table with his knuckles and tipped Morgan a wink. 'One o'clock, okay?' Before Morgan could answer he turned on his heel and was gone. The door to the street swung closed behind him.

For the rest of the morning, Morgan pottered around the bar, cleaning glasses, stacking shelves, serving the occasional straggler who dropped in from the bookie's up the street.

As he went about his work, he thought about Mr Cronin. He had expected him to be back. And he knew what Mr Cronin wanted: he had come to ask him to steal another car. The thought brought a frisson of pleasure. It was like when he took the car the first time – a mixture of fear and excitement. He hadn't known that stealing something could bring such a feeling. It was like a battle of wits, where he had to stay calm, keep his nerve, be cleverer than his opponents – the police and the army. And when it was over, the rush of adrenalin, the feeling of power, the blood pounding in his ears when it was done and he had got away successfully.

What was he going to tell Mr Cronin when he asked? Would he tell him that he had done enough, that he didn't want to get involved any further? Or would he agree? He tried to put the thought out of his mind but it kept coming back. Then he realised that he already knew the answer. He would say, 'Yes'.

He had known for some time. It was a small part that he could play in changing the system and putting something better in its place. That's what they were fighting for, and it was a just cause. He saw again the image of Anto Quinn at the shopping centre, his face red with drink, his breath foul, begging for pennies from passers-by. He thought of his own father, a father he had never known, his mother left alone to raise two small children. He felt his breast fill with sadness.

He hadn't asked them why they wanted the car, but he guessed it was for some job – a bank robbery or something like that. They were constantly pulling jobs and they needed a regular supply of cars, someone like him to steal them. Mr Cronin had said something that had made an impression on him: he had said that not every soldier carried a gun.

But there was something else. At the heart of it was a feeling of pride, that an organisation so powerful and resourceful should come to him to ask a favour made him feel good. He remembered another thing Mr Cronin had said: someone had recommended him, several people indeed. Just hearing Mr Cronin say that had filled him with secret pleasure. For the truth was that few people came to him for anything.

At five to one, Liam came on for his shift. Morgan went out into the store room, washed his hands, put on his coat and got ready to leave. As he went through the bar he stopped at the counter.

'I have to see somebody. I may be a wee bit late. Can you cover for me?'

Liam was a freckle-faced apprentice, eager to please. He nodded his head willingly. 'Sure thing.'

'I should be back about two, half-two at the latest.'

'Take your time,' Liam said and turned away to pull a pint for a customer.

It was cold outside, a sharp wind whipping from the docks and a grey overcast sky which promised rain. Morgan pushed through the lunchtime crowds streaming along Royal Avenue, window-shopping outside the big department stores. When he came to North Street, the crowds thinned out, so he decided to take a short cut through Smithfield and, five minutes later, saw the neon sign of the Bernardo Grill.

Mr Cronin had a window seat. Morgan saw him first, sitting like a sentry with a newspaper spread out before him and his head lifting every so often to scan the street outside. He lifted his hand and waved. Morgan pushed open the door of the restaurant and met a rush of warm air and the smell of cooking.

Mr Cronin got up and began to make a fuss of taking Morgan's coat and folding it carefully on an empty chair beside them.

'You got away all right?'

'No problems,' Morgan said. 'Liam is minding the shop.'

'Good, good.' Mr Cronin fidgeted with his cigarettes. He suddenly pushed forward a greasy menu in a plastic cover. 'Are you hungry?'

'Sort of.'

'They do good pasta here. Do you like pasta?'

'I don't mind.'

'Well, you'll get a good feed here, Sean. You won't need a hamburger on the way home. Not like some of these nouvelle cuisine joints. Know what I mean?'

He threw back his head and laughed, then gave Morgan the menu and concentrated on lighting his cigarette. Morgan examined the printed card before putting it down again on the table.

'I'll take your advice. I'll have the spaghetti.'

'You won't be sorry,' Mr Cronin said and blew out a cloud of smoke. 'What about a wee glass of wine to wash it down?'

'I won't bother. They don't like us to drink when we're at work.'

'I know. They think you'll be dipping into the stock. Don't worry, we'll get you something soft.' He looked around for the waitress, a plump Italian-looking girl, with a smear of sweat on her top lip.

'Do they treat you all right?' Mr Cronin asked when she had gone.

'How do you mean?'

'The job. Are you in the union?'

'No,' Morgan said, 'I'm not.'

'You should get involved, Sean. The union would look after you. The cause of Labour and the cause of Ireland. They're two sides of the same coin. James Connolly said that. They shot him, strapped to a chair. Did you know that?'

Morgan shook his head.

'Oh yes. After the Easter Rising. The British took out the leaders and shot them for treason. Connolly was wounded, but they took him from his hospital bed. They couldn't wait to do away with him, you see, they knew he was a threat. He could unite the working people, Catholic and Protestant. They were afraid of that.'

'I didn't know.'

'I'll bet there's lots you don't know. History, Sean. You should read our history. It's all in there. Divide and conquer – that's always been the British way in Ireland. Keep the people at each other's throats.'

'I have a job,' Morgan said, 'I can't complain. The pay's okay. There's lots of people with no job at all.'

'Who are you telling? Sure, isn't that what's wrong with this damned system? People don't count any more. There's no such thing as human dignity.' Mr Cronin shook his head sadly. 'We'll just have to look after one another, Sean. We'll just have to take care of ourselves.'

When the meal arrived, Morgan looked around the restaurant. It was almost full, mainly business people, but here and there couples, and near the back a family with a baby in a high chair. He waited till the waitress had moved out of earshot before speaking again. 'What did you want to see me about?'

Mr Cronin looked up from his plate and wiped his mouth with a napkin. 'I might have another wee job for you.'

'Another car?'

Mr Cronin looked around, then lowered his voice. 'No, the same car. It's getting fixed, souped up. It'll do over a ton when it's ready. Would you like to drive it?'

Morgan immediately felt afraid. This was a shock; not what

he had been expecting at all. This sounded much more dangerous.

'Drive it where? What for?'

'A wee job.'

'What sort of job?'

Mr Cronin shook his head and smiled. 'Lord, Sean, you ask an awful lot of questions. It's just a job we have in mind. But it's important, not a job I would ask just anyone to do.'

'What would be involved?'

'Driving the car. That's all.'

'And would there be any danger?'

'Sure, everything you do is dangerous. Stealing the car in the first place was dangerous. You could walk out of here and get knocked down by a bus. Danger is everywhere, it's all around you.'

'I mean real danger,' Morgan said. 'I've never been asked to do anything like this before.'

Mr Cronin suddenly reached out and grasped Morgan's wrist with a bony hand, 'That's because nobody trusted you, Sean. But I trust you.'

'I need to think about it.'

'That's okay, just take your time. I'll send somebody for you.'

Mr Cronin finished his wine and raised his hand for the bill.

'Tell me something,' Morgan said as they got ready to leave, 'why are you doing this? You have your business to think about. You don't need to put yourself at risk by getting involved in things like this.'

Mr Cronin gave him a strange look, as if the answer was so obvious that it was unnecessary.

'What about all the injustice, Sean? all the discrimination? the fact that we're treated like subversives in our own country? Somebody has to do something about it. Somebody has to give leadership.'

The call came a couple of days later on a bright Saturday morning that forced Morgan out of bed before his mother had time even to start making breakfast. The early sun had woken him, filtering through the curtains and flooding the little bedroom with light. And then, as he considered whether to go back to sleep, he heard the radio go on in the kitchen. He got out of bed, went into the bathroom and started to shave.

He had the day off, but he had things to do. The car in the front garden, sitting majestically on eight breeze blocks, was being fixed for a friend. He'd had it now for weeks and the inquiring phone calls were getting more strident. Also, his mother was complaining that the battered skeleton was lowering them in the eyes of the neighbours.

He found her in the kitchen, where she seemed to have taken up permanent residence, fussing about the cooker, preparing his breakfast. 'What's wrong with you?' she said. 'Not able to sleep?'

'What do you mean?'

'I usually have to beat the door down to get you up.'

'I'm just feeling energetic,' Morgan said, 'that's all. Nice bright morning. I thought I'd get that car fixed and out of your road. That should make you happy.'

'Get rid of it,' she said. 'The neighbours are complaining. This place isn't a garage, Sean. You need a licence for that sort of thing.'

She poured him a cup of tea and handed him the morning paper, then turned again to the cooker. He watched her as she worked, the grey head, the glasses stuck with sellotape, the patched cardigan thrown carelessly across her shoulders. What sort of life had she had? Scraping, saving, worrying. His father gone since he was a baby, his only memory the stern face staring from the portrait on the sitting-room wall. Only a few years into her marriage and her husband was dead and she was left with two young children. No wonder she fussed. She could leave nothing to chance; it was her way of staking out the boundaries of the possible. All the way through primary school and secondary school and even now that he had grown up and got a job, she still continued. It had become part of her nature, so ingrained that she couldn't stop. On impulse he got up and kissed her cheek. 'You know I love you,' he said.

He caught her by surprise, but he could see that she was pleased.

52

'Do you?' she said. 'Sometimes I wonder.'

'I do, I love you. I just wish you wouldn't worry so much. I can look after myself, I'm not a baby.'

'I know that, but it's dangerous out there. There's plenty of people to lead you astray.' She blinked behind her glasses. 'Plenty of people with fancy talk and, when you look around for them, they're gone.'

Morgan snorted. 'C'mon,' he said, 'for god's sake, Ma, I'm not stupid.'

He shook out the paper and tried to change the subject.

'Where's Margaret? Still in bed?'

'She had a late night,' his mother said.

'Is it this fella she's got?'

'Uh-huh.'

'Is it getting serious?'

'Looks like it.'

'So there'll only be you and me left.' Morgan said and stood to give her a hug.

'That's right,' his mother said, 'we'll just have to learn to get along.'

He put on an old pair of overalls, got out his toolbox and went into the garden to work on the car. Over several weeks, he had stripped it down and replaced the engine, working with parts he could cannibalise from other cars in scrap-yards and garages around town. Now he had to rebuild it.

He loved this work. He loved anything to do with cars, driving them, repairing them … it was what he would have liked to have done full time, had he managed to get an apprenticeship. But when he left school and began to search, there were no openings. Garage owners would look at him and shake their heads. Some said they would get in touch if anything turned up, but they never did.

After a while Morgan gave up looking for an apprenticeship and took the first decent job that came along, as a trainee barman. But the experience left a bitterness which surfaced now and then when he thought of those pitying looks and the shaking heads.

Shortly after two o'clock, Morgan noticed a young lad of

about fifteen making his way along the street as if unsure of his bearings. He was dressed in faded jeans and anorak and, as he approached, seemed to be counting the doorways and looking for a particular house. A little collie dog trotted at his heels.

When he came to Morgan's garden he stopped. 'I'm looking for Sean Morgan,' he said. 'Is that you?'

Morgan put down a spanner and wiped his hands on a rag. He studied the simple face with the light down on the upper lip and the eyes that weren't quite sure of themselves.

'And who are *you* exactly?'

'I've a message for Sean Morgan.'

'Who from?'

'Mr Cronin,' he said with sudden assurance as if mention of the name bestowed a measure of authority on himself.

'That's me,' Morgan said. 'What's the message?'

'You've to be at the Pike Club in Beechmount Street at eight o'clock tonight. Do you know where it is?'

'Yes.'

'Mr Cronin said to take the bus and not to come by car. He said that's important.'

'What else did he say?'

'Just that it's a private meeting and you're to keep it to yourself. And be on time.'

Morgan suppressed a smile. 'Is that all?'

'That's all.'

'All right,' Morgan said, 'you can tell him I'll be there.'

'Slán,' the young lad said and turned away. Morgan watched him, more confident now that he'd carried out his task. He walked with a jaunty stride till he disappeared at the top of the street, the dog still trotting at his heels.

5

Megarry was late. The clock on the dashboard said eight-fifteen, but it was slow. Since he had left home, the sky to the east had brightened, the dismal grey transformed to soft pinks and yellows. Now it was bathed in a cold blue light which promised a fine day. He turned on the car radio and fiddled with the dial, trying to get a time check, but all he got was a couple of rock stations and a news show whose host never paused, even for breath. He gave up and switched the radio off.

They had called this meeting of the Security Committee at the last minute. At least that was Drysdale's excuse when he rang him the previous evening. Megarry had been about to go to bed, and Kathleen's frown when the phone went had warned him to be brief. He suspected that they'd forgotten about him altogether and realised their error only when it was already late. Drysdale's arm had then been twisted to get him on board.

He had no agenda, but security meetings were always the same and he knew from past experience what shape this one would take. The Secretary of State would probably begin, and would give them a rundown on the latest political developments. Megarry could see the owl-like figure brushing a lock of hair from his broad white forehead and staring blindly at the far wall, his mouth opening and closing like a trap-door. There were talks of some sort going on and the Secretary would

55

enthuse about them with bland references to bridge-building and compromise. Megarry would sit at the polished table with the others, watching this well-meaning man going through his paces, trying to convince them that there were answers to the problems which had consumed them for the past twenty-five years. He always sounded optimistic, but Megarry suspected that deep down he was tired and that he had no solutions at all; that behind it all there was a weariness, an incomprehension and a sickness that gnawed at his heart.

When he finished they would applaud politely and then the Commander of Land Forces would take over and give them a rundown on the security situation: arms seizures, arrests, the latest on the paramilitaries. This was the bit Megarry dreaded, for attention would focus on him, wanting to know this and have answers to that. Mostly their opinions were facile, the fruit of some counter-insurgency course attended at military college in England. Once the point-scoring began, he had no option but to grit his teeth and listen, while these twenty soldiers and civil servants parsed and analysed the successes and failures of his department – mainly failures.

As he turned the car on to the Lisburn road, the thought occurred that Drysdale might have persuaded them to change. He had given Megarry a promise. Come back and there will be no more interference; I've got a guarantee; from now on you run your own show. They might even have learned some humility from the Prescott affair: one of their own, a trusted lieutenant, exposed as a killer, and the information hushed up for fear that it would damage the service. In any normal organisation, there would have been lessons drawn, but Megarry knew he wasn't dealing with normal people. Many of them were egomaniacs.

The traffic began to build up as he approached the suburbs of the city, but mostly it was going the other way, commuters travelling to the shops and offices and factories in Belfast. He looked again at the clock and saw that it was now eight-thirty. Drysdale had told him nine o'clock, a new departure for security meetings. 'The idea is to set the agenda for the week, get us off on the right foot, so to speak. An early start will mean that we'll be well finished before lunch, so the whole day isn't wasted.'

'Whose idea is this?' Megarry had asked.

'Barrington's. He's a new adviser to the Secretary. I think it should work.'

Megarry put his foot on the accelerator and watched the arrow edge forward. Having agreed to go to the meeting, he wanted to be on time, to give them no excuse to complain. He suddenly realised that he was sweating, the perspiration dampening his armpits and collar. He took out a handkerchief and mopped his face.

The congestion in Lisburn was worse that he had expected, a slow procession of cars and lorries packing the narrow streets of the town. Megarry felt the tension start to rise. He tapped the dashboard with the palm of his hand and waited for a gap in the traffic. This was just what Kathleen had warned. The pressure, the stress, the tyranny of deadlines: he was back in the middle of it again. The car began to feel uncomfortable and he realised that he had been driving with the heater on since leaving home. He wound down the window to let in some air.

This was the life-style that had almost killed him, rushing around trying to beat the clock, drinking too much, smoking, no exercise. He took a deep breath and felt a searing pain, across his chest. He heard a voice in his head saying, 'Slow down, slow down.' He looked around desperately for somewhere to park and saw a van start to reverse from a builder's yard. He waited, then pulled in and stopped, and sat in the car for ten minutes until he felt the tension pass away.

There was further delay at the security barrier on his way into HQ, and he waited while a bunch of bored squaddies checked every car before letting it through. When his turn came, he showed his identity card and got out with his arms spread to facilitate the body search. A sergeant with a Scottish accent apologised and then hoovered the car with an electronic scanner before giving him the all-clear. When he finally got to the car-park it was five to nine.

Drysdale was waiting just inside the door as he had said he

would. The early morning sun sparkled off the buttons on his uniform tunic. He took Megarry's hand and pumped it vigorously as if he hadn't seen him for months. 'You know, I was thinking,' he said, 'I could have given you a lift. It was only after I put the phone down that the thought occurred to me.'

'I needed the car,' Megarry said. 'I've some calls to make, so it's all the same.'

Drysdale's eyes brightened. 'How's the case going? Getting anywhere?'

'So-so. It's slow. I'm still only making inquiries.'

'Ah,' Drysdale said and nodded his head sagely, then changed the subject. But he looked pleased. 'Have a nice weekend? Do anything interesting?'

'Not much,' Megarry said. 'Kathleen has me doing odd jobs for her around the house, you know all those things that build up and never seem to get done. Yesterday we went for a drive down along the Ards Peninsula and had dinner in Killinchy.' He stopped. 'Do you know that neck of the woods at all?'

'Sure. I used to work down there. I was stationed at Newtownards.'

Megarry could see that Drysdale wasn't interested in the small talk so he used a gap in the conversation to ask about the security meeting. 'What's this all about, Jack?'

'About? The usual. I'm sorry you didn't get more notice. The thing is to go in and sit down and just pick up as if you'd never been away. Concede nothing. Understand?'

They were walking along a corridor with little framed pictures of scenic views adorning the white walls. A door opened and a secretary came out with a bundle of papers under her arm. The two men stood aside to let her pass.

'Why should I want to concede anything, Jack? I thought we'd all agreed that I'd done nothing wrong.'

'Of course, of course, that's not what I meant. But in case you get some bastard trying to pull rank or something. Just stay calm, all right? I'm not anticipating any problems, but you know what these meetings can be like.'

Drysdale looked uncomfortable. He picked at an imaginary thread on his tunic.

'Do you have an agenda?' Megarry asked.

The other man shook his head. 'As I told you, the whole thing was organised in a rush. I don't even know who'll be here.'

'And they asked for me specially?'

'Of course, Cecil. You were always part of the team. Now that things are getting back to normal, I thought you'd want to attend.'

Drysdale managed a weak smile. They stopped outside a door with a printed notice saying: MEETING IN PROGRESS. DO NOT DISTURB. Drysdale turned the handle and they went in to a warm room with a long polished table, chairs and glasses neatly in place and a subdued buzz of conversation.

There was another table in a corner with cups and saucers and the rich aroma of coffee. Clustered around it was a smattering of neatly tailored uniforms and anonymous grey suits. A few heads went up when the door opened and Megarry thought the murmur of conversation dropped for a moment before resuming. When he turned, a thin man was peering at him over half-moon glasses.

'Superintendent. You *are* looking well. You must have taken my advice.'

The man stuck a skinny finger under Megarry's nose and grinned. 'What is it? Golf? Did you do what I said?'

Megarry looked for Drysdale but he was gone. He tried desperately to remember the man's name. 'No,' he said, 'I've just been taking it easy.'

'But you've lost weight. You look so much better. More relaxed. More at ease.'

'Thank you,' Megarry said. He suddenly remembered who this was: a civil servant in the Department of Defence. The last time they'd talked, the man had tried to get him to join a golf club.

'You're obviously managing your time better,' the man said. 'That's the key to it. You're a manager. You have to delegate. Once you've grasped that concept everything else falls into place.'

'You're right,' Megarry said. Was it possible this man hadn't heard what had happened to him? He looked across the room

59

and saw Drysdale chatting vigorously to a figure in a red waistcoat. He turned to excuse himself but the civil servant had moved away and at that moment there was a rustle of papers and a strong voice rose above the hum and asked them to take their seats.

The speaker was a tall man with silver hair and a neat pin-striped suit. He stood at the top of the table and waited patiently for them to file into place.

Megarry saw a leonine head, dark flashing eyes and a handsome face that looked almost boyish despite the white hair. He didn't remember seeing him before.

'Barrington,' Drysdale whispered 'He's the new guy.'

The tall man took a glass from the table and tapped it softly to bring the meeting to order. 'Gentlemen. You are most welcome.'

In that moment, as he spoke those few words, Megarry realised a truth that had been blindingly obvious all these years. He looked around the table and saw the serried ranks of middle-aged male faces. Not one single woman. That's what we've become, he thought. Indeed, that's what we've always been: a male club, seeing the problems of the world through middle-aged male eyes. No wonder we get things wrong.

Barrington was wiping his mouth with a handkerchief. 'Firstly, let me thank you all for coming. Particularly at such short notice. I appreciate that you all have busy agendas, so we won't detain you longer than is necessary. The Secretary of State unfortunately cannot be with us this morning. He has asked me to convey his apologies.'

His glance shifted to an older man in uniform sitting by his side.

'The Commander, Land Forces, is however with us and has agreed to open the proceedings. Gentlemen, the Commander.'

Barrington sat down and poured some water into his glass. There was a shuffling of papers and a squat man in uniform rose to his feet. He had a ruddy face and a neat military moustache. He looked almost blimpish, but Megarry knew that behind the façade was an agile mind and a razor wit.

The Commander tugged at the edges of his tunic and let his

eyes drift around the table until they came to rest on Megarry. The room fell silent.

The Commander coughed. 'Before we begin, there is something I would like to say.' He looked directly at Megarry. 'We have an old colleague among us again. Superintendent Megarry of RUC Special Branch has been out of action for some time. I know I speak for you all when I say that we have missed his lively contributions to our debates. Superintendent Megarry is a man at the very frontline of the war. He has spent most of his career fighting terrorists, and probably no one at this table understands them better than he does. I'm delighted to see him back on board once more.'

Megarry felt his ears burn. He looked around at the upturned faces, bent towards him like so many white balloons. Then he became aware of a few hands clapping. He saw Barrington and the Commander, even Fleming, a tormentor from the past, getting up from their seats, the applause building to a tumult.

His chest tightened and he felt a tremor in the muscles of his neck. Was this really happening? Were these the same people who had baited and harried him all those years, who had dumped all their frustration on him, blamed him and his men for every setback, as if they were colonial hicks who could do nothing right?

Drysdale, whispered, 'Say a few words.'

He looked out over the sea of faces and then got slowly to his feet. The applause died away and one by one they sat down again.

'Gentlemen,' Megarry began, 'I am genuinely moved. In the long years I have been among you, I have witnessed many battles fought in this room. More often than not, I have been on the losing side. Decisions have been taken here that I have not agreed with. Criticism has been levelled which I have found unjust and unfair. Sometimes I have left this room feeling hurt and angry.'

He stopped and took a deep breath. 'But I have never doubted that at the end of the day, we have all been on the same side. That is the side of law and order, the side of decency against the forces of murder and destruction. I am delighted to be back here again and I look forward to working towards the common goal. In my book that means only one thing – the defeat of terrorism.'

He sat down and the applause started up again. He felt Drysdale nudge his back and, when he turned, saw his beaming face.

'Brilliant,' Drysdale said. 'Powerful stuff. By God, Cecil, you missed your vocation. You should have been a politician.'

The Commander was addressing them again, his voice droning in a dull monotone. Megarry listened as he detailed arrests, the seizure of arms, the small change of gossip from the army of paid informers. It was the same as he had always known it: a series of music hall acts, each called upon to give a turn. Nothing had changed despite Barrington's reforming ways.

And yet, as he listened, he felt a warmth creep over him. He was a member of a club, a fraternity. They had welcomed him back and seemed to mean it. Maybe they had liked him all the time.

The Commander was coming to the end of his address. Any moment now, Drysdale would be called on to give his report. Megarry watched Drysdale's hands fidget with a bundle of papers on the desk, arranging them, rearranging them, waiting his turn. He had read that this was the sign of a tidy mind.

The Commander was talking about the dangers of kidnapping, warning them to be vigilant. 'Needless to say, this is something we have always to guard against. International terrorists have used it as a tactic from time to time with varying degrees of success. And I don't have to spell out for you the difficulties such a development would pose for us.'

Megarry knew all this. It was the stuff of countless conferences and seminars and cropped up as a topic every couple of months. But why was the Commander referring to it now? 'I want to stress that this is simply rumour, just the vibration that the geiger counter picks up from time to time. I simply bring it to your attention because I believe that we can never afford to relax, never afford to drop our guard. The terrorist never relaxes, he is constantly seeking ways to probe our defences. We should be at least as alert as he is.' He sat down at last.

Barrington rose to his feet and looked past him to the RUC chief sitting at his side. Megarry didn't turn, but heard the chair scrape on the floor, and Drysdale's nervous expletive muttered under his breath.

Megarry felt in his pocket for his cigarettes and then saw the NO SMOKING sign. That had gone up since the last time he was here. He put the cigarettes back and settled down to listen.

There was a crush of bodies on the way out, people toting briefcases and bags, shaking hands, making appointments for lunch or dinner. Megarry made his way to the edge of the throng, where he could wait for Drysdale. He found an ashtray and lit a cigarette. When he looked up he saw a man with weak eyes and a sallow face standing beside him. Fleming. He had a fawn overcoat slung across one arm and he shifted it to the other arm, as if to cover his unease.

'That was a fine speech you made.'

Megarry examined him. The last time they had spoken, they had roared down the telephone at each other and Fleming had threatened to have him taken off a case.

'Thank you,' Megarry said coldly.

'Yes, indeed. A very fine speech. We *are* a team, you know. That's basically what we are. We should pull together.'

'I believe that too.'

Fleming nodded and his fingers strayed to a small brown moustache. He took a breath and Megarry could see he was having difficulty with these few words. 'I wanted to tell you that I think I may have misjudged you in the past and treated you unfairly. I want to apologise for that.'

'There's no need,' Megarry said. He felt a wave of something approaching sympathy for this man standing before him like a penitent. 'There really is no need. We all say things we regret.'

'But I tried to damage you. That was unfair. You see at the time I thought ...'

'Look, it doesn't matter any more, it was the cut and thrust of the job. You thought you were doing the right thing. I don't hold that against you.'

'Well then, we'll put it behind us, shall we?'

Fleming extended a bony hand and Megarry grasped it. 'Welcome back, Superintendent. I believe you're working on the Great Northern Bank robbery. How's it going?'

Megarry glanced up sharply. 'Where did you hear that?'

Fleming looked flustered. 'I can't remember. Someone told me. It's not meant to be confidential, is it?'

'No, but not many people know.'

'We should keep in touch. Give me a ring, I might be able to help.'

It sounded like the replay of an old record. These very same sentiments, almost word for word, he had heard before. Standing here in this very corridor, Prescott had given him his phone number and told him to ring. And there had been a little man with a briefcase waiting for him in the wings, a minder or a bodyguard. It seemed like another age, a lifetime away.

'Thank you,' Megarry said. 'I might take you up on that.'

Fleming had produced a printed business card, with just his name and telephone number and no mention of his position. Megarry put it in his breast pocket.

'We can never afford to relax,' Fleming said. 'That's the key. The terrorist never sleeps.'

He stood awkwardly for a few seconds, then shifted his overcoat again. 'Well then, I'll be on my way. I suppose we'll see you next week. Now that you're back on board, as the Commander put it.'

'I suppose so,' Megarry said. Out of the corner of his eye he saw Drysdale pushing through the crowd, craning his neck to find him. He dropped his cigarette and crushed it.

'Things may be quiet now,' Fleming said, 'but it won't stay that way. I know these devils. Sooner or later, they'll be up to something.'

Megarry got away as soon as he decently could. Drysdale was in high good form and wanted him to have lunch, but he made an excuse and pushed his way out into the cold, bright afternoon sunshine and down to the car-park. He had some pressing business. After repeated requests, he had secured another interview with Glendinning.

He parked the car near the bank and when he was satisfied that there was no danger stepped out into the throngs of shoppers pushing along Cornmarket. This time there was no one to meet him, no pin-striped welcoming committee in the foyer. He told the receptionist of his appointment and made his way up in the lift, wandering along unfamiliar corridors until he heard the voice of Glendinning's secretary and saw her austere figure watching from a doorway. She looked him over, then led him silently into a small office, through another door and into the manager's presence.

He was sitting gloomily behind the big mahogany desk and was clearly displeased. 'This is most inconvenient,' he said.

'Something has come up.'

'Couldn't it wait?'

'I'm afraid not.'

'You don't seem to understand, Mr Megarry. I'm a very busy man. You can't expect me to drop what I'm doing whenever you want to call.'

'You'd like me to catch these people, wouldn't you?'

'Of course,' Glendinning said irritably, 'that's not the point. Everything in its place. I had to cancel a meeting with an important client so as to accommodate you.'

He shuffled some papers on his desk. Megarry stood for a moment, hat in hand, then lowered his frame into a chair without being invited to sit. He took out a notebook and flipped it open.

'I'd like to go back over some of the things you told me the last time I was here. There are aspects of this business which don't seem to make a lot of sense.'

'Like what?'

'Like the fact that you had a lodgement from Collins' supermarket on the day of the robbery and you didn't tell me about it.'

'What?' The manager sat forward quickly in his seat.

'You had a lodgement that day from Collins', quite a large

one, I understand. Fifty or sixty thousand pounds. Why didn't you tell me about it?'

There was a pause which seemed to last for a long time. Megarry became aware of a clock ticking nearby.

'Where did you get that information?'

'From my inquiries.'

'That's highly confidential information. Strictly company-client. Whoever told you that had absolutely no authority ...'

'For God's sake,' Megarry exploded, 'I'm a policeman. I'm trying to get to the bottom of this business. Of course people talk to me. What do you expect?'

'But what's it got to do with anything? What's the relevance?'

'It could be significant. Why didn't you tell me about it when I called here?'

'Because I didn't think it was important. I still don't see.'

'Well, let's put it this way. If professional raiders hit a bank like yours, and these people were professionals, make no mistake and they miss a major lodgement – a lodgement, incidentally, which is a regular feature. Then, I think we're entitled to ask some questions.'

'I don't understand.'

Megarry brought his face close to the manager's and peered into his nervous eyes. 'What were they *really* after, Mr Glendinning?'

'They were after money, surely.'

'Were they?' The policeman sat back and produced his cigarettes. 'Then why did they miss the Collins' lodgement? Why did they leave the jewellery? That doesn't strike me as the behaviour of people who were after money.'

Glendinning shifted uncomfortably. His gaze circled the policeman's face without quite making eye contact. Finally he fixed his attention on the wall above the coffee percolator. 'Maybe they didn't have time.'

'They had plenty of time. They had you all at their mercy. They had the alarm wires cut.'

'Well, *you* tell me then. I don't understand what you're driving at.'

Megarry expelled a cloud of smoke which mingled blue and

grey in the light. 'I don't think that money was their main priority. They were after something else. You realised that too. That's why you tried to conceal the information about the lodgement from me.'

'I beg your pardon?'

'The lodgement, Mr Glendinning. You didn't want me to know about it.'

The manager's face had gone pale.

'This is impertinence.'

'Calm down,' Megarry said.

'How dare you? I have a good mind ...'

Megarry ignored him. 'Those papers the raider took. Why did he concentrate on the files beginning D, E, F and G?'

'He wanted all the files to begin with.'

'But when he realised how many there were, he narrowed it down to that group. What does that tell you?'

'I don't understand.'

'Does it not suggest that he was after the papers belonging to a particular person, but he didn't want to alert you by asking for that person by name? Is that not a reasonable conclusion to draw?'

'I don't see where all this is getting us.'

'You will in a moment.'

Megarry waved his hand to disperse the smoke hanging like a fog above the desk. 'You enjoy a game of poker, I understand. Serious stuff? What sort of stakes are we talking about?'

There was a gasp. This time it seemed the policeman had gone too far.

'Get out,' Glendinning spluttered. He started up from his seat. 'I don't have to sit in my own office and listen to this sort of abuse.' His fingers trembled as he reached for the phone. 'I'm going to report you, Mr Megarry, I'm going to report you to your superiors.'

Megarry's hand settled like a clamp across the manager's wrist. He took the phone and replaced it on the cradle. 'Let's not do anything rash.'

Glendinning stared.

'I know someone's been leaning on you,' Megarry said,

'Probably a gambling debt. I know this someone asked you for information about a client. Personal information that could only be got from the documents taken in the raid.'

The manager opened his mouth but no sound came out.

'Now, I want you to tell me who that someone was. And I want the client's name.'

6

Morgan got off the bus near the cinema and waited for a gap in the traffic before scurrying across the road towards the park. At the railings, he paused to catch his breath. The light was dying and the sky, through the distant trees, seemed like blue glass. Some kids were playing football deep in the park and their cries were carried back to him, echoing on the night air.

A queue was forming outside the cinema, mainly house-wives gossiping as they waited for the doors to open for the evening bingo session. Morgan hurried past them, keeping his head low, and on past the loungers, hanging about in the pool of light outside Donnelly's pub. A couple of drunks were arguing noisily over a carryout of beer and a lone newspaper boy carried an armful of *Belfast Telegraph*s. When Morgan came to Beechmount Avenue, he turned right and entered the maze of narrow streets.

He knew the area well and had no difficulty finding the club – a grim structure with a grey, featureless exterior, bars on the windows and reinforced steel shutters on the doors. He had seen the same building many times in the ghettoes – a functional warehouse with a bar on the ground floor and a scattering of committee rooms above.

Morgan pushed open the door. There was a hum of voices

and, as he stepped inside, a low rattle of drums and a burst of applause.

A function, which looked to Morgan like a wedding reception, was on. Despite the dim light, he saw that the room was packed with sweating bodies, men and women in their Sunday best. As he closed the door, a man in a tuxedo spoke into a microphone and a band began to play. Couples got up to dance.

Morgan made his way to the counter and waited while the solitary barman tried to satisfy the clamour for drink. At last he caught the man's attention. The man bent his head and tried to listen above the din.

'I was to see Mr Cronin here.'

'Mr Cronin?'

'That's right.'

The barman examined him for a moment. 'It's upstairs,' he said at last and pointed to a door at the end of the room. 'Go through there. It's the room facing you at the top of the stairs. Mr Cronin's up there now.'

The man moved away and began to prepare a pint of beer. Morgan checked his watch: five to eight. He edged through the dancing crowd and made his way through a draughty hall and to the top of some narrow stairs. When he got to the room, he paused; he could feel his heart begin to pound. He could turn back now. Turn and go down the stairs and out into the cold night. Nothing would happen. No one would say a word. No one would even know. He could just pick up the rhythm of his life where it had been before Mr Cronin came calling.

Or he could go into the room and get involved in God knows what; set off down a road that could take him anywhere – a road bound to be strewn with hazards, pitted with danger.

Suddenly he felt the same surge of excitement, the same rush he'd felt when he'd stolen the car and the stocky little sergeant had waved him through the roadblock. He reached out and rapped sharply on the door. A voice called, 'Come in.' He pressed down the handle and entered the room.

It was a large committee room and Morgan's first impression was how cold it was, as if someone had forgotten to turn on the heat. Mr Cronin sat at a table beside a window which looked down into the street. There were two young men and a girl with him. They turned and stared, and Morgan could see from the smile on Mr Cronin's face that Mr Cronin was glad he had come.

'Sean.' Mr Cronin got up from his seat and came forward with his hand stretched out in welcome. 'Good man yourself, glad to see you. You'd no problem finding the place?'

Morgan opened his mouth to reply, but Mr Cronin had started to draw him forward into the circle around the table. 'Let me introduce you. This is Queenie.'

A dark-haired young woman in her early twenties smiled up at him. He noticed her blue eyes and the confident way she looked at him. Then Mr Cronin was pulling him away again and introducing the two men.

'And these pair are Peter and Kevin.'

The men stood up and nodded. Then everyone shook hands and sat down again and waited awkwardly for Mr Cronin to continue. Morgan sneaked a glance at the men. They were in their late teens or early twenties and obviously ill at ease.

'Well, now, boys a boys.' Mr Cronin rubbed his hands and examined his watch. 'Eight o'clock. Spot on. Everybody's very punctual. That's a good sign. That's a very good sign. Time-keeping's going to be very important on this operation. Remember that. Time-keeping is vital.' He rubbed his hands again. 'But we'll get to that later. First things first. I want everybody to relax, okay? I want everybody to feel at home.' He sniffed and rapped the table with his knuckles. 'We're going to be a team. That's what we're going to be. Every single one of you playing a part in the overall operation. Every single one of you important. The whole job depending on each individual. Know what I mean?'

Morgan felt a glow of pride. He was part of a team. He was important. He glanced again at the girl and then at Mr Cronin, who was speaking once more. 'I want to say a few words about security. Security is crucial. Security is the most important aspect of this whole operation. I cannot say that often enough. Security is the rock on which this job will succeed or perish.' He paused to allow the information to sink in. 'You have each been

71

chosen because you bring some individual talent. But you also have something in common. You're clean. You have no criminal records. The Brits know nothing about you. That's vitally important. Keep it that way. From here on, as long as you're a member of this team, I want you to adopt a low profile. Don't do anything that would draw attention to yourself. Stay out of trouble. Keep sober. Alcohol loosens the tongue and loose talk costs lives. Remember that.'

He waved his finger in the air, and Morgan noticed that the earlier banter had evaporated. This was serious talking. 'We'll be meeting here regularly while we're planning this operation. You should be careful when coming and going. If you have a car, leave it behind. Use public transport. Cars can be followed and their movements monitored.' His eyes travelled around the group and rested on Morgan. 'That particularly applies to you, Sean.'

Morgan felt his face burn but Mr Cronin was already moving on. 'We don't use surnames in this team. It means that if anyone is caught and interrogated, he won't be able to betray the others. Remember, you can't tell what you don't know.'

Morgan glanced again at the faces, which seemed to be following Mr Cronin as if hypnotised, as if he were a sorcerer who'd stolen their wits, and he found himself falling into line. Mr Cronin's voice was low and coaxing, easing away doubts, dispelling fears.

'Not that there's any danger,' he heard Mr Cronin say, and he remembered their conversation in the Bernardo Grill. 'That's just a precaution. Just in case. Just something we have to go through. Just part of the routine. Now.' He rapped the table again. 'The operation itself. The reason we're all here tonight.'

Mr Cronin lifted a scuffed briefcase from the floor and took out a road map and a photograph. 'When I've finished explaining, you'll realise that nothing can go wrong. It'll go like clockwork, just like taking candy from a baby.'

He lifted the photograph, a grainy picture, obviously taken from a distance and printed up to portrait size.

'Before we start, I want you to have a good look at that.' He handed the picture to Morgan.

72

It was a photograph of a young girl. She was wearing a school uniform and staring into the camera. Morgan reckoned she was about twelve or thirteen, pale face, blonde hair blown back in the wind. He felt his heart skip a beat and thought again of the danger he was getting into. But the others didn't seem to notice; they were pressing forward to have a look.

'Pass it along,' Mr Cronin said. 'I want you to study it closely. Memorise it.'

The party in the bar was breaking up when Morgan finally made his way out of the club. The band had stopped playing and were busy dismantling the equipment and packing away the instruments. The barman was wearily making his round of the tables, harrying the knots of stragglers who were reluctant to let the evening come to a close.

Outside, the night felt fresh and cool. The cloud had shifted and a handful of stars hung in the sky. Morgan hurried through the empty streets, turning over in his mind what he had seen and heard at the meeting. He felt confused: one minute experiencing a burst of excitement, an impatience to get to grips with the operation, then a stab of apprehension, a doubt, a premonition of danger.

Mr Cronin's words kept ringing in his head: This was an important operation – a big job with a lot depending on it – more than Mr Cronin could safely say – more than it was wise they should know. When Morgan had heard that, he filled with pride. They were relying on him. They had confidence in him.

But he also had doubts. Mr Cronin had sounded sure. Nothing can go wrong, he had said, just like taking candy from a baby. But maybe that was just to buoy them up, keep their spirits high. He had returned again and again to security. It was the rock on which the operation would succeed or perish. Why had he stressed security so much if nothing could go wrong?

After a while, Morgan heard the rumble of traffic and began to see the lights of the main road shining in the dark. As he turned out of Beechmount Avenue, he heard footsteps close behind. Alarmed, he spun around to see a figure in a leather jacket almost on top of him. He raised his arm and immediately heard laughter and a woman's soft voice calling his name. It was Queenie.

She was almost out of breath. 'Slow down, can't you?' she said, 'I've nearly bust a gut trying to catch up with you. My god, but you can fairly travel.'

Morgan was embarrassed, 'I didn't know.'

'Are you deaf as well? I've been shouting at you, but you just bowled along with your head down low, all wrapped up in your own thoughts.'

She stopped, panting. 'Where are you going to anyway?'

Morgan told her.

'Well, that's all right then. I've got to get to Clonard. It's the same way. We can travel together.'

She looked into his face and he saw again the confident blue eyes, the nose turned up just a fraction too much, the firm white teeth in the wide mouth. Suddenly she laughed and took Morgan's arm.

'You don't mind, do you? I'll keep you company. C'mon, you can tell me all about yourself.'

'What do you want to know?' Morgan asked tentatively.

'Got a job? What do you do for a living?'

'I'm a barman.'

She seemed impressed. 'Are you now? That's a handy wee number. And do you work days? I thought barmen worked mainly at night.'

'I do both,' Morgan said, 'it's flexible. At the moment, I'm working days. It suits me better. I can attend the meetings.'

'Ah,' she said. 'Of course. That makes sense.'

They had reached the bus-stop. He leaned against the metal pole and examined her in the light from the lamp-post. She was about the same height as he, stocky with broad shoulders like a boy. A thought occurred to him and he put up a hand to stop her speaking.

'Do you think we should be going on like this? After what Mr Cronin said about security?'

She pulled a face. 'He didn't say we weren't to talk to each other.'

'Nevertheless. Maybe we should just go our separate ways.'

She looked at him and he saw an anger in her eyes. 'Hump you,' she said, 'if that's how you feel, I can walk home alone.'

She turned away and, on impulse, he reached out and held her hand.

'No, don't go. I'm sorry.'

She shook herself free. 'You need to get a grip on yourself. Who do you think you are?'

'I'm sorry,' Morgan said again. 'I was only thinking of what Mr Cronin said. About security.'

'What about it? Talking to me isn't going to do any harm. Look, if the Brits ever pick you up, they'll give you such a hiding that you'll tell them anything they want to hear. Just so they stop. That's how they get most of their convictions.'

Morgan found himself repeating Mr Cronin's words. 'But you can't tell what you don't know.'

'You know a lot already. You know enough to sabotage the whole damn thing if you wanted to.' Suddenly she laughed again. 'Relax, for God's sake. It's not going to happen. Who's going to suspect a guy like you?'

His face burned. 'What do you mean?'

'Your legs. The Brits look at you and they think you're harmless. Why do you think Cronin asked you in the first place? He's not stupid. He knew what he was doing.'

The words struck Morgan like a blow.

'He asked me because I can drive. I stole the car we're going to use. I'm a good driver. That's why he chose me.' He found himself blurting out the information, desperately trying to impress her.

'I'm sure you can drive; I've no doubt. But Mr Cronin picked you because he knew you wouldn't come under suspicion. That's the real reason.'

Morgan's heart sank. Maybe what she was saying was true. Maybe Mr Cronin was taking advantage of his disability. The thought made him angry. He felt her hand, cold against his cheek.

'Don't take it personally. I didn't mean to hurt your feelings. He picked me for the same reason, I'm a nurse in the Royal. He thinks that puts me above suspicion as well.'

'And why are you doing it?'

'Because I want to get back at the Brits. I want to hurt them.'

'Why?'

'Does there have to be a reason? I hate the bastards. This is our country and yet we're treated like second-class citizens. You can't walk the streets without getting stopped and searched. You see them swaggering round with their fucking rifles as if they owned the place. Stopping young lads and pushing them up against the wall. This is our country, they shouldn't be here.'

'But that's all negative stuff,' Morgan said.

'So what? It's good enough.'

'What about all the discrimination, the unemployment? All the things that are wrong with the system?'

'What about them?'

'Don't you want to change it? Make a new society, a better world for everyone?'

He thought he saw the shadow of a smile in the corner of her mouth. 'Maybe.'

'There's so much injustice, so many things wrong.'

'And you think it'll change if we get the Brits out?'

'At least we'd be able to run our own affairs.'

She shook her head. 'That's no guarantee of anything.'

'But it's never been tried. Not properly. If the Brits were gone, we could have a society where people treated each other with decency and respect. Protestants and Catholics. No discrimination, no division.'

'You're a dreamer,' she said.

He felt confused, unsure whether she was laughing at him. He began to protest, 'but it takes dreamers. It takes people with some ...'

'Jesus,' she said, cutting him short and looking at her watch. 'I think we've missed the shagging bus. I think the bastard's gone.'

'We can get a taxi,' Morgan said.

'No we can't. We'll walk. C'mon.' She grabbed his arm and pulled him away from the bus-stop. 'It's not far. And it's a lovely night. We can stop at my place. I'll make you coffee.'

Morgan found himself walking. She intrigued him. There was about her some wild disregard, an honesty that excited him.

'Are you sure Mr Cronin would think it okay?' But he knew before he finished speaking what her reaction would be.

'Hump you and Mr Cronin,' she said, with a smile.

7

'Flatman,' said Megarry. 'Odd name, I don't think I've come across it before.'

He sat down at the corner of Nelson's desk and rummaged for his cigarettes.

'Flatman?' Nelson looked confused. 'Who's Flatman? What are you talking about, Cecil?'

'The guy they were looking for, his name is Flatman. First name Marius. He lives in Lisburn. I have his address.'

'You mean the bank robbery?'

'Yesss.'

Megarry leaned over and ruffled the younger man's hair. 'What a bright spark you are, John. You pick things up so quickly. Mr Flatman is the man they were after. It was because of him that the bank was robbed and all those documents taken. Plus the nine thousand pounds. Which, as I suspected, was only incidental.'

Nelson put down a file he'd been reading. 'How do you know this?'

'Glendinning told me.'

'And why didn't he tell us the first time we talked to him?'

'Because ...' Megarry took out a cigarette and tapped it on the box, 'he needed to be persuaded. But he came round in the end. Let's say he saw my point of view. Mr Glendinning has a problem.'

He struck a match and blew out a wreath of smoke. 'He's a gambler. It's a dangerous sideline for someone in his position. It leaves him wide open to pressure. People can lean on him.'

Across the desk, Nelson was clearly impressed. 'And that's what happened?'

'Of course. A man called Maxi Matthews.' Megarry tossed the match into the ashtray. 'Glendinning plays poker regularly, most of his free time in fact. This guy Matthews is one of his partners, and it turns out that Glendinning has built up a sizeable gambling debt to Matthews. It runs into several thousand pounds. Glendinning can't repay that sort of money all at once. So Matthews has him over a barrel. A couple of months ago, Matthews approached Glendinning with a strange request. He wanted to know if the bank had an account for a man named Marius Flatman. This, of course, is confidential information and Glendinning had a big problem. Matthews pressed him, and hinted that the bank authorities might be interested to learn about Glendinning's gambling debt. After much soul-searching, Glendinning agreed to check the files and pass over the information. But like all blackmailers, Matthews wasn't satisfied. A week or so later he was back with another request. Had Mr Flatman any personal documents lodged with the bank in a security account? Again, Glendinning demurred and again Matthews leaned on him. In the end, it didn't seem to Glendinning that it was a big deal, because he had broken the rules by giving details of the client's account in the first place. So he passed on the information that Mr Flatman did indeed have personal documents lodged in their safety vault.'

Megarry paused. 'This story gets weirder. Matthews came back a third time and asked Glendinning if he could extract the documents, or copies of them, but Glendinning decided that enough was enough. He wasn't going in any deeper. He told Matthews that if he didn't back off, he was going to make a clean breast of the whole business to the police. Matthews got the message and left Glendinning alone. Ten days later, what do you think happens?'

'The bank gets hit?'

'Bingo.'

Megarry lifted a folder off the desk. 'I've gone through this list. People who had documents taken in the raid and lo and behold ...'

'Flatman?'

'Exactly.' Megarry flicked the file open and read: 'Marius E Flatman. Permanent Address: St Mary's, Orchard Gardens, Epsom, Surrey. Present Address: Windnook, Ingledale Road, Lisburn, County Antrim. Items taken: birth certificates, self, wife and child; marriage certificate; insurance policies on self, wife and child; insurance policy on premises at Orchard Gardens, Epsom; lease on premises at Ingledale Road, Lisburn; insurance policy on contents ...' He stopped. 'It's amazing. They rob a bank to get this stuff. What for?'

'Mr Flatman must be important,' Nelson said. 'Who is he exactly?'

'Nobody seems to know.' Megarry stubbed out the cigarette and crushed it with his thumb so that the tobacco spilt. 'Most of his business with the bank seems to be conducted by letter. Nobody remembers setting eyes on him ever. Very odd, isn't it?'

'He must be on the telephone, at least,' Nelson said reaching for the book.

'No.' Megarry shook his head.' I've checked. 'There are six Flatmans listed, but he isn't one of them.'

'Are you sure you've been told everything?'

'I think so. In the end Glendinning seemed to be relieved to get it all off his chest. I think he told me everything there was to know.'

'In that case, there's only one person who can help us now. Do you know where we can find him?'

'He runs a snooker hall out beyond Greencastle.'

'Well,' said Nelson, 'what are we waiting for?'

Nelson drove and Megarry sat in the back seat as if he were in a taxi. At intervals he spoke to the younger man's reflection in the rearview mirror. This was an arrangement they had developed over the months before he was suspended from duty. From Megarry's viewpoint it had certain advantages: he could turn the day's events over in his mind, and pull together the threads of an investigation while Nelson negotiated the traffic like a chauffeur. When they stopped for lunch, he could have that extra glass. In the days when he was drinking heavily, this was no small consideration.

It had been a dull morning, heavy and overcast, threatening rain. But the rain hadn't come and now the cloud had lifted and the sun was beginning to struggle through. Megarry wound down the window to let in some air.

'How did you find out that Glendinning was a gambler?' Nelson asked. He stretched his neck slightly in order to observe Megarry, who had slumped back in his seat and closed his eyes as if he were going to sleep.

'Clinch told me.'

'Did he indeed? Hardly the action of a loyal servant, was it?'

'No, it was downright disloyal. But I encouraged him. He's an ambitious bugger, you must have noticed that.'

'And how did you know that Glendinning was being pressurised?'

'I guessed. I knew that someone in there had passed information. Someone in a senior position who had access to clients' accounts. That's why the raiders knew where to go and what to look for. And once Clinch told me that his boss was practically addicted to stud poker, well ... it was only a matter of putting two and two together.'

'So what'll happen to him?'

'I don't know yet. Technically speaking, he's assisted in the robbery of his own bank. I could charge him. But if I did that, the poor devil would be destroyed.'

'Maybe he should have thought of that.'

'Oh come on, John.' Megarry struggled upright. 'It was such a small thing. He wasn't to know where the information was going to end up or what use it would be put to. He was asked a question and a gun was put to his head. Who knows how anyone would react in those circumstances?'

'I thought he was arrogant, arrogant and rude. The way he

treated his secretary, and Clinch too for that matter. He struck me as a very unpleasant man. I haven't much sympathy for him.'

'Sometimes arrogance is a sign of weakness. Sometimes it's a camouflage. Underneath it, Mr Glendinning is a very vulnerable man. I feel sorry for him.'

'You're getting soft,' Nelson said, 'you're losing your edge.'

He watched Megarry in the rearview mirror, wary of how he might react, but he merely leaned back on the seat and Nelson heard him sigh. 'Compassion, John. It's one of the cardinal virtues. You are a young man, you have a lot to learn. Why don't you just drive?'

They left the main road with its trees and fields and turned inland; after a while the car slowed and they entered an estate. It was a dismal place, row after row of porridge-coloured houses, the bleak horizon broken now and then by patches of green where gangs of kids kicked football on the trampled grass. Megarry watched as they passed a supermarket and an off-licence, their walls scarred with obscene graffiti. He put a hand on Nelson's arm and pointed. 'Over there, I think.'

It had once been a cinema. Now it was a snooker hall. The foyer had been ripped out and a phalanx of pinball machines blocked the entrance. A couple of skinheads in training suits and runners watched as they pulled the car into the forecourt.

Megarry scanned the road, then felt for his shoulder holster. He took out a small revolver, broke it open and checked the chamber. He snapped the weapon together again and replaced it in its pouch. He spoke to Nelson. 'The Star Snooker Hall, proprietor Mr Maxi Matthews. I wonder if he's around?'

He opened the car door and stepped into the pale afternoon sun. They had been climbing steadily since they left the city and down below he could see a tug-boat anchored on the blue glass of the lough. On the other side, the Castlereagh Hills brooded, purple and dark.

Megarry bent to speak to Nelson. 'Just keep the engine running. Watch for anything suspicious. If there's any danger, give a blast on the horn. I won't be long.'

The skinheads at the entrance stood aside reluctantly to let him pass and he entered a dark cavern where the overwhelming smell was damp and disinfectant. He waited until his eyes were accustomed to the gloom, listening to the soft clack of billiard balls.

There were rows of tables, each with a long shade pitching light down on to the green baize, but only some were in use. Megarry counted half a dozen before his eyes shifted to a little counter where he saw a skinny man in a torn cardigan, smoking a cigarette and observing him.

Megarry made his way across. The man straightened up as he approached and blew out smoke through tar-stained teeth. 'Are you a member?'

'No,' Megarry said.

'Then you can't play.'

'That's all right, I don't want to play.'

'So what *do* you want?'

'Just looking for someone,' Megarry said. 'I was told he might be here: Mr Maxi Matthews. You know somebody of that name?'

He let his coat fall open so that the butt of the revolver was visible in its leather pouch. The man's attitude changed immediately; he retreated from the counter, putting his hands up before him like a shield.

'I don't want any trouble.'

'Neither do I. My name's Megarry. I'm a police officer. But Mr Matthews doesn't know me … yet.'

'He's n-n-not here,' the man said tripping over the words in his panic.

'When will he be back?'

'I don't know. Sometimes he doesn't come in at all. I only mind the place, I don't know his movements.' The man's hand trembled as he stubbed out the cigarette. 'I can tell him you called.'

'No,' Megarry said, 'that won't do. I need to see him … now. Do you know where he is?'

The man shook his head and Megarry could see the fear in his face. 'I don't know anything. I just come in here and open up and take the cash and so on. I don't want to get involved in nothing.'

'This is important,' Megarry said, 'I might have to bring you in.'

'Please,' the man said,' I can't help you. Maybe if you came back again?'

Megarry became aware of silence in the hall. The billiard players had stopped and were standing in little knots, staring in his direction. The tension suddenly shifted to menace. Megarry felt a draught, a chill like a breeze. He spun round quickly to see a small, fat man in a charcoal suit come through the door.

The man stood for a moment and the bright light from the street filtered past him and into the hall. Then, realising that something was wrong, he made a dash for the entrance.

'Hey,' Megarry shouted and started after him. The players scattered to let him pass. He watched the man's round bottom disappear through the foyer and the doors swing closed behind him.

'Stop,' Megarry shouted, and found himself struggling for breath.

From his vantage point in the car, Nelson had watched the man go into the building.

A few minutes later the doors flew open and the roly-poly legs came bouncing down the steps again and out into the forecourt. The man darted across the yard towards a blue Volvo, hopping like a gigantic bird, his jacket flapping behind him.

Nelson let out the clutch and the car moved to intercept him. The doors of the hall opened once more and Megarry appeared waving his arms. The little man stopped, then began running towards a low boundary wall.

As Nelson swung the car directly across his path, he stopped, sweat shining like oil on his plump face.

'Maxi Matthews?'

The man didn't speak.

'You better get into the car,' Nelson said as Megarry arrived, his white shirt hanging from his waistband and his breath coming in laboured gasps.

'Now, Mr Matthews.' Megarry held out a mug of tea. It was stained brown along the edges and had a chipped handle and a picture of the queen in satirical pose with a rude caption painted in bright letters. He couldn't remember where they'd picked it up.

'Do you take sugar?'

Matthews grasped the mug and shook his head. During the journey from Greencastle, he had sat squeezed in the back seat with Megarry, a revolver close to his ribs, his face turned to the window as the streets of the city flashed by. No one had spoken.

'We need to ask you a few questions, Mr Matthews. Or may we call you Maxi?'

'Call me what you like.'

Megarry bent forward and peered closely into Matthew's face at the little pig's eyes stuck in the fat white flesh.

'What does Maxi stand for?'

'Maximilian.'

'Ah,' Megarry said, as if a vast mystery had been explained. 'Of course. He was a Mexican emperor, wasn't he? I think he met a sticky end. Shot, wasn't he?'

Matthews blinked. 'I don't know.'

'Oh, they did, Maxi. Put him up against a wall. One last cigarette and then Pfff, blew him away. But that was long ago, things are more civilised now.'

Matthews grasped the mug with both hands and took a long drink of tea. Megarry noticed the rings, five of them, silver and gold, pressing tight into his chubby fingers.

'Although I'm not convinced about some of these people you've been knocking around with.'

'What do you mean?'

'I'm not sure just how civilised they are. I understand they get up to some very nasty stuff – robbing banks, blackmail, murder from time to time.'

'I don't know what you're talking about.'

'I think you do, Maxi. Let's start at the beginning, shall we?

You play poker with Brian Glendinning, don't you? He owes you money. Almost three thousand pounds, I understand.'

'What's that got to do with anything? It's not illegal.'

'No, gambling's not illegal, providing you observe certain regulations. That's not what I had in mind. You approached him a few months ago looking for information about a client of the bank – Mr Flatman, Marius E. Flatman.'

'Did I?' Matthews put the mug down on the table and examined his fingernails.

Across the desk, Nelson had a notebook open and a pencil ready.

'I'm told that you did.'

'I don't remember,' Matthews said, without looking up.

'You made the first request on the third of September, that was a Saturday. You made the second request on the eighth of September. You phoned Mr Glendinning at work. He got the impression that you were threatening him.'

'What could have given him that idea?'

'The fact that you referred to the debt and hinted that you might bring it to the attention of his superiors in the bank. Did you say that?'

'He's imagining things,' Matthews said. 'He owes me money. I'm entitled to get my money, aren't I? Just because I mention the subject doesn't mean I'm threatening him.'

'It's the way you put it. Mr Glendinning is an intelligent man. I don't think he'd imagine a thing like this. You know that threatening someone is a serious offence?'

'It would be if I'd done it. I just told you, he's imagining it.'

'All right,' Megarry said wearily, 'what's Marius Flatman got to do with all this?'

'I never heard of him.'

'Glendinning says you asked for information about him.'

'He's lying.'

Matthews looked up. His pig's eyes had an air of confidence; the fear seemed to have evaporated. I'm being too soft, Megarry thought, Nelson is right. I'm losing my edge. This guy is sitting here and he's laughing at me.

Matthews spread his fingers again, like little sausages. On

impulse, Megarry bunched his fist and brought it down hard on the man's hand. For a moment the little eyes popped in disbelief and then, as the pain shot through his arm, he opened his mouth and screamed.

'What's the matter?' Megarry said. 'Something bothering you?'

Matthews had his hand tucked under his armpit and was crouching away from Megarry. Fear was back in his eyes.

'You're after thumping my hand.'

'What?'

'My hand.' Matthews shook his fingers free, and blew on them in an effort to ease the pain.

'I never touched you,' Megarry said innocently. He appealed to Nelson. 'Did you see me thumping anything, John?'

Nelson shook his head. 'Nothing.'

'There you are, Maxi. Nobody saw a thing. You must have imagined it. Same way as Glendinning imagined you were asking questions about Flatman.'

He raised his fist again and Matthews wriggled free of the chair and struggled to stand up. Megarry placed a hand on his shoulder and pressed him back into his seat. 'What are you getting excited about? We haven't started yet.'

'Please,' Matthews said.

'Please what?'

'Don't hit me.'

'Who's talking about hitting you, Maxi?'

Megarry raised his fist once more and watched as Matthews tried to take cover. Slowly he let his arm drop and felt in his pocket for cigarettes.

'Would you like to try again? Like to refresh your memory? Why were you so interested in Mr Flatman?'

'Please,' Matthews said again.

'Yes?' Megarry selected a cigarette and made a fuss about lighting it. He snapped the lighter shut and blew out a cloud of smoke.

'This isn't easy,' Matthews said. He looked from one policeman to the other. 'This is dangerous stuff.'

Megarry pulled out a chair and sat down where he could look into Matthews' face.

'Just tell us, Maxi.'

'But who'll protect me?'

'We'll protect you. What are you worried about?'

'What am I worried about? Jesus.' He shook his head as if he couldn't believe what he heard. 'I'm worried about ending up with my head in a bag down a country lane somewhere.'

'It won't come to that. Just answer some questions. Here.'

Megarry took out the cigarettes and pushed them across the table, but Matthews waved them away. 'I don't smoke.'

'Why were you interested in Marius Flatman?'

Matthews took a deep breath and his chest inflated like a tyre. He expelled it in a slow release through his nostrils and looked again at Megarry, as if trying to make up his mind.

'Because some guys asked me.'

'To do what exactly?'

'To check if he had an account with the Great Northern Bank. They seemed to know a fair bit about him already. They knew I played poker with Glendinning.'

'How did they know that?'

'I suppose I might have mentioned it or maybe they picked it up somewhere.'

'And you passed over the information?'

'Yes.'

Nelson had started scribbling in his notepad.

'Who were these guys, Maxi?'

'Some men who came into the snooker hall.'

'But you know who they are?'

Matthews looked alarmed. 'Jesus, no. How would I know them?'

'C'mon, Maxi. You're telling me that some people walk off the street and you break your neck to get information for them?'

'I know who they represent,' Matthews said, 'but I don't know them. Do you understand me?' He spread his hands and appealed to Megarry.

'Paramilitaries?'

'That's right.'

Megarry sighed. 'So you couldn't identify these people? You couldn't put a name to them?'

'No,' Matthews said. 'No way. I wouldn't know them again if they walked in that door.'

'You disappoint me,' Megarry said.

'I'm sorry about that, but I want to stay alive.'

'Who is Flatman? Why were they interested in him?'

'I don't know.'

'Maxi, I don't like this, your memory is letting you down. You'll have to try again. Who is Flatman?'

Matthews' face twisted once more in an expression of pain. 'Jeeesuss,' he said.

'Who is he?'

'He's a Brit officer.'

'Yes?'

'A big wheel. Senior Intelligence.'

He spat out the information, then folded his arms and lowered his head as if he had said too much.

'A Brit officer?'

'That's right.'

'How do you know this?'

'Because they told me.'

'The men who came into the snooker hall?'

'Yes.'

Megarry exchanged glances with Nelson.

'And why did they want to know about his affairs?'

'So they could confirm who he was. They wanted to be sure they'd got the right guy.'

'Of course,' Megarry said. Suddenly it was blindingly obvious. He pulled his chair closer to Matthews and whispered into his face.

'One last thing, Maxi. What are they planning to do with him?'

Matthews stared at the policeman as if the question showed enormous naivety. He shrugged his shoulders, and the folds of fat around his cheeks shivered.

'I don't know. What do they normally do?'

Harvey was behind a bank of files when they called. His desk was littered with papers, books, boxes, overflowing ashtrays. He looked up and scowled, Megarry guessed that he was still fed up at having Nelson taken away.

'I'm about to close,' Harvey said. He pulled back his sleeve to uncover a hairy arm, and glanced at his watch. 'In fact I should have been gone already.' He started to get up from his chair but Megarry put out a hand to restrain him.

'I need to talk to you. It'll only take a minute.'

Harvey let his gaze travel between the two men, then slowly settled back into his seat.

'Make it snappy. I'm on a work-to-rule until I get a new assistant. I'm working strictly nine to five. This is one guy who isn't going out of here in a box.' He pointed a chubby finger at his chest and shot a disdainful glance at Nelson, who was standing in the cramped doorway.

Megarry sat down in the one available chair. The place smelt dank and airless. The single light bulb cast a gleam on Harvey's head. Harvey took the three phones off their cradles one by one, and let them lie among the rubble on his desk. He looked up, grinned and showed a mouthful of bad teeth.

'What is it you want?'

'You still have contacts in Military Intelligence?'

'I might have.'

'You've done it for me before.'

Harvey shrugged. 'These people come and go. It depends what it is.'

'I need some dope on a guy, name of Marius. E. Flatman. I can give you all the usual details. D. O. B., address, etc.'

'It seems you've got a lot of dope already. What do you want to know?'

'I want to know who he is, what he does. I'm told he might be a senior British officer. I want to know if he's important.'

'How important?'

'Important enough to kill.'

'They're all important enough to kill,' Harvey said. He searched for a pen and paper and pushed them across to Megarry. 'When do you need this information?'

'Urgently.'

'Of course. I shouldn't have asked.'

He took the paper back and examined it. Then he looked up and slowly shook his head. 'You see, this just proves what I've always said. I get starved of resources. Nobody gives a damn. I'm left here struggling on my own while you guys are out there chasing the exciting cases. And *where* is the first place you come when you've got a problem?'

He looked at Megarry and there was a childlike innocence in his eyes.

'Please,' Megarry said.

'Leave it with me,' said Harvey, 'I'll see what I can do.'

They walked up the stairs to Megarry's office. It was now dark outside and from the big window the lights of the city looked like so many stars in the sky. Megarry sat down at his desk and pulled out the whiskey bottle and, with it, two stained coffee mugs.

He was tired. It had been an eventful day. As he sat with the evening coming down over the city, the realisation came to him that he had become drawn into this case which he had embarked upon so reluctantly. Maybe he had known all along that this would happen. Perhaps he should have refused Drysdale's invitation at the outset. Drysdale had been clever, skilfully setting a trap to lure him in. All that sweet-talk about how good he was and how much they had missed him, the promises that he would be left alone, no more interference from meddling busybodies – how long would that last? Perhaps he should have stuck to his decision to take early retirement. It was what Kathleen wanted.

He thought of the life they would have. There would be more time to do the things put aside in the hurlyburly of his career so far. They could travel, there was the garden, reading. Maybe he'd take up bowling, his father's pastime before he had been killed. He thought of those warm summer nights on village greens, the creased white trousers and blazers, the camaraderie. And afterwards on the way home, a couple of restful pints in some old-fashioned country pub. It could be a pleasant life.

Nelson's voice spoke in the darkened room. 'Maybe we should warn Flatman?'

Megarry sat up and unscrewed the cap of the whiskey bottle. 'Of what exactly?'

'That somebody is planning to murder him.'

'But that's only guesswork, John.' Megarry poured a measure into the cup and pushed it across to the younger man. 'All we know for certain is that they robbed a bank to get his personal papers. And he has already been told that by the bank.'

'What about what Matthews said?'

'What *did* Matthews say?'

'He hinted that they were going to murder Flatman.'

Megarry shook his head, 'Matthews doesn't know anything. He was just a runner for these people, a very minor cog. He's not in on the planning.'

'Well, whatever it is, you can be sure it's not good,' Nelson said. He took a sip of whiskey. 'If I was in Flatman's shoes, I'd like to be told.'

'Slow down. You're jumping to conclusions. If Flatman really is a British officer, then he lives with murder all the time. Just like you and me. Presumably he takes the same precautions.'

'Nevertheless ...'

'Nevertheless nothing. We can't scare the wits out of some poor devil without good reason. And if he *is* a member of the security forces, I want to be on firmer ground before I approach him. I don't want to go barging in making a fool of myself.'

He finished his whiskey and lifted the bottle again.

'But we can't just sit and wait for it to happen,' Nelson said.

'Nobody said that. You're not listening. I said I wanted to be on firmer ground. We know nothing about this man – what he looks like, what he does. Why he's living at a private house and not in barracks where they normally live. We don't even know for sure that he's a British officer. We only have Matthews' word for that.'

He poured a generous measure and held the bottle out, but Nelson waved it away.

'In fact, there is something you can do. You can go to Lisburn and check him out.'

'Do what exactly?'

'Keep an eye on him. Watch the house. See if you can find out a bit more about him. You could go tomorrow morning, early, before anything stirs. Log everything that moves. In and out. Times, details. If anyone leaves, follow them. Wait until they're safely back home again. And be discreet.'

He searched his desk until he found Flatman's address. 'Take field glasses. Get the canteen to make you some sandwiches in case it's a long day and take a mobile phone. I'll be here. If you need to report anything, give me a ring.'

He sat back once more and closed his eyes, and for a moment it seemed that he had dropped off to sleep. He thought again of the bowling tournaments, of his father sitting beside him in the passenger seat while Megarry drove through country lanes white with hawthorn blossom, the air heavy with the scent of cut grass. He had been killed before Megarry had a chance to say how much he loved him, the words he once thought would be so hard and would now find so simple. And his death had changed Megarry's career, set him off on a course that had dominated his life. Maybe Kathleen was right, maybe the time had come to finish it all, to draw a line and close the book.

He opened his eyes and saw that Nelson was observing him.

'You know, John, as I get older, I find that there are fewer certainties. Things appear more complicated. There are more surprises.'

Nelson said nothing.

'I had a strange experience today. I went to a security meeting for the first time in months – since before my suspension. They gave me an ovation.'

'Maybe they were glad to see you.'

'But it was so unexpected. Normally these people kick me around like an old boot. They blame Special Branch for everything that goes wrong. It's like throwing Christians to the lions. There's one guy there, name of Fleming, one of those real know-all types. Head full of shit he learnt in some military college. He's been a real bastard in the past, and today he came up to me and actually apologised.'

He took a slow sip of whiskey. 'And you know, seeing him standing there with his overcoat in his hand, trying to find the right words, I realised that he was a pathetic figure. I began to feel sorry for him.'

'Sometimes when you've been away,' Nelson said, 'people miss you. They appreciate you more.'

Megarry nodded and drained his drink.

'I'm sure you're right, John. But it makes me uneasy. It's as if the signposts have been changed. A man could get lost. At least in the old days, I knew where I stood.'

8

'How do you want me to cook this, Cecil?'

Megarry stirred himself from behind the folds of the morning paper.

'What?'

'Your fish. How do you want me to cook it?'

Kathleen held up a trout, its cold, dead eye twinkling in the morning light. She tapped a fork impatiently against the grill while she waited for him to decide. This was a new fad. Fish for breakfast instead of his usual egg. Someone had told him that there was less cholesterol in fish, better for his heart. Since his suspension, he had taken a great interest in matters relating to his health, although he was still smoking and drinking.

'Poached I think, thank you.'

He lowered his eyes to the paper again while his fingers found the cup of tea his wife had poured. It was the usual stuff, politicians sounding off about security lapses, police brutality, an overnight attack on a rural station. Nobody injured, thank god.

It made him angry, the constant vilification while every day his colleagues put their lives on the line. He was sick of politicians: the absence of leadership, the lack of vision, the fear they had of stepping out of line with the rest of the tribe or saying something conciliatory that might be seen as weakness.

Occasionally it frightened him when he read something dangerous and realised that the speaker had meant every word of it, that it wasn't just hyperbole. When that happened Megarry found himself despairing that there would ever be a peaceful solution.

The room filled with the smell of cooking fish. Kathleen put a plate down before him, then came and sat down. She had her hair combed back and tied with a velvet ribbon; it made her face look young. The sun through the kitchen window made her skin shine, and the thought struck him that she was still beautiful. After all these years, after all they'd been through together.

She cupped her face and stared at him through her fingers.

'Are you all right, Cecil?'

He put the paper down. 'Of course I am. Why do you ask?'

'Because it strikes me you've become very absent-minded of late. You don't hear what I'm saying half the time, as if there were something else on your mind. It's this case, isn't it?'

'I've just been busy.'

'It's more than that. You've become absorbed. I've seen the signs before.'

Megarry lifted his knife and fork. He took a deep breath. 'Yes,' he said, 'it's the case.'

'Tell me.'

'Well,' he sounded reluctant. She watched him cut a piece of fish and spear it with his fork. 'It's complicated, Kathleen. It's not what I thought. It's more than just a run-of-the-mill bank robbery.'

She leaned forward and stroked his wrist. 'How much more?'

'It's not about money after all. It's about people.'

He saw the disappointment in her face and rushed to reassure her. 'Look, I explained all this. I've given them no commitments. I said I'd examine this case, that's all. I've given no guarantees about anything.'

She shook her head. 'You've taken the bait, they've trapped you, just as I knew they would.'

'No,' he said, 'it's not like that. I'm doing this for myself. Because I want to.'

'Did you ever find out who asked for you to take the case?'

'No, I never did.'

'Maybe they knew what they were doing, whoever it was. Maybe they knew their man.'

'Maybe,' Megarry said. He wiped his mouth and stood up from the table.

'Are you going in today?'

'For a few hours. I won't be long.'

'We've got dinner with the Drysdales, remember.'

'Damn,' he said, 'I'd forgotten all about that. What time?'

'Eight o'clock.'

'I'll get home in plenty of time. Don't worry.'

'I won't,' she said, 'he's *your* boss.'

Nelson was awake at six thirty, having gone straight to bed and set the clock after he had dropped Megarry home. He lay for a few moments in the cold room, the jangle from the alarm beating him into bleary-eyed consciousness, then he got up and pulled the curtains to see a sky, black as ink, with not a single star. It was not an auspicious beginning, it threatened rain.

He pottered around the tiny bedsitter, assembling clothes: warm jumpers, stout shoes, a waterproof jacket. He set the kettle to boil, went to the bathroom and ran the shower until the water got tolerably warm. When he returned, he made coffee from a jar and some toast, then took out a road map and plotted his route to Ingledale Road in Lisburn. He checked his watch and saw that it was now six fifty. The roads would be empty at this hour. He would reach Lisburn in twenty minutes. He finished his meal and turned off the cooker and the lights. Outside the air felt cold and damp; a faint yellow blur brightened the sky over the lough. He started the car at the first attempt.

There was little traffic. He met a handful of lorries and an early-morning bus. On the outskirts of Lisburn, he ran into an army jeep with sleepy-looking soldiers huddled for warmth in the back. He kept his distance and waited until they turned off on the Saintfield Road, then accelerated into the town. It was slowly coming awake. One or two shops were open, their lights casting a warm glow into the empty streets. He stopped at a newsagent's where he bought a paper and then, on reflection, a couple of chocolate bars. He checked a bakery window and made a mental note to return later in the day if he needed provisions. When he turned the car into Ingledale Road the hands on the clock showed ten past seven.

It was the kind of road he had imagined it would be – a long avenue of solid houses with iron gates and sweeping drives, forbidding and silent. He couldn't envisage laughter here, or the shouts of children. The trees along the footpath had shed their leaves and the branches poked like fingers towards the bleak morning sky.

He found Windnook at last, an elegant double-fronted house set austerely atop a rolling lawn, with a grey slate roof and smoke curling from a chimney, an old-fashioned wooden garage and a single car outside the front door. He looked around for somewhere to park, and at that moment the stillness was broken by the barking of a dog. It was an eerie sound, an urgent howl bound to draw attention. He drove at once to the top of the road and turned to survey the scene once more.

As luck would have it, there was a house across the street from Windnook with a FOR SALE sign in the garden; possibly it was empty. If he could park in the driveway, it would give him a view into Flatman's house. He drove slowly back again, got out and opened the gate silently. The dog had stopped barking – gone indoors or back to sleep. He reversed the car into the driveway and turned the engine off. Just in front of him was a gnarled eucalyptus tree, its peeling branches drooping to the ground. It would provide cover. He crouched down in the passenger seat and took the glasses out of their leather case.

He had trouble focusing at first. A flash of green splashed with black, slowly emerged as a lawn and a driveway. As he grew more competent, he was able to focus on the house itself, then the windows and finally the front door. He could see now that the car parked outside was a Ford Escort. As he continued to focus the glasses, he saw something stir in the back seat of the car and realised, with a start, that it was a human arm. He crouched closer and studied the Escort again. The arm was slowly withdrawn, and then a few seconds later a head appeared, the tousled head of a man waking from sleep. Nelson watched him stretch his arms and yawn and bend below his line of vision. When he surfaced again, there was another head.

There were two of them; they'd been asleep in the car. Nelson felt his pulse begin to race. He saw the car door open and one of the men put his legs out on to the gravel of the driveway and stand up. He looked about him for a moment and then began massaging his face vigorously with his open palms. Nelson glanced at the dashboard – almost eight o'clock. It was bright now, a dull leaden brightness from a cloud-filled sky. Here and there along the road he could see lights burning in the windows. He focused the glasses on the house once again and saw that the two men had left the car and were leaning on the bonnet smoking cigarettes.

Their nearness startled him. One of them turned and Nelson ducked at once, fearing that they would spot him, then realised that he was yards away and was hidden. He watched the men again, studying their clothes. Both were dressed in anoraks, jeans and heavy roll-neck sweaters and one of them wore a woollen hat like an angler. They looked to be in their late twenties or early thirties, well built and athletic. These men, sleeping in the car in the driveway of the house, had to be guards of some kind.

He heard the purr of an engine and another car turned into the street. He lowered his head below the windscreen and held his breath. This was a more modern vehicle, a Granada. Nelson watched it drive to the gates of the house, pull in and park. Another two men got out, similar in dress and age to the men who had been sleeping in the Ford Escort. One of the men did some quick exercises on the pavement, bending and stretching and touching his toes. He had a khaki knapsack slung across his back like a hiker.

The two men who had been guarding the house were coming down the drive. Nelson watched them stop and speak to the new arrivals and one of them threw his head back and laughed.

They talked for a while, then shook hands and the first two got into the Granada and drove off leaving the new men behind. Nelson took out a notebook and began entering the details in a log, each event marked against the time.

At eight o'clock he rolled up the windows and turned on the radio, keeping the volume low while he listened to the news. There had been another murder overnight – a double killing at a farmhouse in Tyrone, a father and son. Nelson felt his stomach tighten into a knot; he thought of the widow and the family, the grief, the loss, the certain denunciations, the funerals in some windswept country graveyard. Then, inevitably, another murder somewhere else and the cycle started again. He looked at the grey morning and felt gloom descend on him. There was too much killing, too much shedding of innocent blood, as though they were all being dragged helplessly into a pit of depravity, murder feeding off murder. He listened until the newsreader had finished the report and then switched the radio off.

At ten past eight he heard another noise, a low humming sound; a milk-float sailed into the road and came to a halt a few yards from his car. He kept his head down as a schoolboy jumped down from the back and ran to the gates, setting down cartons and bottles of milk. A few minutes later, he heard the noise of the float's engine recede into the next street.

Nelson trained the glasses on the house once more. If Mr Flatman had a job somewhere, sooner or later he would have to leave for work. It was much brighter now and he could see the house and gardens clearly. The house was old, maybe a hundred years old, with ivy climbing the red brick towards the roof. On the first floor, just below the eaves, was a row of windows and he guessed that these were bedrooms. One of the windows was open, the flimsy white curtain hanging limp. He hadn't noticed it before; it was an indication that someone in the house had now got up.

Nelson allowed the glasses to trace the gravel drive and the steps down to the lawn, where someone had whitewashed the stones to make a path. To the right of the lawn was a rose garden, with a handful of blooms still in flower, and beyond that a wooden gate leading to another lawn and what looked like a tennis court. He swung the glasses back, until suddenly his vision filled with the blonde hair and soft face of a young girl. She must have come out of the house while his attention was on the garden. He adjusted the lens and studied her: she was wearing a maroon-coloured overcoat and scarf, maroon beret and white knee-length socks. Slung across her shoulder was a brown school satchel. Nelson calculated she was about twelve or thirteen. She came down the steps of the house and began chatting with one of the new men who had come on duty, but it struck Nelson that it was a formal conversation. There was nothing animated, no banter, none of the carelessness to be expected in one so young.

As he watched, there was more activity – The heavy front door opened and a tall man in a fawn overcoat appeared. He stood for a moment surveying the scene before him, then it seemed to Nelson that he said something, for the girl turned away and the man she had been speaking to stood smartly to attention and saluted. He then strode briskly to the garage and began to pull open the doors.

The tall man began talking to the girl. Nelson tried to get a fix on his face – thin, pale, with a mousy moustache like a smudge mark on his top lip. They seemed to be arguing, for the man kept waving his finger while the girl hung her head. It struck Nelson that he was reproaching her for something, perhaps for talking to the man who had gone to open the garage doors.

A shiny black Mercedes emerged and reversed to the front of the house where the driver got out and held open the passenger door. The tall man bent down and slid into the car; the girl followed. The driver settled into the driving seat.

At the same time, Nelson became aware of more activity on the road outside. He put down the field-glasses to see two BMWs pull into the avenue, drive past the house, then turn and come back. This time one stopped slightly in front of the gates, the other a little behind. The Mercedes was now coming down the drive. It swept through the gates and out on to the road sandwiched between the other two cars. There was a brief blast of a horn and the convoy moved off up the road in quick processsion. Nelson looked at his watch; it was eight thirty.

He waited until they had turned at the top of the avenue and were no longer in sight, then he eased his own car out from its hiding place and began to follow. When he reached the corner of the road, he could see the procession accelerating towards the centre of town. He put his foot down and started in pursuit. The traffic had built up and he had difficulty catching them, but when they stopped at some lights he was able to manoeuvre behind a delivery van which provided cover.

Nelson kept his distance as they went through the narrow streets of the town, slowly now because of the traffic. At the first junction, the convoy turned right and Nelson followed. The traffic began to thin out and he realised that if he had to tail them much further, it would only be a matter of time before they spotted him. They were heading away from town and out into the countryside. He passed fields with sheep and cattle, standing like pale ghosts in the grey light. A cluster of buildings came into view, modern flat-roofed structures resembling a small village, with smoke rising like a cloud from a central chimney. Nelson could see a road leading off to the left, heavy gates and what looked like a security barrier. As he watched, the cars turned off one by one and drove down the road towards the buildings. He would have to make a decision: to follow them in the certain knowledge that they would see him or to continue on the present road.

There was a hoarding at the side of the road. It stood on stilts and carried an official crest and the message in large letters. HM MINISTRY OF DEFENCE: RESTRICTED ACCESS. Nelson slowed down and watched the last car turn off towards the security gates. A soldier with a rifle came out from a bunker and bent to identify the driver. Nelson had no option but to continue driving out into the grey countryside.

It was after eleven when he finally contacted Megarry.

'Where've you been?'

'What?'

'I've been ringing you since nine o'clock. Nobody seemed to know whether you were even coming into work today.'

Megarry sounded impatient, 'I got delayed. Where are you?'

'Lisburn. I've been here since seven o'clock.'

'Anything to report?'

Nelson tried to control his excitement. 'We've got a big fish here, Cecil, a *very* big fish. Security guards on the house, a convoy into work. They're not in uniform so I assume they're SAS. I think this guy is ver-ry important.'

Megarry gave a low whistle.

'He works at the Ministry of Defence. I watched him go into work, but had to turn off because I couldn't follow them any further.'

'What's he look like?'

'Tall, thin, small moustache, dresses in civvies. But he looks like a soldier. These guards were saluting him.'

'Did they see you?'

'I don't think so. I stayed well behind. But if they're SAS they'll spot anything out of the ordinary.'

'Where are you right now?'

'Top of Ingledale Road. I can't get any closer to the house. There's nowhere to park. It's too dangerous.'

'There was a short silence, then Megarry said, 'You did good work, you did very good work. Now listen carefully. I want you to stay there until he gets home. Just note the traffic in and out of the street.' A further pause. 'And anything else you think is important.'

'When will I see you?'

'Tomorrow morning, nine o'clock in my office. I've an engagement tonight, I'm going to be tied up.'

'Okay.'

'Are you all right?' Megarry asked, 'you have enough food? is there anything you need?'

'I'm all right,' Nelson said and switched off the phone.

'Bushmills, Cecil?'

Drysdale raised an eyebrow, then quickly held a hand up

before Megarry could reply. 'Don't tell me, I know it off by heart.'

He took the policeman's coat, then struck his palm against his forehead, as if he had just committed an enormous gaffe. 'God forgive me, Kathleen. My manners have gone to hell. What would you like?'

He looked embarrassed. Megarry caught a whiff of alcohol on his breath and guessed that he'd been drinking already.

'It's all right,' Kathleen said, handing him her stole, 'I'm used to it by now. Living with Cecil, you know.' She smiled at Margaret Drysdale, whose downturned lip expressed mock horror. 'I'll have a sherry, if it's not too much trouble.'

'At once,' Drysdale said. He clicked his heels and hung the coats on a rack, then headed towards the kitchen.

'Come in here,' Mrs Drysdale said, indicating a brightly lit parlour; a fire was crackling in the grate. 'It must be cold out there. I heard the forecast, they're expecting frost tonight.'

'Are they, by God?' Megarry stood before the fire and rubbed his hands together furiously, then turned to his wife. 'Nothing in the garden that needs protection? From the frost, I mean. I take it all that stuff's been moved into the greenhouse by now?'

'What stuff, Cecil?'

'All those daffodil bulbs, or is it tulips? You know, that sort of thing.'

He looked around the parlour; it was clearly their best room – chintzy settees, carpets, Waterford crystal on top of a sideboard beside graduation pictures of the children. But it was cold. He could feel a chill in the room as if it were rarely used, and a faint odour of must.

'Daffodil bulbs stay in the ground, all the year round.'

'Well, there are things you take in. I know you do it every year.'

'Not daffodils.'

Megarry shrugged, 'You know I'm hopeless at gardening.'

Margaret Drysdale smiled. 'One gardener per family, I always say. That way there are no rows. I do the gardening here, Jack hasn't time. I expect you're the same, Cecil.'

'I just never got the hang of it,' Megarry said, spotting Drysdale in the doorway with a tray.

'I find it therapeutic,' Mrs Drysdale continued in a soothing voice. 'It relaxes me, I like to see things grow.'

'And it's good exercise. All that bending and lifting – and the fresh air. It should keep you fit.' Drysdale was beside them with the drinks. 'Ahhh. Here's a man with the right idea.'

'One sherry?' Drysdale grinned and held out the tray like a waiter. 'Gin and tonic? Bushmills, ice and water?'

'Are you having something, Jack?' his wife asked.

'Of course. I have a glass of wine.'

Megarry saw a glance pass between them, as if the question of who'd be drinking what and how much had been discussed in advance.

Drysdale put the tray down on a table and addressed the others. 'Why don't you sit down? Why are you all standing around like Brown's cows?'

He smiled and indicated a settee closer to the fire. Megarry took a sip of whiskey and lowered himself, taking care not to spill anything.

'Did you go in today?' Drysdale began. He sat beside Megarry and clasped his hands. Across the room, the women already had their heads together. What do they find to talk about? Megarry wondered. They haven't seen each other for months. At least we have work, Drysdale and I.

'I went in for a while,' he said. 'I'd some paperwork to catch up on.'

'Making progress?' Drysdale spread his lips in a thin crease.

'It's hard to say. This isn't an ordinary case, Jack. It's not straightforward.'

'Of course not, that's why they asked for you. They wanted the best guy. There are times, Cecil when I think you're too modest for your own good. You're not ambitious enough. Where's the fire in your belly?'

Megarry ignored the remark.

'Who exactly did ask for me? You never told me.'

Drysdale took a deep breath and sucked his teeth, he gave the impression that he was wrestling with some great matter of state. He's tipsy, Megarry thought. He had a few before we came.

'Well, the Commander was very positive. And several others. There seemed to be general agreement.'

'What others?'

'Fleming for one, he pushed very hard for you.'

'Fleming?' Megarry put his glass down. 'But he threatened to have me taken off the McCarthy case. Did you know that? He made a lot of trouble for me, Jack, he's been one of my chief tormentors.'

'Nevertheless ...' Drysdale played with the rim of his glass. 'He recommended you. He spoke very highly of you.'

'Did he indeed?'

Megarry thought again of the pale face and the weak eyes afraid to look directly into your face. Maybe I've been unfair, he thought. He remembered the man offering his hand after the security meeting. 'I may have misjudged you in the past,' he'd said. That statement alone must have taken a certain amount of courage – to admit he'd been wrong.

'There was a sort of a consensus,' Drysdale continued. 'You know the way you sometimes feel matters have been decided in advance. That maybe there'd been a caucus before the main meeting. I got the distinct impression that their minds were already made up for you.'

'But it was only a simple robbery, Jack. Why should the Security Committee interest themselves? It was only a minor thing.'

Drysdale shrugged. 'Search me, but that's the way it was.'

Megarry sat forward in his seat. 'You ever run across a guy called Flatman?' he asked. 'Marius Flatman? Senior guy, possibly Military Intelligence?'

Drysdale blinked, 'I don't think so. Why do you ask?'

'Because I think you should know him, I think we both should. He's the type of man should be on the Security Committee by all accounts.'

'Who is he?' Drysdale asked.

'I'm not sure. A man of that name had papers taken in this

raid, personal papers. He's something big in the intelligence services; some people may be targeting him.'

Drysdale's face flushed. He sat his glass down carefully on the table. 'That's very interesting.'

'I'd prefer if you kept it to yourself for a while. I don't want to start a scare, and I am only speculating. I've nothing solid to go on yet.'

'Tell me more,' Drysdale said.

'Brit. Home address in Epsom, Surrey. Presently living in Lisburn. Working at the Ministry of Defence.'

'I knew it,' Drysdale said. He clapped his hands. 'I knew there was more to this thing than met the eye. By God, Cecil, this is serious.'

'You don't recognise the name?'

Drysdale shook his head. 'I'm afraid not. But then, who knows? To tell you the truth, I long ago gave up trying to keep track of these people.' He gave Megarry a conspiratorial look. 'I don't know who half these guys are any more. And I don't believe half of what I'm told either. God be with the days when everything was straightforward and we all knew who *not* to trust.'

He laughed at his joke and drained his glass. 'Of course, if I were ever asked, I'd deny I said that. But privately,' he waved his hand in a slicing motion, 'that's the way I feel.'

He pointed to Megarry's drink. 'You're getting low. Let me get you a refill.' He looked at the women. 'I'm going back to the bar. Another tincture, anyone?'

Mrs Drysdale stood up. 'I'll get them, Jack, I have to go into the kitchen anyway.' She took the glasses. 'Same again, everyone?' and before anyone could reply, she was out of the room and the door had closed behind her.

Drysdale turned his grey head in Kathleen's direction. 'How are you, my dear?'

'I'm fine,' Kathleen said, straightening her skirt.

'You look so good ... your face, your figure.' he glanced momentarily towards Megarry. 'You look so ... so youthful.'

'Thank you.'

'Yes,' Drysdale said, 'you look young. Whereas I am feeling

old and decrepit. Worn down, worn out.' He threw his head back and sighed. 'Ah bliss it is, to be young.'

'Not for everyone,' Megarry said from the settee.

'What?' Drysdale and Kathleen both turned towards him.

'I'm thinking of that outrage last night. Father and son murdered in their beds. The young fella was engaged to be married. Not much bliss in that household today.'

'You're right, of course you are,' said Kathleen. 'We get so selfish, so easily. We forget other people's troubles so quickly.'

'There's too much of it,' Drysdale said. 'And we're too bloody lenient. You know my views on this sort of thing Cecil.'

'I know them, but I don't necessarily agree with them.'

'Why are law and order dirty words these days? That used not to be the case. How have we lost the propaganda war?'

'I'm not sure your method works, that's all.'

'We should string them up,' Drysdale said with emphasis. 'I make no apology for saying that. They kill, and they should be killed in return. It's in the Bible: an eye for an eye, a tooth for a tooth. If those little rats knew they faced the hangman, they'd think twice before going out and shooting someone.'

Megarry closed his eyes. How often had he heard this diatribe? Or a variation of it? Every barfly in Belfast had a version of it. Now here it was straight from the mouth of the Chief of Police.

Drysdale's voice droned on ... 'Punishment fit the crime'. An old memory returned to Megarry. He saw again a man sitting on a staircase with a heavy revolver cradled in his hands, his finger curled around the trigger. The man raised the gun. There was a loud report and a flash and the hallway filled with the bitter smell of cordite. Megarry's colleague fell backwards, blood spurting like red ink on the walls and his clothes. The man's blood was running down the back of his own hand and dripping on to the floor.

He shook his head and the vision dissolved.

'It also says, "Vengeance is mine, says the lord." I think you'll find that somewhere.'

'What's that, Cecil?'

'The Bible. You quoted it at me. I was quoting it back. The

108

bottom line is that it doesn't work, it just perpetuates the violence. Makes martyrs, brings new recruits. I may be wrong, but that's the way I feel.'

Somewhere in the hallway a phone was ringing. The door opened and Margaret Drysdale was back with the tray of drinks. She put it down carefully and said to Megarry, 'There's a call for you.'

'For me?' Megarry looked surprised.

'Yes. You'll find the phone halfway down the hall, beside the coat-rack.'

He found the phone as she had said, lying sideways on top of a directory. 'Hello?'

'It's me, Harvey.'

It took him a moment to recognise the voice. 'Yes,' he said, 'what is it?'

'I thought this was urgent. Otherwise I wouldn't have disturbed you. This guy Flatman you asked me to investigate.'

'Oh,' Megarry said. 'Of course.'

'The news is not good.'

'What do you mean?'

'He doesn't exist.'

'*What?*'

'I checked like you asked, but it drew a blank. There's no record of him, not here anyway.'

Megarry shook his head. The voice on the phone sounded blurred. Was Harvey drunk too? Was there nobody sober?

9

In the days following the meeting at the Pike Club, Morgan began to be uneasy. The more he thought about what he'd agreed to do, the more unhappy he became. What bothered him was a feeling that he was being used. It stemmed from what Queenie had said. He remembered the words she had used. 'The Brits look at you and they think you're harmless.' This had hurt him. He also began to worry about the morality of the operation, as Mr Cronin had now taken to calling it. Despite the enthusiasm of the others, he had doubts. He tried to put them out of his mind, but they kept returning. One evening, he confronted Queenie with them.

'These things happen,' she said, in the cold matter-of-fact way that Morgan found fascinating. 'This is a war, after all. It's them or us. If you start getting scruples, you start to lose.'

'But how does that make it right?'

'I didn't say it was right in itself, but you have to see things in the overall context.'

'Which is?'

'Look,' she said. 'They've got more manpower than us. Better weapons. They've got everyone on their side: the judges, the church, the media, armies of bloody informers. If we're going to win, we've got to be more determined, we've got to be more ruthless. We can't afford these debates about right and wrong. Anyway, no harm will come to her.'

'How do you know that?'

'Because that would defeat the whole purpose of the exercise. Think about it. They need her in one piece for God's sake, if they're going to trade her or swap her, or whatever it is they're planning to do with her.'

She had a way of making Morgan feel foolish. The answers came rolling off her tongue without effort, yet she was an ordinary working-class person, like him. She had no fancy education, no university degree.

They were sitting in the kitchen of her flat after listening to Mr Cronin go over the details of the plan once more. Morgan was getting sick of it, he knew it by heart.

'I'm fed up,' he said. 'Mr Cronin treats us like kids.'

He thought of the long session in the cold room above the hall, Mr Cronin with the road map spread on the green baize and a pointer like his teacher used to have, getting each one of them to go through the paces over and over again.

'It's necessary, so that everybody knows what they have to do. We only get one shot at this. We can't afford to make mistakes.'

'But I could do it in my sleep, for god's sake. How long have we been at it now?'

'Six days.'

'It seems more like six weeks.'

She put her hand on his wrist and stroked the hairs on his arm. 'Why are you so impatient, Sean? Why don't you slow down, just take things as they come?'

'I want it done, because it's there. Waiting. It's like an examination, or a birthday. Everything is circling towards it. It's the most important thing in my life right now, and I want it over so that I can relax, go back to living my life.'

'But your life will never be the same. You know that, don't you?'

'Why do you say that?'

'Because this will leave its mark on you. You can't get involved in something like this and pretend it never happened.

In years to come you'll remember it. Even if you drop out and never do another job.' She withdrew her hand. 'If you're not sure about it why did you agree to take part? Why didn't you just say no? No one forced you.'

It was the question he'd asked himself over and over since that day Mr Cronin had taken him for lunch in the Bernardo Grill. It was the question that lay at the heart of this whole business. At times he was racked with doubt, at others he convinced himself that it was all right, that nothing would go wrong, that no harm would come. Still, he envied Queenie her certainty, her conviction that what they were doing was not only right but necessary.

'I have doubts from time to time,' he said.

'You're tense, that's all. You shouldn't worry about it. Put it out of your head.'

She moved closer to him and he smelt her scent. She took his hand and he felt a strange tingling sensation.

'You take all the cares of the world on your shoulders, Sean. You can't do that, just focus on one thing. Don't try to see all the angles, that only confuses you.'

He realised that he could kiss her, he could just reach out and take her in his arms. It would be the most natural thing. But suddenly she pulled away, shaking her head so that her dark hair fell down into her eyes and he realised that she was laughing.

'And for God's sake, stop worrying. No one will get hurt.'

'How can you be so sure?'

'Because that's the whole point. I've just explained it to you.'

'Tell me something,' he said. 'Your name – Queenie. It's an odd name for a republican.'

'I didn't choose it, it was given to me. And anyway, it's only a nickname.' Her mouth curled in a smile. 'My father gave it to me when I was just a wee girl. He used to sit me on his lap when he'd had a few drinks and call me his little queen.'

It was a perfect explanation – everything about her was fascinating – her looks, her attitude, her personality. Now her name; he repeated it. 'My little queen.'

She reached out and stroked his cheek.

112

'Yes,' she said.

The following evening, when the training session had ended, Mr Cronin asked Sean to stay behind. He sat at the table while the others filed out of the room. The thought occurred to him that Mr Cronin had heard about his visits to Queenie's flat. Strictly speaking, it breached security; they were supposed to disperse when the sessions were over and go their separate ways. And Mr Cronin was hot on security; from Day One he had lectured them on the need to obey the rules, to do nothing to put the operation at risk.

But when the door had closed and the last of them had filed down the stairs, Mr Cronin drew Morgan to the window and pulled the curtain aside. 'C'mere. I want to show you something.' He pointed into the street to where a couple of kids were leaning on a brand new Carina, parked awkwardly on the footpath. They were dressed in jeans and anoraks and one of them had a silver earring. Morgan reckoned they were about fourteen or fifteen.

'Recognise either of them?'

'I don't think so. Should I?'

'I thought you might know them. I was watching them earlier. They've been running that car round and round the block. They can't even drive, for god's sake. Where do you think they would get a car like that?'

'I'd say they stole it.'

'That's what I thought.' Mr Cronin took a deep breath and Morgan saw that he was angry. 'Well, it'll have to stop, Sean. We'll have to do something about it, before somebody gets killed.'

'It's widespread. I'm surprised nobody's told you before. There's nights when the Murph is like Brand's Hatch with all these kids driving stolen cars.'

'Is it now?' Mr Cronin let the curtain drop. There was a note in his voice that made Morgan uneasy. 'Well now; we can't have that. We've got a responsibility to the community. What if one of those wee bastards was to hit a child or an old person?

113

They wouldn't stand a chance. What about the people whose cars are getting taken, haven't they got some rights?'

'The kids have nothing to do all day. Hanging around street corners. No jobs. Stealing cars gives them a kick.'

'I'm sorry for them,' Mr Cronin said, 'but we can't allow them to take it out on their own community. It's anti-social. Don't you think the people have enough to put up with, without having those wee fuckers terrorising them? Apart from anything else, it brings the Brits in. Gives them an excuse to come poking around, pretending to be looking after the people, trying to get on their good side. Know what I mean?'

'Of course.'

'We'll have to take some action, make an example of some of them. A short sharp, shock – something that'll teach them a lesson. Put that joy-riding out of their heads once and for all.'

Morgan felt a shock of fear.

'What do you mean?'

Mr Cronin hesitated, then tapped his nose with a bony finger. 'Well, I'll put it to you this way, Sean. If one of those wee bastards was to have his knee-caps blown away, he wouldn't be able to drive a motor-car. Would he now?'

Morgan was stunned. Mr Cronin had this facility of shifting from mood to mood: now he was cold and logical, seeing only the problem and how it could be tackled. There was no place for emotions.

'We owe it to the people. They look to us for protection. Life is hard enough for them ...' He stopped in mid-sentence and shook his head. 'Honest to God, Sean, it would break your heart. The people are trying to make the best of their lives, trying to take a pride in their own communities. We can't let those wee bastards drag it all down.'

He moved back to the table and took out a packet of cigarettes. Morgan noticed how quiet everything had become. Mr Cronin fumbled with a light, then shook out the match and expelled a cloud of smoke.

'Are you happy?' he said at last.

The question caught Morgan by surprise. 'Happy?'

'Yeah. I've been watching you this last while. It strikes me there's something bothering you. Why don't you get it off your chest?'

'There's nothing bothering me,' Morgan lied.

'Are you sure? If you're not happy, you should tell me. I don't want people on this operation who are not happy. It spreads. It can affect morale.'

'I'm happy enough,' Morgan said. 'I'm just impatient. I want to get on with the job.'

'But we're not ready.'

'We're as ready as we'll ever be.'

Mr Cronin shook his head and blew out a wreath of smoke. 'I don't mean us, necessarily. There are other people involved, remember. We're only part of a bigger operation. The whole thing has to be co-ordinated.'

'But why do we have to go over the same rigmarole night after night? I could do it in my sleep.'

Mr Cronin looked up sharply. 'It's not rigmarole, Sean. Everybody has to know exactly what's expected of them. The way to get things perfect is to repeat them over and over again.' He sniffed and tapped ash off the end of the cigarette. 'Let me tell you something that I've never mentioned before.'

Morgan realised he was about to hear something important.

'When I first joined the organisation, years and years ago, we used to go on training camps in Donegal. We'd be out in all weathers, in the dark, in the rain. One of the exercises was to dismantle a rifle blindfolded and put it together again. We had to know every part of that rifle, just by the feel and the touch, and to know where each part went. The only way we were able to do that was to repeat it over and over until we got it right. Until we could do it in our sleep.'

'I'm sorry,' Morgan said. 'I didn't mean to criticise the training sessions. It's just that I'm all wound up. I want to do the job now.'

'You'll have to relax,' Mr Cronin said and punched his shoulder in a playful way. 'We're almost there, just a few more days. First the dummy-run, and then, before you know it ... D-Day.'

Talk like this brought the excitement back. Morgan felt the adrenalin flow.

'This is a big job, Sean. I mean big. Verrry big. There's an awful lot involved here – far-reaching implications for the whole organisation. We have to get it right first time, there'll be no second chance. Know what I mean?'

'Why did you pick me?' Morgan said suddenly.

Mr Cronin hesitated and his eyes seemed to search Morgan's face. 'Why did I pick you? Because you're the best driver I could find. You came highly recommended. Several people spoke on your behalf. I've explained all this to you, Sean.'

'Had it anything to do with my legs?'

'What?'

Mr Cronin's eyes filled with horror. 'Your legs? What in the name of God, are you talking about?'

'I thought maybe you picked me because I wouldn't be suspected, because they would think that someone like me ...'

'Mother of God, don't say another word. Whatever put that notion into your head?'

He put his arm around Morgan's shoulder and pulled him close as if he were a child. 'We take you for granted, Sean. We don't realise what goes through your mind. We don't realise the cross you have to bear.'

Morgan felt Mr Cronin's breath hot against his skin. 'I picked you because you are the best. There was no other reason. Because you are the best and because I thought you believed in what we're trying to do. Get the Brits out, build a new order, a decent society where people will be treated with some human dignity instead of being kicked around like dogs.'

The words were like balm. They reassured him, dispelled the doubts Queenie had sown with her wilful, careless talk.

'I picked you because you are your father's son.'

Mr Cronin crushed out the cigarette and ground it with his thumb. 'When I look at you, I see a valued member of the team, someone I can trust, someone I can rely on. Believe me, there's not many I can say that about.'

Mr Cronin released him and there was a silence between the two men. Morgan felt tears at the back of his eyes. The little

116

speech had reassured him and he felt ashamed that he had ever doubted.

Mr Cronin sat forward and clapped his hands. 'I tell you what, why don't you go down and see the car?'

Morgan's heart leaped. 'Is it ready?'

'Yes. It's been resprayed, souped up, new engine. You wouldn't know it, the owner wouldn't know it.' Mr Cronin laughed and Morgan remembered those had been the very words of the man in the garage when he had first delivered the car.

It was a slack morning in the bar and, as luck would have it, Morgan was scheduled to have the afternoon off. He spent the time cleaning and stacking shelves and serving the occasional customer who dropped in, and longing to get down to Smithfield to see the car.

At half eleven a delivery of beer arrived and Morgan had to go down to the cellar to supervise. When he started work at the bar, he had made it a point of principle that he wouldn't shirk any of the heavy physical work that had to be done. He wanted no exceptions made for him, and insisted that he be treated exactly as the other staff.

By twelve thirty, both Liam and Joe, an older man, had come on duty, so Morgan was free to go. He went into the store room and had a quick wash. When he came back, Liam was cutting sandwiches, ready for the lunchtime trade.

'Everything okay?' Morgan asked. He liked Liam. He was just out of school, eager and willing. He hadn't yet learned to be cynical.

'As okay as it will ever be.'

'I'll be off then. I have to see a guy over in Smithfield.'

'About a car?'

Morgan smiled, 'How did you know that?'

'Sure, what else would it be? Cars are the only things you're interested in.'

He ruffled the youngster's hair, then raised his hand and waved to Joe. 'Don't work too hard.'

It was a mild day but a low mist hung over the city and

seemed to trap the air. When he looked north, he could see the tops of Cavehill and Divis and above them a watery sun struggling to break through. He made his way along Donegall Street and into Royal Avenue, past the *Telegraph* office and then the Central Library where a bunch of schoolkids were congregating on the steps, furtively puffing cigarettes.

As he approached Smithfield, his spirits rose. Making his way through the crowds, he wondered what sort of a job they'd made of it, what improvements they'd done. He remembered what Mr Cronin had told him about souping it up and putting in a new engine, but he wanted to see it for himself, for professional reasons. He had picked it in the first place, gone into the North Belfast suburbs and stolen it. He felt it was his car, his own personal property.

He pushed along Gresham Street, past the hawkers selling fruit and vegetables and into a warren of alleys running away towards Carrick Hill. He took the paper from his pocket and studied the map Mr Cronin had drawn for him. Cricket's Lane was an entry just off Smithfield Square. He would find it easily enough. He began to fold the paper, then, on impulse, rolled it in a ball and dropped it into the nearest bin.

The place was locked when he arrived. Morgan searched the black anonymous door looking for a knocker or some way to draw attention to himself. High on the wall he saw a button. He reached up and pressed and heard a bell ringing somewhere inside the building and, in a short time, footsteps. A pimple-faced youth in dirty overalls put his head out the door, fixing Morgan with an impudent eye.

'We're closed,' he said, 'what do you want?' He had crumbs on his chin; Morgan had interrupted his lunch.

'Jim McKeever?'

'Who are you?'

'Mr Cronin sent me.'

'Oh.' The youth's attitude changed at once. 'Is it about the car?'

'Yes, I've come about the car.'

'You'd better come in.'

The youth stepped away from the door and Morgan

followed him inside. The place had no windows; what light there was came from a series of bulbs in sockets along the wall. He had entered a narrow warehouse. He smelt a noisome smell like ground corn or flour and when he looked closer he saw racks with bags stacked as high as the ceiling. Near the back of the warehouse, where the light didn't quite penetrate, he made out the contours of a car covered in white drapes.

'You're not taking it, are you?' The youth continued to observe Morgan with a hint of suspicion. 'Mr Cronin said I was to mind it till Thursday.'

'Mr Cronin told you right. I just want to see it that's all, make sure that everything's okay.'

'I haven't touched it,' the youth said, 'not since they brought it in.'

'When was that?'

'Saturday afternoon.'

Morgan did a quick calculation. The car had been here for three days. They had moved it successfully through the security barriers that ringed the ghettoes. Now when the time came for the operation, it would be simple to drive away from the city centre. They were unlikely to be stopped and questioned, or even to raise suspicion.

'Well then,' the youth said. He started to walk up the warehouse towards the shadowy slope, past a stove with a teapot burnt black from use and the half-eaten remains of a sandwich. The boy began to pull the sheets off the car, and Morgan's heart began to pound. The cloth slipped away: the blue Toyota Sprinter had been transformed into a gleaming turquoise model.

'Nice job, eh?' The youth stood aside and grinned foolishly as if he were personally responsible for the work.

'Sure,' Morgan said. His eyes took in the new licence-plates, the tyres, the bright new mirrors; he ran his fingers along the bodywork and felt a buzz of excitement. Then the thought struck him that perhaps they'd done too much, made it look too new. In their determination to disguise the car, they might have made it more conspicuous.

He put a finger under the bonnet and lifted it to reveal a mass of tubes and coils and shining plugs. A whole new engine had been installed, a souped-up engine capable of doing well over 100 mph if he remembered what Mr Cronin had said.

'Do you want to switch it on?' the youth asked, 'try it out?'

'What?'

'I've got the keys. You can start it, if you want.'

Morgan opened the door reverently and got into the driving seat. He stretched his legs to reach the brakes and the clutch. He turned the key and the engine trembled into life with a cold clean energy that travelled through him. He closed his eyes and felt his body shake in sympathy. He pressed the accelerator and heard the exhaust roar, the sound and smell filling the narrow room.

'Do you want to take it out?'

The youth was shouting at him through the window. Morgan switched the engine off and opened the door.

'What did you say?'

'I asked if you wanted to take it out. Go for a spin? I'll be here for a while yet.'

'Take it out?' It was as if the boy had spoken his own thoughts. What had Mr Cronin said? Go down and check the car; make sure everything's okay. He hadn't said anything about taking it out. But on the other hand, he hadn't forbidden it. And how was Morgan to check the car unless he took it for a drive? But then he felt a chill of fear, as if the youth had suggested something dangerous, something forbidden that could have terrible consequences.

'I'll be here until five o'clock. There's a full tank of petrol.'

Morgan looked at his watch. It was five to three. He could take it for a quick spin, ten or fifteen minutes. If there was a problem that required attention, wasn't it better that he should find it now, when there was time to fix it?

'I'm not sure,' he said.

'Suit yourself.' The boy shrugged and started to turn away. Morgan made up his mind. 'All right,' he said, 'open the main doors.'

He secured the seat belt and began to reverse the car. He

could see daylight flooding in from the alleyway outside, hear the embattled noise of traffic.

At the door, he stopped.

'I'll be twenty minutes. Don't go until I get back.'

The boy looked offended. 'I told you I'm here until five, but then I have to close. Them's my instructions.'

Morgan backed the car into the alley. At the top of the lane, traffic was passing along the street. Where should he go? North into the hills above Ligoniel? If the mist had cleared, he would be able to look down over the whole city. He drove to the end of the lane and joined the stream of cars heading along North Street, when he had an inspiration. Why not drive the car along the route the operation would take, the route they would travel on D-Day? Why not do his own dummy-run? He could do a test run on the car and, at the same time, reconnoitre the route. He settled deeper into the driving seat and the traffic around him fell away as the car rushed forward. The power surged out of the engine and into him, welding him as if he and the car were one.

He passed the BBC building, Shaftesbury Square, the University. The earlier doubts eased away, and soon he was in tree-lined suburbs. He slowed down and began to look for landmarks. On his left, the Barrington Inn, then the Rugby Club and the Avalon Hotel. He began to count the avenues, Eglantine, Columbine, Woodbine. He remembered the training sessions in the cold room above the Pike Club, Mr Cronin with his pointer and the road map spread out. Slow down, watch out, brake. Any moment now.

He tumbled on it before he expected: the gates of the school looming in the grey afternoon mist and, just beyond, the newsagent's shop with its sign for Cadbury's chocolates. That's where she would be waiting, unaware, unconcerned, innocent of the approaching danger.

His heart began to beat. She came here every day. She would be with a group of pals and they would have to detach her. He rehearsed in his mind what they would do.

He would slow down and stop the car. Wearing dark glasses, Queenie would get out to ask directions. She would call the girl by name and as a woman, she would put the kid at ease. Then quickly, Peter would appear from behind with the gun and force her into the car. It would be over in a flash.

He would drive to Finaghy, where another car would be waiting, and transfer her. The others would disperse, and he would take the Sprinter back to the ghetto where it would be burnt together with every shred of evidence that could link them to it.

Gradually, his excitement subsided and he realised that he was leaving the city behind; he had forgotten to turn. The houses were thinning out and suddenly he was in the countryside, among green fields and cattle, the smell of turf burning from a chimney somewhere. He pulled into a lay-by, turned off the engine and sat thinking.

Now that he had driven the car over the route they would take, he felt peaceful, satisfied. But he knew that it wouldn't last. It was like a drug; he would want it again. He'd keep on wanting it until they did the job, once and for all.

What would happen then? Even then, would he feel that quick tingle along the nerve ends when he thought of stealing a car?

He checked his watch: twenty past three. He had been gone almost half an hour, but it was all right. He could be back in Smithfield in twenty minutes, well before the deadline the boy had mentioned. He started the car and decided to return by a different route. He turned on the radio and the car filled with the jaunty sound of traditional music, and he tapped his hand to the rhythm. Before long, he was at the outskirts of the city-centre. Somewhere a church bell chimed the half hour.

On his left was an hotel, a big modern structure of glass and steel. On his right were a couple of pubs. A boy in a cap was selling evening papers and two men were coming out of a bookie's shop. For some reason the music stopped and the car fell silent. As he bent to examine the radio, he heard a dull rumble like thunder, and the car lifted off the ground. He knew at once that it was a bomb. The street filled with smoke and falling masonry – a sheet of glass, the size of a window, floated in slow motion and smashed into tiny pieces on the road before him. A woman screamed, a child called for its father. Then everything was pandemonium, dust, screaming, the deafening clamour of alarm bells.

He realised that his was the only vehicle still travelling on the road and panic seized him. He thought of pulling in to stop, but what of the car, the operation, Mr Cronin? In the distance was the sound of a fire-engine, wailing like a lost soul.

Out of nowhere, came the upraised hand, the bottle-green uniform of the RUC man walking out in front of him, commanding him to stop. Morgan put his foot on the brake and cold terror washed over him.

10

Megarry was in his office by ten to nine. Driving into work through the quiet streets, the trees bare of leaves, the suburban gardens gaunt and spare in the winter sunshine, his mind had been fixed on one thing only – Harvey's phone call telling him that Flatman did not exist.

If that was true – and Harvey's contacts were good and usually reliable – then who was the man living in Ingledale Road whose house was guarded by plain-clothes soldiers and who drove to work in a convoy of cars? And why had someone gone to the trouble of robbing a bank to get his personal papers?

He left the car in the car-park and took the lift, stopping at the canteen to get some coffee. Nelson was sitting in the office, his feet on a chair and a newspaper spread across his lap. He stood up immediately but before he could speak, Megarry raised a hand to silence him. 'I want Harvey in on this.'

He lifted the phone and listened to the gentle purring sound until Harvey came on the line. 'Can you drop down?'

Harvey groaned. 'I've got someone with me.'

'Get rid of him. I need you here, *urgently*.'

He put the phone back on its cradle, took the lid off the polythene cup of coffee and turned back to Nelson.

'Now,' he said, 'tell me about yesterday. What time did you get away?'

Nelson settled beside the desk and tried to compose himself. His face glowed with excitement.

'Twenty past six.'

'By which time Mr Flatman was safely back home?'

'That's right. I waited until the cars had driven into the street and parked at his house. They changed the guards again at four-fifteen. They seem to work in relays.'

'These guards, were they armed?'

'Not that I could see, but I assumed they were carrying short-arms.'

'You think they might be SAS?'

'They looked the type – young, fit, athletic.'

'And the cars?'

'Two BMWs, front and back. Bullet-proof glass, I would guess. Flatman was in the middle car. Brand-new Mercedes, with a driver who looked like the others. Stocky, crew-cut, medium build. Tough-looking character.'

'And you followed them to the Ministry of Defence?'

'That's right. They got there just before nine. I watched them going in through the security check-point.'

'Anything else I should know?'

Nelson shook his head. 'I don't think so.' He held up a thin folder. 'I made out a report for you – everything that entered the road, times, vehicle registrations. I wrote it all down.' Megarry opened the file and let his eye scan the columns painstakingly copied in Nelson's spidery hand. He'd even got the number of the milk-float.

'You did good work, John, very thorough. That's exactly what a stake-out should be. I compliment you.'

Nelson beamed.

'But what would you say if I told you that Flatman doesn't exist?'

Megarry waited for the other man's reaction. Nelson gave a nervous laugh, then began to protest, 'That's nonsense. I saw him, for God's sake. Tall, thin, military bearing. I told you that I followed him to work.'

'You followed *someone*. How do you know it was Flatman?'

'Because he is the man living at Windnook and the papers

125

taken in the bank raid give his name as Flatman. Who else could it be?'

Megarry didn't reply. He lifted the cup and caressed the white polythene.

'I got a phone call last night from Harvey. I asked him to check out Flatman, remember? The army has no record of anyone with that name serving in Northern Ireland.'

'There must be a mistake.'

'I don't think so. Harvey's information is usually spot-on.'

'I don't understand that,' Nelson said, 'but I'll tell you one thing. Whoever is living in Ingledale Road is big. Whether or not he calls himself Flatman, he's important. Important enough to have a security guard on his house and an escort to and from work. This man is not some mickey-mouse civil servant.'

Nelson was given to impetuosity, to rushing to conclusions. He hadn't yet learned to take things slowly, to consider all the possibilities, to weigh up all the evidence.

'Slow down,' Megarry said, 'I'm not disputing what you saw. But certain things are not adding up.'

There was a tap at the door and Harvey came in. With a sullen look, he lowered himself into a chair and rolled his eyes. 'I'm a very busy person. I have a mountain of work to get through and no one to assist me.'

Megarry took out his cigarettes and offered them, but Harvey shook his head.

'I wanted to thank you for the help you gave me with Mr Flatman.'

'Is that all? You dragged me down here just to thank me?'

Harvey started to get out of his chair but Megarry motioned him back. 'I also want to put some questions to you.' He fumbled with a lighter and blew out a cloud of smoke. 'The mysterious Mr Flatman – your informants tell you there's no record of him?'

'Well now, we might as well get this right.' Harvey looked from one man to the other. 'They say there's no *present* record of him.'

'What does that mean? Nelson asked.

'It means that there *was* a Marius Flatman. He was a colonel in the East Anglian Regiment, but he's no longer listed as a serving officer.'

'In Northern Ireland?'

'Or anywhere, for that matter.'

'Is he dead?'

'No, not dead. Disappeared. They were able to trace his career until about two years ago. He did a lot of travelling. Trouble spots mainly, Nicaragua, South Africa, The Middle East, anywhere there was a bit of bother, Colonel Flatman would turn up. His last recorded position was as lecturer at Cranbourne Military College in Surrey. It's an officers' training school, he taught counter-insurgency studies. You know what that's shorthand for dirty tricks, psy-ops, black propaganda, that kind of stuff.'

Megarry leant forward in his chair. 'What exactly was he doing in those foreign places?'

'The record simply says that he was on secondment.'

'To what?'

'I don't know, but I could use my imagination.'

'What happened after Cranbourne?'

'The record stops. He hasn't been transferred. He hasn't been killed. He hasn't died. He hasn't resigned. But he's not teaching there any more. Officially he doesn't exist.'

Megarry considered for a moment. 'Maybe there are two of them?'

'Two Marius Flatmans? Are you kidding? It's a very unusual name.'

Harvey took out his handkerchief and made a fuss of mopping his brow. 'Well, if you've finished with me now, I'd better get back. I have someone waiting.'

'We're not finished with you,' Megarry said, 'we have to get to the bottom of this.'

'But I've told you all I know.'

Megarry sighed deeply and crushed out his cigarette. 'About ten days ago, there was a raid on the Great Northern Bank in Chichester Street. They made a point of taking certain documents lodged there for safekeeping, including those relating to a Mr Marius Flatman. The documents gave an address in

Lisburn and' he held up a finger, 'another address in Epsom, Surrey, where Cranbourne College is located.'

Harvey gave a low whistle.

'Nelson spent all day yesterday staking out the house in Lisburn and it turns out that Mr Flatman has enough security to look after the Queen. And to cap it all, he works at the Ministry of Defence.'

'But why all this deception?' Nelson asked.

'I think that's fairly obvious. Whatever he's engaged in, they want to keep it secret. Maxi said he thought he was in Intelligence, didn't he? They've given him a new name and removed him from the official record so that nobody knows he's serving here.'

'But the people who robbed the bank know about him. They took those papers so that they could confirm his identity.'

'Yes,' Megarry said, 'that's what worries me.'

'Hadn't you better warn him?' Harvey asked. 'Tell him that these guys are planning to murder him?'

'We don't know that.'

'What else could it be?'

'He's too well guarded.'

'Kidnap?' Nelson said. 'Maybe they're planning to kidnap him, hold him for ransom?'

Megarry remembered a blimpish figure, a ruddy face, the neat military moustache bobbing like a trap-door as the Commander of Land Forces addressed the Security Committee, warning them to be on their guard. What was the phrase he had used? The vibrations that the geiger counter picked up from time to time?

'No,' he said.' They'd have the same problem – he has too much security. They'd never get close enough to kidnap him.'

He got up from the desk and walked to the window. The sun had given way to sullen cloud and a light rain was starting to fall. In the distance, through the mist, the green snout of Cavehill drooped over Glengormley. He stood looking out over the city, the rooftops glistening in the soft rain. In the yard below, a car started up, the exhaust burb-burbing before the engine caught. He turned back into the room.

'What about his family? Those documents that were taken mentioned a wife and child, didn't they?' He looked at Nelson. 'Is he living alone? Does he have anyone with him? Did you see anyone else in the house?'

'There was a girl,' Nelson said, 'a young girl about twelve or thirteen. She went with him in the car.'

'To work?'

'Yes.'

'Any other children? What about a wife? There must be a woman in the house if there's a child.'

'I didn't see her.'

'It could be the girl,' Megarry said. 'If it's a ransom they're after, the authorities would pay up just as quickly and it might be easier for them to grab her.'

Harvey had taken out his handkerchief and was once more mopping his brow. 'Can I suggest caution? I think you're on the right track, but if you go to the authorities with what you've got, they'll laugh in your face. And they won't thank you for blowing Flatman's cover. You need more evidence. They'll make mincemeat of you, if you get this wrong.' He got up from his chair. 'I think I'll have that cigarette now.'

For a moment, Megarry said nothing. Then he spoke to Nelson. 'You'll have to go out there again. Concentrate on the girl. She has to go to school somewhere, follow *her* this time. Don't let her out of your sight. Take a camera and get some pictures. Find out if there's a wife or other children. See if they've got security ...'

The phone rang. Its shrill tone seemed to fill the room. Megarry grabbed it and spoke angrily. 'Who is it?'

He recognised the voice at once.

'It's Fleming. I thought I'd give you a call. You know, I meant to say to you when we last spoke, that we should really have lunch. I feel I owe it to you.'

'I'm very busy right now,' Megarry said.

'We're all busy, it's the nature of the job. But sometimes a bit of lunch can help to focus things. I'd be grateful if you could find the time. Is it the case?'

'The case?'

129

'That has you so busy? Is that why you've no time?'

'Partly,' Megarry said.

'How's it going? Making progress?'

'A bit.'

'Look, why don't we have lunch? We can talk it over, sometimes another viewpoint can be helpful. I'll make a reservation and call you back. I'll take you to my club. Tomorrow suit?'

Megarry was about to refuse, then he saw again the nervous figure in the hallway with his overcoat draped across his arm. To turn him down would seem callous, ungrateful. The man had apologised, after all, and was trying to make amends.

'All right,' he said reluctantly. 'Tomorrow will be fine.'

The Records Office was at the very top of the building – a narrow room with columns of grey filing cabinets standing like soldiers in solemn ranks. Next door, a sparkling new extension housed two massive computers and a bank of terminals.

Megarry preferred the old ways when everything was on paper, when a file meant what it said, a cardboard envelope with typed details, easily read and digested. Now the accumulated intelligence of years of police work was being transferred to computer disc and a small company of older men in white coats worked from early in the morning until late in the day feeding information into the gleaming machines. For Megarry, the change meant scrolling through lists of statistics, inputting commands, staring at a screen while pages of information flashed before his tired eyes. He remembered with fondness the old pieces of paper that he could feel with his hand, that he could leave aside and refer back to if necessary. The new way was supposed to represent progress, but in many respects he thought it deficient.

He took the lift, rattling and creaking to the seventh floor, then waited while it shuddered to a halt and the ancient steel doors swung open to reveal a long tiled corridor, subdued lights and a silence broken by a strange humming sound. He walked along the corridor, his eyes taking in the new paint, the glass, the spotless cleanliness. He compared it to his own room, to Harvey's poky little den with its boxes, files and the smell of cabbage from the canteen, and it occurred to him that the police authorities cared more for their costly computers than for the staff who had to use them.

As he got to the end of the passage, the humming grew louder, and he realised that it was coming from a large machine in the middle of the room. As he examined it, he noticed a thin man with grey hair who peered at him nervously from behind a pair of wire spectacles.

'Superintendent Megarry?' he asked nervously.

'Sam.'

'You rarely come up here any more. We feel abandoned, as if we've been banished and no one cares for us.'

'But you have this cushy job, Sam, nice cosy office, no risk, no danger, no driving around in the cold and damp. Some people would kill for this.'

Sam shook his head. 'I preferred what I was doing before. Bloody computers. You can't talk to them. We're all bored to death.'

He backed into the office and Megarry followed. He stood still to take in the sterilised room with its shining machines and rows of desks and terminals. In the middle of the floor someone had put a houseplant in a tub, but its leaves were wilting and it seemed unhappy. Two detectives looked up from a screen and nodded in recognition.

'You were looking for stolen cars,' Sam said as he showed Megarry to a desk. 'Where did you want to begin?'

'How far back do they go?'

'As far as you want.'

'How many cars get taken every week?'

'Do you mean in the whole of Northern Ireland?'

The man's question caught Megarry off guard. Would the kidnap gang go to the trouble of stealing a car in some distant town – Dungannon or Derry perhaps – to allay suspicion? Or would they simply take one here in Belfast?

'Let's just concentrate on Greater Belfast. Why don't we start there?'

'Well now,' the man said and pulled nervously at his fingers, 'you could be talking dozens. Forty, fifty, maybe even sixty a week. I'd need to check that.'

'But most of them would be recovered, right?'

'About seventy-five per cent.'

'Well then, Sam. Why don't you just get me a list of the cars taken in the last six weeks and not recovered?'

Megarry sighed. Sam wasn't the brightest. He'd been a good enough cop in his day, plodding, meticulous, but without initiative. Now he was approaching retirement and they'd transferred him up here. It was obvious that his heart wasn't in this work.

Sam bent to the terminal and tapped in a series of commands and a menu flashed up on the screen. He tapped more keys and a list appeared. He adjusted the brightness, stepped back and rubbed his hands.

'Now,' he said, 'that's what you're looking for. But there's one other thing. There's cars that get stolen and are never reported to us. Just remember that. There's stolen cars out there that we know nothing about.' Megarry thanked him, waited until he had gone, then began to trawl through the list. The cars had been coded according to make, description, date of theft, date of reported theft, registration number and location. There were rows and rows of them, many more than he had thought. For a moment he felt the hopelessness of the task; it was a long shot, trying to trace a stolen car. They could steal them anywhere, even outside the state.

Maybe he was wrong and they hadn't stolen a car at all. Maybe they had simply gone out and bought a new one and changed it beyond recognition, then hidden it until such time as they were ready. He sighed, drew a line in his notebook, and started to scroll through the material on the screen. The listed cars were mainly Mazdas, Volvos and Opels, taken no doubt by joyriders for an evening's sport, but now and then there was a more expensive car, a BMW or a Mercedes. The cars had been taken from all manner of places, from outside pubs and restaurants and shopping centres. Often from outside the victim's front door.

He thought of the type of car they would need: Something

132

fast so that they could get away quickly; something large enough to hold several people; something that wouldn't stand out or draw attention. He decided to make a list of half a dozen vehicles. He knew from experience that a longer list would be counter-productive. No one would read it. People were bombarded with statistics nowadays and their attention span could stretch only so far.

He began by discarding any car over three years old on the grounds that the gang would go for something fairly new. From time to time he entered the registrations of possible vehicles until in the end he had more than twenty. He started in again working on model, size, age, engine capacity, even colour. He found this part particularly difficult. As he drew a line with his pen through a rejected vehicle, the thought would occur that this might be the very car the gang had taken. Several times he reconsidered and added a previously discarded car to the list. After two hours, he had it down to eight.

He switched off the terminal and went in search of Sam. He found him in a little kitchen at the rear of the office drinking tea.

'I need a typewriter,' Megarry said.

The man put down his cup and Megarry followed him into another room where there was a typewriter. He inserted a clean sheet of paper and typed with two fingers: URGENT PRIORITY. STOLEN VEHICLES. STAFF ARE REQUESTED TO REPORT SIGHTING OF THE FOLLOWING CARS.

He appended the list and took it off to the telegraph room. A young constable in shirt sleeves stood quickly to attention. Megarry gestured him back into his seat and gave him the material.

'I want this faxed to all stations,' he said, 'at once.'

11

'Out of the car.'

The policeman's voice was cold and formal. Morgan looked into the ruddy provincial face, reached for the seat belt and began to unhook himself. Out of the corner of his eye, he could see other policemen closing in to give cover to their colleague, fingers curling on the triggers of their guns – neat bottle-green uniforms, grey flak-jackets, the faces stern and uncompromising. It came to him that they thought he was the bomber.

He tried to still his rising panic.

'Where are you coming from?'

'Malone Road,' Morgan stammered.

'Did you not hear the bomb?'

'Yes.'

'Why didn't you stop?'

'I don't know. I was dazed. I just kept on driving.'

'Up against the wall.'

Arms pushed him roughly, feet kicked his legs apart, then hands running along his spreadeagled body as he was frisked for weapons.

'All right,' a voice said, 'he's clean.'

More questions. There were two of them now and they fired queries in relentless sequence. 'Where are you going?' 'What were you doing?' Morgan had barely time to answer one question when another came hurtling at him.

'Name and address?'

He started to reply, then Mr Cronin's advice in the cold room above the Pike Club swam back into his head. Keep calm. Think before you answer.

'Sean Morgan, 42, Ballykelly Way.'

The two men exchanged glances at the mention of the ghetto address.

'And who owns that car?'

'I do.'

'Can you prove that?'

'Yes. There are papers in the glove compartment.'

'Occupation?'

'Barman.'

'Barman?'

'That's right,' Morgan said.

'Where do you work?'

He saw some more RUC men examining the car, opening the boot, feeling along the upholstery. One of them had a walkie-talkie; he spoke into it and kept glancing in Morgan's direction. Eventually, one of the policemen settled into the driver's seat and switched on the engine.

'What's going on?' Morgan asked.

There was no reply. Instead someone poked him in the back, 'Get into the jeep.' An RUC man pointed towards a blue personnel carrier parked a few yards away.

'Are you arresting me?'

'Get into the bloody jeep.'

It was a short drive to the station. Morgan sat in the back of the carrier, across from one of the policemen with a gun. Nobody said a word as they careered through unfamiliar city streets, glimpsed in a blur of fading light. The jeep slowed, banter was exchanged with someone on sentry duty and they went over a ramp into the station compound.

'Out,' the policeman said.

Morgan climbed down from the back and looked around. It was a bleak yard with a few vehicles parked neatly against a wall, some cars and a couple of personnel carriers. During the journey, he had tried to reassure himself that everything would be okay. They would check the car and find it was clean. Ditto with himself. He just had to keep his nerve, and they would realise they had made a mistake and let him go.

'This way.' It was the policeman who had first detained him, a big, thickset man with a red face and a strange country accent, Tyrone or somewhere like that. He seemed to be in charge. Morgan followed him through a door and along a corridor until they came to a small room, painted a depressing grey. It contained a table and some chairs but no windows. The only light was a naked bulb on the ceiling.

'Empty your pockets.' The man produced a large envelope and held it open while Morgan put in his money, keys, wallet, and other personal belongings.

'Watch.' The man pointed to Morgan's wrist and he put it the watch as well.

'Now,' the man said, 'sit there and wait.'

The door banged shut with a finality that scared Morgan. He sat alone in the narrow room, his mind teeming with possibilities. Why were they holding him? What did they know? He thought of Mr Cronin and the others in the room above the Pike Club, patiently going over the details of the operation. Maybe someone had squealed, someone further up the line? He dismissed the idea at once. He must stay calm, keep his nerve. Whatever else happened he must say nothing about the operation or give any hint that would place it in jeopardy.

The door opened; the policeman was back. There were three others with him. One stood Morgan against the wall and took his photograph, another took his fingerprints, a third took swabs from his hands. Then two of them began to question him again, the ruddy-faced policeman and a small grey-haired man in a suit. They took it in turns, like a team. Name and address again? Date of birth? Schools? Family? Ages? Occupations? Then the questions to trap him. Where was the shopping centre? How would you get to the church? Where was such and such a street? They doubled back. Date of birth again? School? Mother's name? Back and forth the questions went. Why didn't he stop when he heard the bomb? Where was he coming from? What was his business?

Morgan felt his head beginning to reel. He tried to remain calm, to follow Mr Cronin's advice. Don't get flustered. Don't panic. Think before you answer. The detective with the grey hair was leaning across the table.

'Where did you get that car?'

'I bought it.'

'You bought it? On your salary? How much do you earn?'

'What's that got to do with anything?'

'It's got everything to do with it. Don't you get cheeky with me.' The man glared at Morgan. 'It's not looking good for you. You didn't stop at the scene of an explosion. You can't give a satisfactory account of your movements. I can tell you something, sonny.' He leaned so close that Morgan could smell his breath. 'We're checking that car to see if it was stolen.'

He sat back in triumph and Morgan's fear returned. Was it possible for them to trace the car after all the work that had gone into changing it? He tried to stay calm, to fight back the rising panic.

The first detective reached out and put a hand on his colleague's shoulder. 'Calm down, Dave. He may be telling the truth.'

'The truth? He wouldn't know the truth if it bit him on the leg.' But he lowered his voice, got up and left the room.

'He's upset,' the first man said. 'We've just heard that four people were killed in that explosion. Just blown away like that.' He made a puffing sound with his lips and opened his hand, as if he were letting a butterfly go. 'Who would do a thing like that? What do they hope to achieve?'

'I don't know.'

The man pulled out a packet of cigarettes and offered them, but Morgan shook his head.

'Killing people solves nothing. All it does is add to the sense of grievance, the desire for revenge. It's a vicious circle. It has to stop.'

Morgan bent his head and let the words roll over him. He'd been warned about this routine. It was intended to soften him up, to make him feel guilty. But he hadn't planted any bombs. Why should he feel guilty?

'That man there,' the policeman nodded towards the door, 'he had a brother killed in an explosion a few years back. He goes berserk when something like this happens. But don't you worry, I won't let them harm you.'

He lowered his voice and Morgan thought of the confessional, the priest whispering, the confidences spilling out in the darkened box. 'If there's anything you want to get off your chest, you can tell me. You can trust me. I'll look after you.'

'I know nothing about it,' Morgan said.

'Nothing?'

'I was just out for a drive, honest.'

The man took a deep breath and sat back. He looked disappointed. 'You know it will go hard for you if you don't co-operate. We're only human beings. If you make our lives difficult, we can make your life difficult. On the other hand ...'

He blew out a wreath of smoke. Morgan caught the smell of the tobacco and regretted not taking the cigarette he'd been offered. 'But I can't tell you something I don't know,' he protested. 'I was just out for a drive. I'd nothing to do with the bomb. I would have stopped the car only I was so terrified that I didn't know what to do. That's why I kept on driving.'

The man nodded, and Morgan thought that he had convinced him. He seemed like a decent guy, but they were trained to be like that – the good cop and the bad cop. It was all part of softening him up and getting him to tell them what they wanted to know.

'What are your views on politics?' the man suddenly said.

'Politics?'

'Yes, you know what I'm talking about. Have you any political views?'

'No,' Morgan said, shaking his head. 'I'm not interested in that stuff.'

'Don't be daft, of course you're interested. Ever attend meetings? Ever go on demonstrations?'

'No, I keep my head down. I mind my own business. I don't bother with anything like that.'

138

'But you'd know who was involved, wouldn't you? You'd know their names?'

'Involved?'

'You know what I mean – the people who run the paramilitaries in your area.'

'No, I don't know anything like that.'

'C'mon,' the policeman said, 'you live in the middle of one of the biggest terrorist dens in the city, and you mean to tell me you don't have any idea who's involved in it?'

'I just told you. I keep to myself. I mind my own business.'

'There could be money in this.' The man narrowed his eyes and put a finger against his nose. 'Easy money and no risk. All you'd have to do is keep us informed about what's going on. There's loads of people doing it. You'd be surprised.'

'I'd be no use to you, I don't know anything.'

'Even small things,' the man went on. 'Insignificant things. Things that you mightn't think important. It can all fit into a pattern. It can become part of the jigsaw.'

Morgan tried to blot out the man's voice. He was talking now of regular payments. No risk. Loads of people doing it. People you'd never suspect. 'We could tell you who to watch. Give you a special number to ring. You wouldn't even have to meet any of us. And every week a cheque. Think about it, it's money for jam.'

He was interrupted by the door opening again. The man with the suit and the grey hair was back. Morgan watched as they conferred in a whisper, and tried to read their faces for what was happening. Were they going to detain him or let him go? He wished he knew what time it was, but they had taken his watch and there was no clock and he wasn't sure how they might react if he was to ask them right out. They were looking in his direction, then the first man threw his head back and laughed. He got up slowly and approached Morgan.

'You're a lucky man,' he said, 'your car's clean and you're clean. You're free to go.'

Morgan felt his heart leap. He started to get up, but the policeman put a hand on his chest. 'Let me give you a piece of advice.' He bent close and looked into Morgan's face.

'Next time you get caught up in something like this, you stop. Understand?'

'Sure,' Morgan said, 'I hope it never happens again.'

'Well then,' the policeman said, 'come on and we'll get your things.'

He led Morgan back along a corridor. There were lights burning and windows, and it was now dark outside. They stopped at an office where an older man in uniform was sitting behind a desk. He seemed like a jovial type, with a fat well-contented face. 'Cup of tea?' The man raised his eyebrows, 'You must be parched.'

'No, I'm all right.'

'You're sure? I've got the kettle on.'

But Morgan shook his head. He wanted to get away as fast as he could.

'Suit yourself.' The policeman reached into a drawer and took out an envelope. 'Here's your stuff.' He emptied the contents on to the desk. 'Just make sure it's all there and then sign these.' He pushed a piece of paper across and handed Morgan a pen. Morgan looked closely at the form – a clearance to say he hadn't been harmed while in police custody. He scribbled his signature and the man produced two more documents. 'For your belongings. And this one is for the car.'

The man spread the forms flat on the desk and Morgan signed.

'Right,' the first policeman said, 'come with me.'

They went down another corridor and out into the yard again. It had been raining and the night air was damp. Morgan felt his spirits rise.

The policeman led him to the car and pulled open the door. The keys were still in the ignition. He held out his hand. 'No hard feelings. It's a job. We had to do it.'

'I know that,' Morgan said.

The man nodded, then walked to the barrier and waited while it was hoisted. Morgan drove through, taking care not to give any impression of haste. At the gate, he rolled down the window and waved goodbye. A voice in his head urged him to flee, to get away fast in case they changed their minds. In case a phone rang somewhere and someone said, 'Hold him.'

But nothing happened. The barrier clanged down behind him; the policeman was walking back across the yard towards the office – already putting Morgan out of his mind, thinking of the next task, the humdrum little jobs that awaited him.

Morgan switched on the lights and accelerated. He was free; excitement rose in his breast. The police had come so close, but he had outwitted them, just as he had outwitted them when he'd stolen the car all those weeks ago. He had stuck to his story and they'd been unable to beat him down.

He checked the clock on the dashboard and saw that it was almost eight o'clock, over four hours since the police had stopped him.

A terrible thought hurtled into his head and the euphoria drained away. The garage in Smithfield would be closed: he had nowhere to leave the car.

12

The cars and lorries thundered past, illuminating the damp night with their headlights. All around, Morgan heard the noises of the city – the roar of traffic, the sound of a boat horn near the docks. These sounds had comforted him in the past, reminded him that he was part of a community, that there were people here who cared for him. But tonight the sounds brought him no solace. All he felt was cold and fear that he had taken the car without permission and had nowhere to garage it.

He tried desperately to think what to do. He couldn't take it home; a brand-new car would draw attention and Mr Cronin had specifically warned that vehicles going in and out of the ghettoes were being monitored by the Brits.

He thought of driving back to Smithfield. Maybe the warehouse would still be open. Maybe the boy would have stayed on, waiting for him to return. But he knew it was hopeless. He remembered what the boy had said, 'I'm here until five, but then I have to close. Them's my instructions.'

He realised that if he continued to sit by the side of the road he would arouse suspicion. A passing army patrol would report him, or might even stop and question him, and the whole business would start all over again. He decided to move.

He took his watch from his pocket and strapped it on his

wrist – eight o'clock. The meeting in Beechmount would be starting now. They'd wonder where he was. Mr Cronin would probably wait for a while, then begin without him. But Mr Cronin wouldn't be pleased. Since he had attended these meetings in the cold room above the club, no one had ever dared to be late.

Morgan started the engine and drove to the end of the road. There was a roundabout, but instead of turning right for the city centre, he continued out of town until he saw the neon sign for the Cherrytree Inn. He pulled into the car-park and locked the doors and started towards the welcoming lights flooding out from the lounge, listening to the ominous sound the gravel made as he crunched it underfoot. He needed a drink – brandy or whiskey, something strong to calm his nerves and help him think. Then he remembered that Mr Cronin had warned them all against alcohol. He'd said that loose tongues cost lives. Morgan pushed into the warm interior of the bar and made his way to the counter. When he caught the barman's eye, he ordered coffee and sandwiches.

The lounge was filling up, couples holding hands and whispering over their glasses; at the bar were a bunch of rowdy students from the nearby university. Morgan listened as the laughter rolled across the room and when he looked up he could see smiling faces in the mirrors around the bar. Everyone was happy; everyone but him. He cursed himself for taking the car. If he had just done as he was told, gone down and checked it to make sure that everything was all right; if he had simply done that and left it there, he wouldn't have been caught, he wouldn't have been interrogated. He wouldn't be stuck with the car on his hands …

Mr Cronin would be furious. They would probably have to call off the operation, scrap all their plans. The weeks of work that had already gone into the project would be wasted. It had far-reaching implications for the whole organisation. Morgan had let them down. They had put their trust in him and he had failed them. Those people who had spoken on his behalf, who had recommended him, how would they feel when the job had to be aborted because of him? Because of his arrogance, because of his impatience, because he couldn't resist the stupid impulse to take the car out before they were ready?

Someone was speaking to him. He looked up as the barman set down his coffee and a sandwich in a cellophane wrapper. 'That's one fifty please. Will that be all?'

'Yes.'

He found some change and paid the man, then tore the paper from the bread. The sight of the food made him realise how hungry he was. He hadn't eaten anything since breakfast, more than ten hours ago. He began to stuff pieces of bread into his mouth, turning the dilemma over in his mind. Maybe things weren't all bad, maybe there was a bright side; the police had let him go after all. But then the hopelessness of his situation swept over him and he felt the fear and loneliness return.

He bought another coffee and sat stirring the spoon round and round in the cup. The police had been friendly towards the end; the cop with the red face had even tried in a ham-fisted way to recruit him as a tout. They wouldn't have behaved like that unless they believed him. And if they believed him, then why did he have to tell Mr Cronin about his arrest? What was the point?

He felt his spirits rise. He could make up a story, invent some explanation for having the car. He could say he'd taken it for a drive to familiarise himself with the route and when he got back into town had found security checks all over the place because of the bomb. By the time the roadblocks had been lifted, the garage was closed.

This was half-true. There *was* increased security, the place was crawling with police and military. Mr Cronin was bound to have seen it on television. If Morgan could find somewhere to leave the car, even for twenty-four hours, he might get away with it.

There was a break in the talk and someone laughed. It was a high-pitched nervous giggle which silenced the voices around, scattering the fragments of conversation like dying leaves. He knew someone who laughed like that: Bates. Bates was an old school friend, a single man who dropped into the bar some evenings on his way home from work. He lived on his own in a sprawling flat in Charlemont Street, up near the City Hospital. Morgan had been in it once; a wild party that had spilled out of the bar at closing time with six packs and carryouts and a man who played a tin whistle. Bates had a garage which he never used. Bates might do it.

Morgan turned the idea over. Bates was reliable – a slow, plodding, steady type who could be depended on to keep his mouth shut. And he was sympathetic. One or two comments he had passed from time to time in the quiet of the snug had convinced Morgan that Bates's political feelings would be close to his own.

It was half past eight. If he was lucky he might catch Bates before he went out and still have time to get to the Pike Club. He got up from the stool, pushed through the crowds surging around the bar and made his way to the car-park. The night air was like a damp cloth. A handful of stars were in the sky and a pallid moon hid behind a bank of clouds. Morgan settled into the driving seat, turned on the radio and tried to blot out all memory of the day's events.

Mr Cronin was sitting on his own at the big table with the baize cover. There was no sign of the others. He had been playing solitaire with a pack of cards and an ashtray was overflowing with crushed butts.

'You're late,' Mr Cronin said without looking up, 'we had to go on without you.'

It sounded like an accusation, although the voice was friendly enough. Morgan sat down. 'I got delayed. There was a bomb in town. You might have heard about it. They had security checks all over the place.'

'I heard about it,' Mr Cronin said. 'It's terrible: four people dead. What good will it do?' He made a tutting sound with his tongue and shook his head. 'I'm not sure I agree with this bombing business. There's too much risk, too many things can go wrong. Innocent people get killed.'

He began to deal out the cards. 'But why should a bomb detain you, Sean? You could have taken a bus or a taxi.'

'I had the car.'

145

The words sounded like a pistol shot in the quiet of the little room. Mr Cronin stopped dealing. He lifted his head so that his eyes were staring into Morgan's face. '*Our* car? The car for the operation?'

'Yes.'

'You had it out?'

'Yes. I took it out for a drive. Remember you told me to go down and check it over?'

'But I didn't tell you to take it out. I just meant for you to satisfy yourself that everything was okay.'

'I had to take it out. How was I supposed to check it if I couldn't take it out?'

'But you had no permission.'

'I didn't think I'd need permission. It was only meant to be a short drive around the town. How was I supposed to know they'd plant a bomb?'

Something in Morgan's manner alerted Mr Cronin. 'Where is it now?'

'It's safe.'

'Safe? What does safe mean? Is it back in Smithfield?'

'No, that's the whole point, that's what I'm trying to explain.'

Morgan felt his heart hammering. He wanted to hurry on, to explain himself, to show how innocently things had tumbled out of control.

'I couldn't get through. By the time they'd lifted the security barriers, Smithfield was closed.'

'Jesus Christ,' he heard Mr Cronin say. 'I don't believe this. I don't believe I'm hearing this.' He gripped Morgan's wrist and squeezed it so hard that the skin turned white. 'Where is it? Where have you got it?'

Morgan shook his arm free. 'It's in a garage in Charlemont Street. Near the Lisburn Road. It'll be all right.'

'Will it?'

'The garage belongs to a friend. He's okay, we can trust him.'

Morgan tried to explain: safe, reliable, sympathetic. But Mr Cronin wasn't listening. He was shouting, his lips and mouth flecked with spittle like snowflakes. He banged the table and the cigarette butts spilled from the ashtray in an ugly mess.

146

'That car doesn't belong to you. It doesn't belong to me. That car belongs to the organisation. Do you know what the penalties are for abusing organisation property?'

'I'm sorry,' Morgan said weakly, 'that's not what I meant to do.'

'Sorry? What good is sorry? You know what you've done? You've jeopardised months of planning. You've put the whole operation at risk. You've ...' He ran out of words, and shook his head sadly from side to side. 'Jesus, Sean, how could you be so stupid?'

'The car is safe,' Morgan said again. 'This guy is reliable. I'd go bail for him.'

'Reliable? You don't know what you're talking about. We know nothing about him, he could be anybody.'

'He's a friend, he's okay.'

Mr Cronin sighed. 'You've so much to learn, Sean. How reliable will he be if the Brits come and beat the shit out of him? Or if they offer a reward and he's short of cash? Will he stay reliable then? In this business you trust only your closest comrades. You obey orders. You maintain discipline. Discipline. Do you understand? This is an army, not a bloody gang of tupenny-hapenny hoodlums.'

He searched his pockets until he found a packet of cigarettes. 'You disappoint me, Sean. I had high hopes for you. I thought you understood the nature of this war, the odds we're up against. I thought I could rely on you. Didn't I talk to you enough times about security?'

Morgan lowered his head. This was what he had feared. The shame of failing them, of letting them down after they had invested their trust, Mr Cronin and the others who had recommended him. He had betrayed them all.

'What will happen?'

'I'll have to report it, it's the rules. Somebody else will have to decide.'

'But the car is safe. It's even closer to the route. In some ways where we have it now is better. There's no need to call the operation off, there's no need for that.'

Mr Cronin had opened his briefcase and taken out a notebook. 'What's this man's name?'

'Jim Bates.'

'And what's his address?'

Morgan told him and he wrote it down.

There was a silence, then Morgan spoke again. 'What will I do now?'

'Go home. This will take a couple of days. We'll meet again on Thursday. Maybe we'll know by then.'

Mr Cronin locked his briefcase to indicate that the meeting was over. Morgan said, 'I'm sorry, I meant no harm.'

'I know that,' Mr Cronin said wearily, 'but you were selfish, you didn't think. That's all it takes, just one selfish person to screw up the whole thing. Just one. Know what I mean?'

Morgan took the bus home. It was filled with drunks returning from a party. He sat at the back and felt depression settle over him like a cloud.

This morning when he had gone to work filled with anticipation because he was going to see the car again, he had been barely able to contain himself. He couldn't wait for lunchtime to come, so that he could get round to Smithfield to see what sort of a job they had done. Morning seemed a different age.

A dull ache throbbed at the base of his spine, a slow drip, drip of pain, insinuating itself into his consciousness. A cold sweat broke across his forehead. He recognised this pain, he'd had it before. It was a bad omen.

The man beside him began to sing in a loud cracked voice that rattled along the bus: 'And it's no, nay, never. No nay, never, no more / Will I play the Wild Rover, no, never, no more.'

He sang out of tune and every so often nudged Morgan to encourage him to join in. 'You're a long time dead,' he kept saying, 'why don't you enjoy yourself?'

Morgan ignored him, and eventually the man fell asleep and started to snore, while someone else took up the refrain.

The bleak outline of the shopping centre came lurching into view and then the grey steeple of the church. He rang the bell and waited till the bus had jolted to a halt before walking unsteadily up the aisle and getting off.

The estate was bathed in a bright yellow light, the glare from a hundred street-lamps. Here and there music played, there was laughter, a dog barking in the night. At the off-licence a gang of skinheads were morosely drinking cider. They stood in silence as he walked past, and then he heard a snigger and a drunken laugh and someone shouted an obscenity at his departing back.

His mother was sitting at the kitchen table in her torn cardigan, watching the flickering images on the corner screen. It was as if she hadn't moved since morning. She rose automatically and went to the sink to fill the kettle, turned her head and watched him over the rim of her broken spectacles.

'What kept you?' she said, 'you're usually home earlier than this.'

'Am I?' Morgan felt his temper begin to stir. Barely in the door and she was beginning her interrogation. Then he remembered that she would soon have enough to worry her. He spoke softly: 'I didn't realise.'

'Wasn't this your half-day? What have you been doing with yourself?'

'Nothing much. Played a bit of snooker in the club. Met a few people.'

There was a soft plop as the gas ignited.

'You only come home when you've nothing better to do,' she said. 'Gallivanting around the place. What does that say for me? You'd think this was some sort of boarding house, the way you carry on.'

Morgan turned wearily and began to climb the stairs. He had made up his mind what he was going to do. All the way home on the bus, he had been thinking about it. He knew that the risk was small, but it was a risk and he had to cover it.

At the top of the stairs, he stopped. His mother was still talking, the sound floated up.

'I worry about you, Sean,' she was saying, 'you've no idea. All this gallivanting. I never know where you are, what you're doing. I don't like it, not one wee bit.'

149

13

For his second visit to Ingledale Road, Nelson decided to leave earlier than before. He wanted to give himself time to secure a good vantage point, now that he knew the hazards of surveillance in such a confined space, with a permanent guard on Flatman's house. As things turned out, it was as well that he did.

He took with him a camera which he got from the Stores Office on Megarry's instructions. It was fitted with a telescopic lens and a device which allowed him to take photographs even when the light was poor. The person who gave it to him, a thin man in a tweed jacket smelling of pipe tobacco, spent a great deal of time explaining how it worked. Nelson learned later that he was a scientist on secondment from the RUC forensic department.

He also took a couple of warm pullovers, a bundle of music tapes for the car stereo, the fieldglasses he had used on his first visit and a pack of sandwiches from the canteen. By half past six, he had locked up the flat and was edging the car out of the garage and pointing in the direction of town.

The morning was cold and wet, with the sky dark and threatening. Only the street-lamps gave light to the deserted roads. He put the heater on, and the wipers to clear the windscreen, and headed north until he came to the motorway.

Fifteen minutes later, he was on the outskirts of Lisburn. He slowed as he approached Ingledale Road, prepared to swing into the street when he saw something which made him brake urgently.

The two black BMWs were already in position outside Flatman's house. For some reason, they had come early. Nelson quickly changed gear and drove on, cursing softly as a voice on the radio began to give the weather forecast. He turned the radio off, took the car to the top of the road and found a cul de sac where he pulled in and stopped. He would have to revise his plans; he couldn't drive into the street without being seen by the occupants of the cars. If he was going to watch the house and take photographs, he would have to make his way on foot. He checked the time: just after seven. He locked the car and got out, taking the fieldglasses and the camera. In the breast pocket of his anorak he had a small torch and a notebook and pen. The earlier rain had eased off; he pulled a woollen hat over his ears and prayed that the weather would hold.

Across the street from where he had parked was a large house with a sprawling lawn running down to a low wall. Nelson scaled the wall and entered the garden, then slowly made his way to the back of the house, where he climbed a fence into another garden. He moved carefully, trying not to make any noise in case he wakened a dog or set off an alarm. As he pushed through shrubbery and hedges, his clothes began to get damp. Once he felt something give way underfoot and he saw little shards of broken glass where he had trampled on a cold frame. He came out on to another lawn, where he could make out a belt of trees, their stark branches thrusting against the morning sky. He saw the bright glare of street-lights and, when he came closer, the outline of the cars standing sentry at the gates. He was in a garden directly across the street from Flatman's house.

He edged closer through the wet grass until he came to a hedge of griselenia, where he squatted and raised the field-glasses: dark chimney stacks, the slate roof and, just below, lights burning in the upstairs rooms. He lowered the glasses and saw the Ford Escort he had seen the last time and two men in khaki jackets chatting and smoking beside the garage door. He had a perfect view of Flatman's house and the hedge gave him cover. He checked his watch: twenty past seven.

For a long time nothing happened. The sky gradually brightened, but it seemed to get colder and he felt his leg begin to cramp. He shifted his position and massaged it, but this brought little relief.

Finally there was a stir of activity – one of the guards pushed the garage doors open and prepared to take out the Mercedes. Nelson primed the camera. The morning was brighter by now, but he activated the light-intensifier as he had been instructed. The front door of the house opened and the thin military figure of Flatman appeared in the doorway. Nelson pressed down on the camera and there was a gentle whirring as the film unwound. Immediately another figure came into the frame, someone he hadn't seen before, a tall blonde middle-aged woman in a pink dressing gown. As Flatman began to descend the steps to the drive, the woman leaned forward and kissed him gently on the cheek. Nelson pressed again and photographed her. He trained the camera on the door of the house; Flatman disappeared and the frame went empty. Then it was filled again with the girl, the same fresh-faced young girl of his previous visit. She bent her head to adjust her scarf against the damp morning air. Nelson waited until she was looking straight towards him, then pressed once more.

Flatman and the girl went down the steps and got into the car. Nelson continued to press the button, photographing Flatman, the girl, the guards, until the vehicle began to move down the drive. He put the camera carefully into an inside pocket, then started back the way he had come, hoping desperately that nobody and nothing would raise the alarm. He had completed the first part of his task.

His car had a thin coating of condensation fogging the windscreen. He wiped it, then settled into the driving seat and started in pursuit of the convoy. He caught up with it in Bridge Street, moving slowly through the traffic. Nelson adopted the same tactic as last time, staying as far back as possible. The first BMW turned off to the right and the others followed. Then they were in the countryside and the rooftops of the Defence building came into view.

Nelson dropped farther back and let the gap between himself and the convoy open: he knew where they were going and could afford to take his time. One by one, the cars turned off and drove towards the security barriers at the gates of the complex. Nelson drove on for about a quarter of a mile until he came to a lay-by protected by a belt of hawthorn bushes. He turned the car so that it was pointing the way he had come, turned off the engine and settled down to wait. Yet again, he checked his watch: quarter to nine. He turned on the radio and fiddled for a music station; when he looked up the Mercedes was coming out through the gates. The two BMWs remained behind.

Nelson raised the glasses: there was just the driver and the girl, ensconced in the back seat. The car cleared the security check again and turned back on to the road for Lisburn. When it was almost out of sight, he engaged the engine and began to follow. This time the Mercedes took a detour into Belfast. The road began to fill with traffic and Nelson fell back, allowing several cars to fill the space between them. The sun came out and danced and sparkled on the sidelights of the car as they left the countryside and entered the outskirts of the city. The Mercedes left the central lane and began to slow down. Its indicator flashed as it came to a stop at the gates of a school. Nelson saw a wave of red blazers, and a cluster of young girls running around a playground. A sign hung limply from a metal frame: MOUNTPLEASANT SCHOOL FOR GIRLS.

There was a garden centre across the road, with black plastic pots and garden furniture like pavement tables in the sun. Nelson waited for a break in the traffic, then swung his car across and stopped.

Caroline Flatman got out and waited on the pavement until Bennett had eased the car away and beeped the horn; it was a little ritual they had. She lifted her hand and gave a tiny wave and saw him watching her in the wing mirror as the car joined the main stream of traffic on the road into Belfast.

There were times when she felt like a prisoner. The constant guard, the eyes keeping watch on her every movement. She understood exactly how her mother felt when she complained about the security on the house: they had no privacy. What did they think she was going to do, for God's sake? Run off with a stranger?

She began the long walk up the drive to the school. She didn't trust Bennett – all the way from the Defence complex he had plied her with chit-chat, asking her questions about school and what she did, and about boys, particularly boys. From time to time she wondered if Bennett got some pleasure from these interrogations, but she knew that it was much more mundane. He reported directly to her father, and she had heard them often enough sharing information as Bennett drove him into work. Bennett was a stool pigeon: he was making sure that she didn't step out of line. It was as simple as that.

At the top of the drive was the redbrick of the school, and the sun shone through the naked branches in a pale golden haze. Something in the sight moved her, and she remembered a poem she had learnt for Mr Boyd, the English teacher. The words came tumbling into her head: 'I saw the Master of the Sun. He stood / High in his luminous car, himself more bright …'. She remembered learning the poem, pacing the floor of her bedroom with her eyes closed until she had it by heart. She wanted so much to please him, to get things right. And later at her desk, bending over her so close that she could smell his aftershave, he had patiently explained what the poem meant. It had been like a revelation – the beauty of the lines, the imagery.

She thought of sunny days at their house in Epsom, mornings when she had cantered across the downs on her mare Romany, the breath from the animal's nostrils hanging white in the cold air. And later when the weather grew warmer, sitting in the garden, the charcoal smell of the barbecue, her father uncorking the bottles of Frascati, dewy from the fridge.

Those had been good times, when he taught at the College, in the years before Northern Ireland: the picnics, the trips to the cinema, the tennis parties, Tom Evans hanging about always wanting to partner her. In his silly way he must have admired her. She blushed when she remembered how she had teased him, laughing with the other girls at his gauche behaviour, his awkward efforts to impress, the way he followed her around with his big doggy eyes.

It had all started to fall apart when her father got his transfer. She remembered the afternoon he came home and told them, the shock on her mother's face, which she tried to hide. There had been a shower earlier and the flowers in the garden were heavy with rain, their leaves hanging limp and flat along the grass.

'It will only be a short posting,' her father had said, 'four years max, maybe less. We won't notice it going by.'

'And then what?' her mother asked.

'Then something else. I don't inquire about these things. I'm a soldier, I do as I'm told.' He walked to the cabinet, got out the whisky and poured a large drink, then stood for a long while looking out over the damp lawn.

For a few days the subject wasn't referred to and then, as they were finishing dinner, her mother brought it up again. 'Have they told you when you're going?'

Her father laid down his knife and fork and pushed his plate into the middle of the table. 'A few weeks. They have to find a replacement for me at the College.'

'What about Caroline and me?'

'How do you mean?'

'What's going to happen to us?'

He smiled as if the question was so silly that it hardly required an answer. 'You'll stay here where you've always stayed.'

'Couldn't we come with you?' Her mother reached out and took his hand. 'We could rent a house. We'd all be together. I hate it when you have to go away. Please Marius, let us come with you.'

'You must be joking. You want to come and live in Northern Ireland? Are you out of your mind?'

'Why not?'

'Do you know what it's like? Bombs going off, people getting murdered in broad daylight. Good God woman, I never heard of anything so ridiculous.'

'But it isn't all like that,' her mother pleaded. 'There must be safe places, where life goes on normally. We could live somewhere quiet. We'd be together, we should be together.'

Her father had laughed then, a tinny laugh with a hint of nervousness. 'You never suggested this when I was posted abroad before.'

'But those were impossible places – Nicaragua, for God's sake. Northern Ireland is different.'

'It's not, it's just the goddamned same. Just as dangerous. If anything, these bloody Irish terrorists are more sophisticated than most of the others I've had to face.'

'But we'll miss you, Marius.'

This time he guffawed. 'I'm not going to Australia, you know. It's only an hour's plane ride away. I can be home most weekends, work permitting, and we can talk on the phone every day.'

'But it's not the same thing. We should be together.'

'No,' he said firmly. 'It isn't possible. The authorities wouldn't allow it. Think of the security considerations.'

'At least you could ask them. If they're so keen for you to go, they should make some allowances for your family.'

Her father didn't reply. He got up and walked out into the garden and the issue hung in the air for days, like a bad smell that wouldn't go away. But her mother didn't give up. Caroline could see how determined she was, how she badgered him on every occasion until in the end she wore him down as water wears a hole in a stone. He surrendered with bad grace and much huffing and puffing and it was all settled after innumerable phone calls and a trip to London. He came back with a long face that was meant to indicate suffering and sacrifice, and over dinner he made it clear what the circumstances would be.

'They insist on round-the-clock security. That means that none of us will be a free agent. You must tell them each day where you plan to go and what you plan to do. They will vet the arrangements. If you wish to go shopping, you will be accompanied by a plain-clothes guard. Ditto with social engagements. We'll have to find a school for Caroline and the same strict security will apply to her. Oh, and one final thing.' He paused. 'We have to change our name.'

'Whatever for?' Her mother laughed.

'Because it's part of the conditions, to do with my work. I can't explain it all, but while we live in Northern Ireland we will be known by an alias. I suppose we'll all get used to it after a while.'

He shrugged his shoulders, 'Do you still want to go?'

'Of course.'

He looked at the two faces smiling with enthusiasm across the broad dinner table and his own face broke into a grin. 'Well then, on your heads be it.' He went to the kitchen and came back with a bottle of champagne and three glasses.

They came to Lisburn at the end of August, at the fag-end of a blazing hot summer which quickly faded into rain and damp, and were given a house on the outskirts of the town, selected and approved by the authorities. It came with a twenty-four-hour security guard, as her father had warned – soldiers with blackened faces whom they sometimes surprised in the shrubbery beside the tennis court.

14

From the broad bay windows of the teachers' common room, Raymond Boyd had a view out over the playing fields, the rolling lawns, the drive, the rose garden and the little wood at the back of Mountpleasant School. He thought it was a wonderful place, it had every facility – language laboratories, libraries, science rooms, gymnasia, even a computer lab. In the months he had spent here, he had often stood at this window and thought what a far cry it was from the overcrowded pre-fab where he had been schooled in the mean streets of the Lower Falls.

It was all thanks to Mr Cronin, another in the long list of favours done for his family over the years, stretching back to the time when his brother Tommy had been caught with a gun. Tommy hadn't been involved in anything; he was just a gullible kid who had been asked to hide a weapon and had been found out when someone informed. He got twelve years in prison.

The episode had almost broken their mother's heart, but Mr Cronin had been on hand from the moment of Tommy's arrest. He had arranged a solicitor, gone with them to court for the numerous hearings, and when the trial was over he had arranged loans of money, credit from his shops and presents at Christmas. He had been a guardian angel to them. Whenever they tried to thank him, Mr Cronin brushed it aside in his usual self-effacing fashion. 'We have to look after each other. Sure isn't that what we're here for?' He would shrug his shoulders and rub his hands in that exaggerated way he had. 'If we don't do it, who will? Know what I mean?'

The teaching job had come about in the same off-hand way. It was not what Raymond Boyd had intended; had things worked out the way he had planned, he wouldn't be in Ireland at all. He would be in New York, studying journalism at Columbia University. He had been accepted as long ago as May and in the weeks that followed all the formalities had been completed. He had posted off his acceptance form and settled down to enjoy what remained of the summer. But as the weeks went by and he heard nothing more, he began to grow uneasy. At first he put it down to the mail. Maybe the US system wasn't as efficient as their own. The weeks turned into a month and then two months, and panic began to set in. Eventually, he decided to telephone and the news he received from the registrar was devastating. He wasn't enrolled as a student; the university had never received his acceptance form. He tried to rescue the situation, but it was too late, the class lists were closed. He would have to apply again next year.

He felt totally demoralised. Everything he had hoped for seemed to lie in ruins. For the first time in his life, events had slipped out of control, fate had turned against him. It was while he was in this dark mood that he ran into Mr Cronin one evening in the Pike Club, standing at the bar in his Crombie overcoat with a glass of Guinness before him. When he saw Boyd he waved him over. 'Boys a boys. I didn't expect to see you. I thought you were heading off to America to become a famous reporter.'

'I was,' Boyd said, 'but something happened.'

Mr Cronin detected the note of despondency. 'Did you not get the grades?'

'No, nothing like that. They lost my acceptance form.'

'Oh dear, that's too bad. What's going to happen now?'

'I have to wait another year.' Boyd tried to sound cheerful. 'It'll all work out in the end. It's just that ...', he sighed, 'I had my heart set on it, it's very disappointing.'

'I'm sure it is.' Mr Cronin looked grave to show his concern. 'And what are you going to do in the meantime?'

'I don't know, go on the dole, I suppose.'

'Can you not get a job? You've got a degree, haven't you?'

'Of course. But you see, everything's nailed down for another year. I'm too late now.'

Mr Cronin took a sip from his glass and silence fell between them. Boyd felt embarrassed: this was what lay ahead, awkward explanations, pitying looks from people who wouldn't believe that it was a simple error. Maybe he should take himself away somewhere, go to London maybe, get some sort of job until the time came to apply to Columbia again.

His thoughts were interrupted by Mr Cronin. 'What sort of degree have you got?'

'English Literature.'

'Do you think you could teach?'

'But I've just explained, all the jobs are gone. You have to apply months in advance.'

'But this has only just come up,' Mr Cronin said, 'I learnt about it the other day. A girl I know was teaching at this school on the Lisburn Road. Posh sort of place, I believe. Anyway, she got a better offer so she gave in her notice. Last minute sort of thing. Not very considerate of her, I know. Now they're frantic to get a replacement.' He sniffed. 'It might be nothing at all, but you could give her a ring. Here.'

He took out a notebook and pen and wrote down a number.

'Now what can we get you to drink? We can't have you standing there looking like a washed-out rag.'

Boyd got the job, a temporary contract with the possibility of a permanent position if both sides were happy. But Boyd knew that it would never come to that; he had reapplied to Columbia and been accepted. He had sent the documents by registered mail, and this time nothing had gone wrong. In a few weeks he would leave for New York.

He had been amazed how quickly he had settled in and how much he enjoyed the work. He discovered that he had a talent for teaching and the pupils liked him. When he went into the class in the morning, he could tell from their faces that they were genuinely pleased to see him.

The English girl had proved a problem though – she was bright but there was something about her. She seemed unsettled, and the other girls ignored her. She had made only one or two friends. He decided from the start to take an interest in her. Partly, he saw her as a challenge, and partly it was concern – she was a visitor. He wanted her to settle down and get good results. He gave her extra work and coached her along until in no time at all, she had caught up with the rest of the class and was easily holding her own. But the more he did for her, the more she seemed to want, and it worried him. She began to confide in him, to pour out little secrets. He tried to discourage her, but it was almost as if she needed a father confessor, someone she could trust.

One afternoon she said something that surprised him. At first he dismissed it, putting it down to her schoolgirl imagination, something said to impress him, to make herself appear important. But when she repeated it about a week later, he began to examine her in a new light. She told him that she lived in a house in Lisburn, with a twenty-four-hour security guard. And most surprising of all, she said that she was using a false name, all her family were. They had to do it because of the nature of her father's work, but their real name was Flatman.

One evening in the Pike Club, in an unguarded moment, he mentioned her to Mr Cronin. 'What did you say her real name was?'

'Flatman.'

Mr Cronin sniffed. 'That's interesting.'

Boyd felt a little prickle of fear and regretted mentioning her. He tried to change the subject, but Mr Cronin brought him back.

'What does her father do for a living?'

Boyd started to protest. 'She's only a kid, for God's sake. She's probably making it up, you know what kids are like.'

'Why don't you find out?' Mr Cronin said. 'Ask her about her father.'

'But it's none of my business.'

'Make it your business. Boys a boys. You want to be a reporter? You've got to learn to be nosy, develop a brass neck. There's no such thing as secrets. Secrets is only news waiting to be discovered. Know what I mean?'

Boyd watched her now as she came along past the rose garden, the morning light filtering through the fine hairs on the crown of her head so that it shone like silver in the sun. She had her eyes down and her gaze fixed on the path before her, but as she neared the window she saw him. She raised her hand and her face spread in a smile. There was something in that smile, a quality of innocence, a measure of trust, that touched him. She would do anything I asked, he thought and, all at once, the gravity of the responsibility bore down on him. He lifted his hand in a little gesture and returned her greeting.

Boyd left the window and walked out into the corridor just as she came through the door. She seemed to carry a scent of the morning with her, a freshness he could smell. Her cheeks were flushed and her eyes were bright. She stopped and opened her satchel with a great show of excitement. 'I have it,' she said, 'I finished it last night.'

She reached into her bag, took out a folder and thrust it into Boyd's hands. It was a project he'd set her, an essay on Wordsworth and the Romantic poets. It was something extra, a little bit of private work to help her along.

He took the folder, opened it and saw the rows of neat handwriting, the careful underlining in red ink.

'That's excellent, Caroline. I'll read it during my break.'

She stood back and he could see the pleasure in her face.

'Did you find it difficult?'

'No, I enjoyed it, it was interesting. I love Wordsworth. I think the poems are so moving.'

As Boyd flicked through the manuscript, he became conscious of giggling from a group of girls walking past in a huddle of red blazers.

'I'd better go,' he said quickly.

He saw the look of disappointment on her face. 'Have you a free period today?'

162

'Yes,' she said eagerly, 'in the afternoon, half past two.'

'Come and see me in my room, I'll have read it by then. We can discuss it.'

'Half past two,' she said in a loud voice and strode away down the corridor, past the bust of the founder and the glass case where the school trophies stood on display.

The lunch with Fleming had run on much longer than Megarry had anticipated. The service was leisurely, rather than slow or inefficient, and despite his protestations about work, Fleming seemed in no hurry to get away. It was quarter past three before Megarry escaped.

He drove quickly across town, left the car in the compound, and took the lift to the third floor. As he went along the corridor he heard the phone ringing inside his office. His first thought was that it was Nelson, calling from Lisburn with intelligence about the Flatman girl. He fumbled with his keys and unlocked the door; the ringing sound was louder. Megarry lifted the instrument and clamped it to his ear.

'Cecil?'

He realised, with disappointment, that it wasn't Nelson; it was an older voice, the tone calm and assured, like the voice of a confident lawyer.

'Who is this?'

'It's Dave McConkey, Church Street station.'

The name meant nothing to him. 'What can I do for you, Dave?'

'You sent out a list of cars.'

Megarry caught his breath. 'That's right.'

'We may be able to help you.'

There was a racket from the yard below, the sound of a truck unloading and voices shouting encouragement. 'I can't hear you very well. Hang on a minute.'

He got up and closed the window. 'Now,' he said, 'start again. What did you just say?'

'The cars, Cecil. We might have seen one – The Sprinter. You had a Sprinter on the list?'

'Yes, we did.'

'We may have had a sighting.'

He remembered McConkey now. Plain-clothes detective. Bad temper. Got himself into trouble a few years back for ill-treating a prisoner and they'd been lucky to avoid a court case.

'This might be nothing,' McConkey was saying, 'but then, you never know. We had a guy in here a few days ago. Morgan, Sean Morgan. He was driving a Sprinter. It was the day of the bomb in the Plaza Hotel.'

'What colour was it?'

'Turquoise. Yours is blue, but ...'

'He could have sprayed it.'

'I was going to say that,' McConkey said. 'Odd colour, turquoise. I don't think I've seen one like that before.'

'Tell me more.'

'The registration's different, but you'd expect that too. If the car was nicked, that is.'

Megarry pulled a notepad over and got out his pen. 'What's his name again?'

'Sean Morgan.'

'I take it you checked him out?'

'Of course, as a matter of routine. He was clean. We had to let him go in the end.'

Megarry's fingers beat a small tattoo on the desk. 'Give me the number.'

'Is it something big? Some sort of a big job you've rumbled?'

'I don't know,' Megarry said warily, 'it's just something I'm working on.'

'Well, if it *is* something big, they're not going to use some guy with a record, are they? They're going to use somebody clean.'

'I know all that,' Megarry snapped, 'just give me the registration number.'

'I'm only trying to be helpful.'

'The best way to be helpful is to give me the goddamned number.'

McConkey gave him the information and Megarry wrote it down. 'What else have you got?'

'Mug-shots, prints.'

'Get them over to me fast, will you? Send a messenger. Where does this guy live?'

'West Belfast – Ballykelly Way. Do you know it?'

'I'll find it.'

'There's one more thing.'

'Yes?'

'He's deformed.'

'What?'

'He's crippled, Cecil.'

He thought he heard McConkey laughing on the line. 'Is this some sort of joke? If it is, I take a very dim view of it.'

'Calm down,' McConkey said. 'He can walk, he can drive. I saw him. It's good cover. Put it to you this way, who'd ever suspect him?'

'Don't tell me my job,' Megarry yelled, 'just get that stuff over to me fast.'

'Is this all the thanks I get?'

'Thank you,' Megarry said and put the phone down.

He hunted among the papers and files until he found a telephone directory. He flicked the pages and got the section marked Car Distributors. In a few seconds he had the number. A young female voice came on the line.

'Can I speak to the sales director?'

'He's at a meeting right now. Can I say who's calling?'

'It's the police, I want to check a car.'

There was an intake of breath. 'Perhaps you'd like to talk to Mr Hughes. He's the deputy. He's free to talk to you.'

Mr Hughes introduced himself and Megarry began again. 'I'm trying to check a car, a Toyota Sprinter. You distribute that make, don't you?'

'Yes we do.'

'Is there a turquoise model?'

'No,' the man said. 'Blue …'

'No turquoise. You're sure?'

'Absolutely.'

'Anybody else distribute a turquoise model?'

'No, we're the sole distributors.'

'Could you import one that colour?'

'No.'

'You're sure?'

'Absolutely,' the man said. 'There's no such colour in that model.'

'Bingo,' Megarry said and put the phone down.

15

Megarry found Harvey in his little office, behind a wall of files, boxes and bits of rubbish, the detritus of a hundred cases.

Lifting his head above a parapet of papers, he examined Megarry with a defensive eye. 'Can I help you?'

'You're not still on that stupid work-to-rule, are you?'

'I might be, what's it to you?'

'I have a job for you.'

'What sort of job?'

'I have to go into West Belfast. I need someone to ride shotgun.'

Harvey's face spread in a grin. 'What about your partner, Mr Nelson, why doesn't he go with you?'

'He's otherwise engaged.'

'So you come to me?'

'This is important, I really need you.'

Harvey sniffed. 'Where exactly do you want me to go?'

'Falls Road.'

'That's Indian territory.'

'That's why I need someone reliable like you, someone who knows the ropes.'

Harvey's lip curled in a smile. 'You're full of shit, Cecil, right up to here.' He drew a line across his throat and gave a snort.

'Jesus Christ, I'm so goddamned soft, people walk all over me. I'm like a goddamned living doormat.'

Megarry tossed his car keys from one hand to the other so that they made a clinking sound. 'It beats sitting here all day, you said so yourself.'

Harvey got up and reached for his coat. 'Forewarned is forearmed,' he said as he opened a drawer and took out a Luger in a leather holster.

They went along Divis Street, up through Lower Falls until they came to the Royal Victoria Hospital.

'When's the last time you were up here?'

'Fifteen, twenty years?'

'It's changed,' Megarry said. 'It's different now. You know, I started my career here as a rookie. Pounding the beat. This place was teeming with life in those days, street after street of little parlour houses, two up, two down, outside toilets. The people didn't have much, but they had work. The mills were here. And the factories. Now they have nothing but hatred and their sense of pride.'

'You sound like a social worker.'

'I'm giving you the facts. They were decent people. Tough, hard men, women raising big families. But they shared what they had, they helped one another. There were rules. They showed respect, it wasn't a jungle. They've destroyed this place.'

'Who exactly destroyed it?'

'The authorities. They never trusted these people, they always treated them as outsiders. The police were sent in here to keep them under control. Now there's no work, the kids have nothing to do. They hate the police, they hate the army, they feel they don't count, that nobody listens to them. Is it any wonder they're in revolt?'

They came to a junction. Megarry changed gear and they entered an estate lit by the glow of street-lamps, rows of identical houses stretching to the foot of the mountain, brooding, silent and dark in the background. They found the shopping centre, a warren of gloomy boxes with steel shutters and cavernous black interiors. There was a grey supermarket, its walls splashed with graffiti, a butcher's shop, a bookie's, an off-licence bathed in a pool of orange light.

They drove on until they came to the church. A young boy in an anorak was walking a greyhound. Megarry pulled the car over and stopped.

'Hello.'

The boy looked at him suspiciously.

'Can you give me directions? Ballykelly Way?'

'Who're you looking for?'

They boy's eyes were taking in the car, the occupants. I don't trust this little fucker, Megarry thought. He could be trouble.

'Nobody you'd know.'

The boy went on staring. He was about fourteen, dark eyes sunk deep in his face, and an odd tilt to his head. Beside him, the dog shivered in the cold. Megarry wondered if he had misjudged the situation; the kid might be simple.

'Well,' he said again, 'do you know where it is, or don't you?'

'It's down there,' the boy said at last, pointing towards the valley of houses, 'the second street on the right.'

'Thank you.'

The boy didn't reply. He waited until they drove on, then pulled the dog struggling across the road and watched from the other side as they disappeared into the evening gloom.

They found the house easily enough. It had the skeleton of a car propped up on breeze blocks in the front garden, like an abandoned whale washed up on some forlorn beach. Megarry didn't stop but drove to the top of the street, then turned and came back again, his eyes scanning the road.

'Now,' he said to Harvey, 'when I get out, you take my place. Keep your gun handy in case this guy tries to make a bolt for it. If he does, you stop him. Whatever happens, keep your eyes peeled. If anything excites you, bang the horn. Okay?'

'Okay.'

Megarry opened the door and stepped on to the pavement, glancing quickly to left and right. There was no one in sight. He strode up the garden path and grasped the knocker.

He felt an odd singing in his temples and realised that he was excited. Under his shirt, his heart beat faster.

He grasped the knocker once more and rattled it impatiently, then listened as the sound reverberated through the tiny house. My God, he thought, the walls are so thin, they're like cardboard. How can these people have any privacy?

He saw a shaft of light from somewhere at the back of the house, and heard footsteps approach. The door was pulled open and an elderly woman put her head out and watched him over her broken glasses.

'RUC,' Megarry said. He had his identification ready. 'Does Sean Morgan live here?'

'Yes.'

'I'd like to speak to him.'

He saw her eyes flicker. Fear. It was often the reaction he got. Fear or disdain. She pulled her cardigan closer around her shoulders. 'He's not here.'

'Do you know when he'll be back?'

The woman shook her head.

'Do you know where he is?'

'No.'

Megarry felt a surge of anger. She was stonewalling, refusing to co-operate. 'You're not being very helpful,' he said, his voice rising. 'You don't know where he is, you don't know when he'll be back. What *do* you know?'

'He went away.'

'What do you mean?'

'He's left home.'

Megarry heard himself repeating the information like a stupid schoolboy. 'Left home?'

'Yes,' the woman said, 'a couple of nights ago.'

She stood in the doorway with a defeated look, as if he had brought tragedy into her life. Megarry lowered his voice and spoke in comforting tones, the way you would to a child.

'Are you his mother?'

'Yes.'

'Would it be all right to come in for a few minutes?'

She didn't reply, just slowly backed away from him. He

170

followed her in and closed the door. It was like a hundred houses he'd been in; he could smell bacon cooking and the whiff of disinfectant; there was a mirror and cheap carpeting in the hallway, and in the sitting room a colour television and the inevitable picture of Jesus with his bleeding heart.

This is the height of their expectations, he thought. This is luxury, some of them don't even have this.

'What's he done?'

He forced himself to smile. 'He hasn't done anything, Mrs Morgan. I just wanted to ask him a few questions, that's all.'

'What about?'

'Oh, just a case I'm working on.'

'Well, you won't find him now. He came home the other night, packed a bag and said he'd be gone for a while.'

'Did he say where to?'

'Dublin.'

'Did he give you an address? A telephone number?'

She looked at him again over the edge of her glasses, stuck with Sellotape.

'I don't believe him,' she said. 'He hasn't left, he's still around somewhere.'

'Around town?'

'Yes.'

He could see the tears waiting to fall. Women have it the worst, he thought – mothers, daughters, wives. He took her arm and led her to a chair. 'Look,' he said, 'I don't want you worrying, but I have to find him. He may be in trouble. If I can find him, I may be able to stop something serious. Will you help me?'

She was snuffling now. She had a handkerchief in her hand and was dabbing her face. He saw the grey head shaking.

'You could try his work.'

'Where's that?'

'Donaghy's Bar in York Street.'

'You know nothing, Mrs Morgan?'

'I knew he was up to something, he's been acting strange recently.'

'Like what?'

'He changed his shift at the bar. And he used to go off every evening to meetings. But everytime I asked him, he'd deny it.'

'Did anybody call at the house for him?'

'Just people to do with that old car out there.'

'Is it his car?'

'No, he's fixing it for somebody.'

'Does he like working with cars?'

'It's his hobby.'

'Do you know anything about a Toyota Sprinter, turquoise colour? Did you ever see him with a car like that?'

The woman stared at him as if he were mad, then lowered her eyes.

'No,' she said, 'Nothing like that.'

Megarry sighed. I *have* brought tragedy into her life, he thought, I've brought trouble, the way the police always bring trouble. But I've come to the right place, and I've got the right man. Now all I have to do is find him.

'There's something you can do for me,' he said. 'If he contacts you at all, will you tell me? Don't think of it as informing. You might be keeping him out of trouble.'

He tore a leaf from his notebook and scribbled a number. As he reached across to her, his eye caught a photograph beside the television: a black-and-white picture of a young man in an open-neck shirt, an old-fashioned picture in a wooden frame. The face seemed familiar. He lifted the photograph. 'Who's this, Mrs Morgan?'

'My husband.'

'Where is he?'

'Dead,' she said.

He was about to ask her what had happened, but he closed his eyes briefly and it came back to him. He remembered the hallway of a house, a gun exploding, a man falling, the smell of cordite. It was a picture from the past, reaching out to touch him with its cold fingers.

'He's gone,' Megarry said as he settled himself wearily into the passenger seat.

172

'Gone?' Harvey started the engine and rolled his sad eyes. 'You mean we've risked our lives for nothing?'

Megarry felt the burden of the past weigh down on him; was in no mood for Harvey's grim humour.

They drove in silence for a while, the headlights of the car sweeping the empty streets with a yellow beam. Harvey didn't speak again until they were clear of the estate and onto the main road.

'Where will you start?'

Megarry sighed. He had an enormous task, a city of over half a million people.

'He could be anywhere. It's like looking for a needle in a haystack. I don't think it's possible.'

'Don't talk like that. That's not the Megarry I used to know.'

'What do you mean? I have to be realistic.'

The other man grinned at him. 'Look, when we get back to the office, I'll start work on a profile. Contacts, workmates, relatives, friends, schoolmates, people who might be prepared to help him. I'll draw up a list of addresses where he might be hiding. We can send in raiding parties this evening. What do you think?'

'I don't know ...'

'Give it a go, you'd like to catch him, wouldn't you? You'd like to have him sitting across a desk from you now with the lights turned down, pumping him for the names of his accomplices, dates, times, plans. I know you, Cecil.'

'How long would it take to make out this list?'

'A couple of hours.'

'All right,' Megarry said, 'I'll talk to Drysdale.'

'Attaboy, Cecil, don't let the bastards grind you down.'

He found Nelson waiting when he returned to the office. He was excited.

Megarry took off his overcoat and hung it on the rack, then sat down beside him.

'Did you get any pictures?'

'Yes, Flatman, the girl, a middle-aged woman, who I hadn't

seen before and I assume is the wife. They're being developed right now.'

'Any other family members?'

'No, just those three.'

'What about the kid?'

'She goes to school in Belfast, place called Mountpleasant. Upper Lisburn Road. A private school, posh sort of place.'

'And security?'

'Tight as a goldfish's arse.'

Megarry felt a frisson of excitement.

'There's a garden centre across the road from the school with a sort of lay-by. I parked there and waited. The school gets out again at four thirty. The driver was back at four twenty, picked her up and drove her back to Lisburn. It's the same drill as they have for Flatman except there's only one car.'

'Where did the driver leave her in Lisburn?'

'At the house.'

'Did she get off anywhere on the way? Visit anyone, stop at the library, anything like that?'

'No.'

'Did she stay inside the school all the time?'

A brief smile crept across Nelson's face, a smile of triumph.

'No,' he said, 'she didn't.' They get a number of breaks during the day. At eleven o'clock, there's a break of fifteen minutes. A lot of the kids run around the schoolyard or walk in the playing fields. At one o'clock, they get a longer break, forty-five minutes. There's a tuck-shop just down the road from the school. It's a sort of newsagent-cum-confectioner. A couple of the bigger girls went down there. She went with them.'

'What did they do?'

'Hung around. There's a boys' school nearby, pimply youths mainly. You know the routine, drinking cokes, some of the boys smoking cigarettes.'

'How long was she outside the school?'

Nelson consulted his notebook. 'Ten past one till twenty-five past, a total of fifteen minutes.'

'That's it!' Megarry shouted and clapped his hands. 'Don't you see? If they wanted to snatch her, fifteen minutes is plenty of time, more than they would need. The whole thing could be over in a couple of minutes.' He reached in his pocket and dug out his cigarettes. 'She'll be relaxed, off guard. I'll bet she's been told never to leave the school grounds. But they've reckoned without her pals and some harmless flirting. She probably thinks all this security stuff is a load of horsefeathers'.

'But we still have no hard evidence,' Nelson said. 'Maybe we're assuming too much. All we've got is a kid leaving the school for fifteen minutes during her lunch break.'

'There's been a development.'

'What?'

'We have a suspect. I traced a stolen car. The guy who had it has gone on the run.'

There was a polite tap at the door. A young constable came into the room with a large brown envelope in his hand. 'I was told to bring this up.'

Nelson sliced it open. Half a dozen photographs fell in a heap on the desk. He picked one up and inspected it, then handed it to Megarry. 'That's the kid, coming out of the house. That's her again, getting into the car.'

Megarry examined the pictures. The face of a young girl stared out at him, wrapped in a scarf, cocooned against the cold morning. She was a good-looking child with fine features, but she looked unhappy.

'That's Flatman and his wife.'

Nelson handed over another print. A woman in a dressing gown stood in the doorway of a house; beside her, a man in an overcoat. He had a thin face and a little military moustache.

Megarry gasped – a small involuntary intake of breath.

'This is Flatman? this is the man who lives in Ingledale Road?'

Nelson caught the shock in his voice. He took the photograph again and inspected it. 'Well, that's the man who lives there, I'm assuming it's Flatman.'

Megarry examined the print once more. There could be no mistake. Even allowing for the poor light and the fact that the picture was taken at a distance, he recognised him at once.

At ten thirty Harvey phoned him at home.

'I've got the list made out and the teams organised. We're about to go in. Just ringing to let you know.'

'You know the drill,' Megarry said. 'Avoid confrontation. Just in and out. I don't want to read in the morning papers that we've been terrorising the population.'

'Don't worry, I briefed them personally.'

'And you've told the military?'

'Yes, I've done all that. I'll ring you later and let you know the results.'

'Good luck.'

'I'll ring you,' Harvey said.

Kathleen was watching television and Megarry sat with her for a while as an old black-and-white movie flickered to a conclusion. He was tired; the pace of the last few days had been hectic, much faster than he had become used to. Satisfying, he had to admit. An enjoyment, an excitement he remembered from the past.

Eventually Kathleen turned the set off, stood up and yawned.

'I'm turning in,' she said, 'what about you?'

On impulse, he reached out and kissed her softly behind the ear. It took her by surprise. 'Hey, what's come over you?'

He put his arms around her. 'Just the way I feel. I'm glad I came home. You rescued me.'

'No,' she said, 'you rescued yourself. I was just the facilitator.'

'Whatever, I did the right thing.'

'I'm happy for you, Cecil. What's put you in this mood?'

'The case I'm working on. We have a suspect, a young man called Morgan. I knew his father once.'

She looked up sharply. '*Morgan?* You don't mean ...?'

'Yes, I'm sure it's the same man. I saw his photograph today when I interviewed his widow.'

'How long is it, Cecil?'

'Twenty-five years.'

'That's an amazing coincidence.'

She laid her head on his shoulder and he kissed her again.

'You go to bed,' he said. 'I'm expecting some calls. I won't disturb you when I come up.'

He poured himself a large Bushmills, settled down and opened a book. He couldn't concentrate. His mind was on the men in the photographs. One past, one present ...

Shortly after two o'clock, he was woken by the loud ring of the telephone. Harvey. Megarry knew before he spoke that it was bad news.

'This thing is looking like a disaster. We didn't even get a sniff of him.'

'Nothing at all?'

'Oh, they knew him all right, everywhere we called. But they haven't seen him for days or weeks. You know the kind of thing, all innocent. The bottom line is, we couldn't find him.'

'Any trouble?'

'Nothing serious. Just the usual sullen resentment. No violence.'

16

The pain in his back woke Morgan early. It was throbbing again despite the sedative he had taken the night before. It was an omen; although he couldn't explain it, he knew from experience what it meant: something bad was going to happen.

He turned towards Queenie's body curled beside him, knees drawn up to her chest, pale skin showing through the flimsy fabric of her nightdress. She was still asleep, her dark hair like a web across the pillow. From her lips, at intervals, little bubbles of air escaped with a phht-phht sound like a tiny engine.

He lay for a while, watching her sleep, smelling the scent of her skin, the strange female smell he found so exciting. He had never seen a woman like this before, the curve of her hips, the soft putty feel of belly, the roundness of her breasts. It fascinated him. He saw a little blemish on her shoulder, a red birth mark, the size of a coin. He stretched out a hand and touched it and she shivered in her sleep and muttered. He withdrew his hand and she sank deeper into the sheets. The rhythmic puffing of her lips began again.

He had come to her after the meeting with Mr Cronin had left him scared and worried. He had a doubt, an anxiety that troubled him like an itch: what if the police were to change their minds? what if they decided that they wanted to talk to him again, and came looking for him? what if they wanted to arrest him? where would that leave the operation? He had made up his mind to leave home, give up his job and find somewhere else to stay, so that they couldn't find him. He arrived on her doorstep around midnight. He knew that she might not be in, because she worked odd shifts at the hospital, but there was a light burning in the hallway and after the second knock he heard footsteps on the stairs. The door was pulled open and there she was, standing in her dressing gown with the light from the house flooding around her. She took an astonished look at Morgan wrapped in his old gaberdine coat and clutching a sports bag. 'Jesus Christ,' she said, 'you're like a refugee from a jumble sale.'

He felt the colour rise in his cheeks and said, 'I'm sorry if I got you up. Can I come in?'

'Well you can't stand there looking like that, you'll frighten the neighbours. C'mon.'

She bent and took the bag from him. 'You've caught me on the hop. I'm not used to visitors at this hour of the night. What am I supposed to do, open a bottle of champagne?'

Morgan felt a secret pleasure at all the fuss. Queenie led him into the kitchen and put the kettle on for coffee.

'Well,' she said, 'do you want to tell me what it's all about?'

He had been tempted to tell her a lie, to conceal the truth. He could easily make up a story about a row with his mother. But he felt an overwhelming urge to confess, to share his burden.

'I got into a bit of trouble with the car.'

'What?' She turned from the cooker and stared.

'I took it out for a spin and got stopped by the cops.'

'Does Mr Cronin know?'

'Not all of it. He doesn't know about the police.'

'But they let you go?'

'After they grilled me for a couple of hours and took my fingerprints.'

She shook her head. 'I don't trust those bastards. You never know what they'll get up to. Where's the car now?'

'In a garage in Charlemont Street.'

She brought the coffee and sat down. 'You shouldn't have done it, Sean. That was very stupid. Verrry, verrry stupid.'

Morgan had nothing to say. He felt tired. So much had happened in the last twelve hours, and his world had been turned upside down. As if she could read his mind, she took his hand and caressed it gently.

'You're like a big baby with your car. Mr Cronin's as bad with his security.' She tutted. 'Little boys playing soldiers.'

'It's a war.'

'For some it's a game.'

Her bluntness shocked him. How could she talk like that?

'Not for me, I've risked a lot. I didn't have to get involved. Mr Cronin came to *me*, remember.'

'None of us had to get involved, Sean, but each of us chose to. For all our different reasons. And now we're all in it together. We have to look after each other.'

'Why do you say those mocking things? Don't you believe in what we're doing?'

She shrugged. 'Of course I believe, but some of the things we have to do are dirty things. The reality is so much grubbier than the ideal.'

He gasped. She was talking in riddles again.

'I can't help thinking of that poor kid, Sean. I can't help thinking what she'll go through.'

'But she won't be harmed. You said so yourself. Mr Cronin said so. You told me that was the whole point.'

'No, she won't be harmed, but that doesn't mean she's going to enjoy it. She'll be terrified – guarded at all times, moved around from pillar to post in the boot of a car. She won't be able to go for a piss without somebody standing outside the door.'

He felt his temper rise. She had this way of confusing him, of turning logic on its head, of taking contrary views and always seeming to be right.

'If that's how you feel about it, why don't you get out?'

He saw her mouth pucker and an impish look come into her eye, the next moment she started to laugh.

'Why should I get out? I want to hit the Brits, teach 'em a lesson. I told you all this before. It doesn't mean I have to agree with everything the organisation does. I'm not a zombie, I can still think for myself. I know right from wrong.'

180

He felt the tiredness again. Suddenly she leaned forward and kissed him on the cheek. 'You need some sleep,' she said. 'You poor silly eejit. C'mon, it's time you were in bed.'

Queenie gave him a sleeping bag and some cushions in the lounge, where he lay in a bundle between a bookshelf and the television. During the night, he felt the pain in his back. He took some painkillers from his bag and padded to the bathroom for water. As he passed her bedroom, he saw that the door was open.

'Sean, are you all right?'

He stopped and spoke into the darkness. 'It's nothing, just a pain.'

'Where?'

'My back.'

'Is it the floor?'

'I don't think so.'

'The floor is hard, maybe that's what it is.'

He felt stupid talking like this to someone he couldn't see.

'Come here,' she said.

He entered her bedroom where he could make out her dark outline from the light of the street-lamp shining through the curtains. She took his hand. 'Where is it sore?'

'It's all right, it'll go away. I've got painkillers.'

He felt her hand on the base of his spine, gently massaging – a warm sensual feeling mingled with the pain. He cried out, a little cooing sound like a pigeon would make.

'You poor child.'

She kept saying it over and over, 'You poor, silly child.'

Thursday was the day appointed for the dry run, the day they would go over the course as if it were the real thing. Every detail would be the same: times, route, procedure. Everybody knew exactly what they had to do. Morgan would drive the car. Kevin would be the look-out, in place in advance to warn them if there was any danger. They would pull in beside the tuck shop and Queenie would get out to ask directions. She would speak gently, putting the girl at ease, and then Peter would come from behind with the gun and the girl would be bundled into the car.

Morgan would drive away – calmly, speedily. At Finaghy another car would be waiting. They would transfer the kid. Morgan would take the car and the gloves and anything else that would link them to the kidnap. These would be burnt and the evidence destroyed.

He had been looking forward to this day since the training had begun. At nights when he couldn't sleep, he had lain in bed and gone over each step, rehearsing it in his mind until his eyelids had grown heavy and he dozed off. It was almost the climax of all their training; there was only one day more important – tomorrow, when they would carry out the job itself.

But all that had changed since he had taken the car and got stopped by the police. Now he didn't know what would happen, whether the job would be on or off, whether Mr Cronin would have instructions to alter it or postpone it or cancel it altogether. And if it were cancelled, whether he would be blamed because of his indiscipline, what Mr Cronin had called his selfishness.

Queenie had to go into work. She got up at eight o'clock and fussed around the flat, closing doors, running water in the bathroom, trailing in and out of the kitchen. He lay on in bed, listening to the sounds of traffic in the street outside. At half-past eight she came in with toast and coffee.

'How's your back?'

The pain was still there, a worm of discomfort, but it had eased considerably from the night he had arrived. Morgan tried a joke. 'It's better. Whatever you did last night must have cured it.'

She slapped him playfully across the knuckles. 'Don't you get out of your box,' she said.

She was wearing a sweater and skirt and had her hair tied back in a severe bun. He could just imagine her on the ward – thorough and efficient in her starched white uniform. He had never thought of her this way before.

'I finish at one. The meeting's at two. I'll have a bite to eat at work and then I'll make my way across. There's food in the fridge, if you want any, help yourself.'

She bent her head and kissed him on the mouth. He stretched his arms to pull her down, but she struggled free and straightened her hair. 'I'll be late. I'll see you at the meeting.' And then almost as an afterthought, she said, 'Are you afraid?'

'A little.'

'Afraid of what Mr Cronin will say?'

'Yes.'

She smiled her impish smile again and he felt his troubles ease away.

'Don't worry, Sean. Everything will be all right. You'll see.'

He heard her footsteps receding down the stairs and the hall door closing. He lay in the sheets, thinking about her beside him, her body close to his, her special scent. He had never been good with women – he felt awkward and ill at ease in their company, conscious of his affliction, worrying what went through their heads and whether they were thinking of his wasted trunk and his withered legs.

Queenie was the first woman he'd ever had, and the memory of their few nights together filled him with wonder. She had made it all so easy, so natural, as if it were the simplest thing in the world. Then to lie like that, wrapped in each other's arms. He remembered each touch, each kiss, the way she had guided him and showed him what to do, the exquisite pleasure, more intense than anything he had known.

What did she see in him? Was he just some plaything, someone to entertain her until she grew tired and looked for other satisfaction? Would they still be lovers when this job was over?

He fell asleep again and dreamed about the car chase. But it was a fitful sleep and he soon woke. He went into the bathroom and turned the water on for a shower. In a cupboard he found a clutter of bottles filled with oils and creams and strangely scented lotions. He unscrewed the caps and sniffed the contents, feeling as if he were an intruder. He wanted to know everything about her, all the little personal details, all the small, humdrum, day-to-day events of her life.

At ten past one, he was ready to leave. He got down the old gaberdine coat and a cap to hide his face. He hadn't been out of the flat since he had arrived and he was fearful that people would be watching him. This was the same fear he had felt the day he stole the car and the night he attended the first meeting in Beechmount, as if everyone knew who he was and was following him with their eyes. He knew it was foolish, like the fear of stepping on cracks in the pavement, but he kept his head down and his gaze averted as he hurried past the loungers outside the bookie's shop and the kids playing football at the gable end, until he came to the main road and the sanctuary of the bus-stop.

The club looked different in the daylight – brighter, less intimidating, and the warm sun danced off the windows in a thousand spangles of light. There was a function planned for the afternoon, a pensioners' bingo session, and when he pushed open the doors two men were setting out rows of plastic chairs.

He caught the smell of stale beer and cigarette smoke as he went through the bar and out into the dingy hall. When he got to the landing he stopped to take a deep breath. They would be waiting for him, the two boys with their pale, uncertain faces, Mr Cronin, sitting as usual at the table by the window, where he could look down into the street, and Queenie. What would the decision be, to cancel or to go ahead?

As soon as he opened the door, he knew there was something wrong. Mr Cronin turned to look at him and he saw displeasure in his eyes. It seemed to Morgan that everyone else in the room sensed it too; they sat waiting in silence for Mr Cronin to speak. For a moment he said nothing. He was smoking a cigarette and he leaned over and crushed it in an ashtray.

'You made it, Sean.' His voice was cold with none of the banter he used to help them relax.

Morgan started to reply, but Mr Cronin silenced him.

'I got a strange telephone call last night.' He kept his eyes fixed on Morgan. 'Very strange. It was from someone whose house had been raided by the police. They were looking for you.'

'For me?'

'Yes, Sean. Why would they be looking for you? Is there any reason?'

'No,' Morgan heard the denial tumbling from his lips. 'I can't understand it. I was at home last night. I didn't go out.' He felt Queenie's eyes on him.

'Did they not call at your house?'

'No,' Morgan said. The fear was hammering in his breast. Why were the police looking for him? Was it about the car? He even wondered if Mr Cronin had found out that he was now with Queenie and this was his way of testing him. 'Are you sure it was me? There's no mistake?'

'There's no mistake, Sean. It was you all right. There's something else. We've been keeping surveillance on the target. Yesterday a strange man turned up at the school; he appeared in the morning and hung about all day. He waited until she left the premises and then followed her to Lisburn. I had him checked out – he's a Special Branch detective.'

Morgan felt panic wash over him.

Mr Cronin kept his eyes on him, studying his face. 'You're sure you know nothing about this, Sean?'

'No,' Morgan said again, 'nothing.'

Mr Cronin sniffed. 'Well, it means a change of plan.' He turned to Peter and Kevin. 'You lads are being stood down from the operation. You're to go home and forget everything you ever heard in this room. There'll be other jobs for you in the fullness of time. Just lie low for a while and you'll be contacted again.'

They got up reluctantly and left. Mr Cronin waited until they had gone before speaking again.

'Maybe the Special Branch man is additional security. Maybe the cops have got wind of what we're planning. But one way or another, it's too dangerous to continue with the operation as scheduled.'

He snapped the locks on his briefcase, took out the road map and spread it on the table. 'It doesn't matter,' he said. 'We're going ahead anyway, but we're going to do it differently.'

He lifted the pointer.

'What about the dry-run?' Morgan asked cautiously.

Mr Cronin lowered the pointer.

'There won't be one. We haven't time. We're doing it today. We're snatching the girl this afternoon.'

Megarry was up early and into the office before his usual time. There was an envelope on his desk. It had come in overnight and he knew what it contained. He cut through the flap and the sealing tape, and took out Morgan's picture and fingerprints.

He held the photograph to the light. A young, frightened face stared out at him and he thought how they always looked the same in these pictures, as if they were against a wall waiting to be shot. He remembered the face of the man sitting on the stairs in that little house, all those years ago, a gun cradled in his hands. The eyes were the same, the nose, the bend of the jaw, the low sweep of hair across the forehead.

Now that man's son was hiding somewhere in the city, waiting until it was time for him to get behind the wheel of the stolen car and execute their plan. No doubt he thought he was doing right – striking a blow for justice or freedom, something like that. No doubt he believed that by taking the girl they could achieve some good, put right some wrong.

He visualised the ripples in the pond, the energy spreading out in waves and never dying; the antiquity of the quarrel, father to son, generation to generation. Old ghosts were stirring, old memories, events that had convulsed Megarry's life and shaped it.

He didn't hear Nelson come in, but when he turned the young man was standing in the doorway with his scarf in his hand. He looked at Megarry with apprehension. 'How did it go last night?'

'Not good.'

'Nothing?'

'Not a sniff, as Harvey said.'

'What're you going to do?' He started to take off his coat, but Megarry was holding up a hand. 'Keep it on,' he said, 'We're going out.'

'Where to?'

'Donaghy's Bar.'

They found it easily enough, in an alley at the bottom of York Street, at the back of the cathedral. It was an old-fashioned pub that once did a thriving business from traders and shop-workers and retained its charm. It hadn't opened yet, so Megarry rapped on the window until the curtains were drawn and a querulous face peered out.

'Police,' Megarry mouthed and held up his identity card. The face disappeared and there was a rattle of bolts and locks as the door was pulled open to reveal a skinny man in a barman's long white apron. He had a bald forehead and a little ring of curly hair that got thicker as it approached his ears.

'Does Sean Morgan work here?'

The man stared, his eyes moving from one policeman to the other. At last he said, 'He's not here now. He hasn't been in to work since Tuesday.'

'Are you his boss?'

'Yes.'

'Can we talk to you?'

'Of course.'

They followed him into a long bar with tables and chairs, and stools propped against the counter. Near the end of the room, a young boy with a broom was sweeping the floor; another man was polishing glasses and stacking them on a shelf. They both stopped as the policemen came in.

'Well now,' the skinny man said, 'can I get you gentlemen a cup of tea?' His eyes strayed to a row of bottles behind the bar, 'or maybe something stronger. A wee snifter of whiskey perhaps? It's a raw morning out there.'

'It's too early,' Megarry said, taking out his cigarettes.

'Tea then?'

'Tea would be fine.'

The man motioned to the boy and settled down on a stool beside the policemen. He lowered his voice and spoke in a confidential tone. 'My name's O'Rourke. I'm the manager here.' He hesitated, 'Is Sean in some kind of trouble?'

Megarry looked up and saw his reflection in a mirror. JOHN POWER, it said. PREMIER WHISKIES. He remembered another bar

187

with a similar legend, a dark, crowded place near the docks. He had done so much business there, interviewed so many informers, the crush of bodies and the peals of laughter giving cover while secrets passed from hand to hand. In the end it had become too dangerous. One drink too many, then the false sense of security and the chatter would be shattered by the roar of gunfire and the crack of breaking glass. Now he picked with care the places where he drank, a table near the back, a view of the door so that he could see the assassin's face whenever he came.

'No,' Megarry said. 'Just a few questions. Did you know he'd left home?'

The man nodded his head, 'I was told he'd gone to Dublin for a few days.'

'Who told you that?'

'His sister rang in.'

'Has he ever done that before?'

'Not that I remember.'

'When's the last time you saw him?'

'Monday.'

Nelson interrupted, 'You said Tuesday.'

'Tuesday, I was off. He was here Tuesday, but I didn't see him.'

'Tell me about him,' Megarry said.

The man puffed out his cheeks. 'What's there to tell? He's a good worker. Does his share of the dirty jobs. Cheerful most of the time. He does have a wee tendency to temper, but he get's on well with everyone. Very good with the customers.'

'He's a cripple, I understand.'

The man looked shocked. 'That's putting it a bit strong. He had a back injury when he was a child. His legs are deformed, but he can walk all right and it doesn't stop him doing the hard work.'

'This trip to Dublin, it was a bit sudden, wasn't it?'

The man rubbed his hand across his bald head as if he were polishing it. 'I suppose it was, in a way. There was no warning. At least I heard nothing about it. And if he was going to tell anyone, I suppose he would have told me.'

'Who was the last person to talk to him?'

They were interrupted by the boy with the tea. He set down a tray and three cups on the counter. The manager reached out to detain him. 'Liam, you were here on Tuesday?'

'Yes.'

'Did you talk to Sean?'

The boy nodded.

'These gentlemen are making some inquiries about him; they're police officers. Did he mention anything about going to Dublin?'

'No,' the boy said, 'nothing like that.'

Megarry caught the scared look in his eye. He spoke quietly. 'We're just making a few inquiries, nothing to worry about. Just tell us what you can remember.'

'Well,' the boy began, glancing nervously at the three faces, 'it was a quiet morning. He'd a half-day off and he was looking forward to it. Trade was slow so we tried to catch up on a few things.'

'Like what?'

'Stacking shelves … a bit of stocktaking.'

'You said he had a half-day?'

'Yes.'

'Did he say if he'd anything planned? anything special? Did he say where he was going? Can you remember?'

'Oh yes,' the boy said, brightening up, 'he said he was going to Smithfield.'

'Smithfield? Did he say what for?'

'To see some fella about a car.'

Megarry and Nelson exchanged glances and started rapidly down the room. The skinny manager shouted after them, 'Hey, what about this tea?'

Jim McKeever put down the tabloid he was reading when he heard the banging on the door – an imperious rapping, a barrage of sound, loud, urgent, causing a flicker of fear to ripple through him. Wiping his hands on a rag, he started towards the door, where shafts of daylight filtered through the cracks from the street outside.

'I'm coming,' he said, 'calm down.'

The noise came again, thumps and bangs and shouts warning him to open up. He stopped and looked down the dim warehouse floor. Near the back, where the light cast shadows on the stacks of flour, he thought he could still see the car, shimmering beneath its ghostly white drapes. But the car wasn't there any more, only the drapes. The cripple had taken it and hadn't come back. If it was the car they were looking for, McKeever wouldn't be any use to them at all.

The voices seemed to be right beside him now, rattling in his brain. 'Open up. If you don't open that fucking door, we'll break it down. You've been warned.'

'Okay, okay,' McKeever said. He had only been doing a favour for Mr Cronin, minding the car while the boss was away. He hadn't asked any questions, but he'd known something about it wasn't quite right.

'Hold your horses. I'm coming.' He reached up and found the lock. As he turned the key, the door came crashing in on him. He saw the police uniforms, a flash of green and silver buttons. One of them grabbed his arm, twisted it up his back and forced him against the wall. Another shouted in his ear, 'Where is it?'

'What?'

'The car, the goddamned car. Talk, or I'll break your fucking neck.'

McKeever felt the pain shoot along his arm like a blade of lightning.

'I don't know what you're talking about.'

'Don't lie to me.'

'I'm not lying.'

Fingers grabbed his hair and pulled his head back from the wall. 'I'm giving you one last chance.' The breath was hot in his ear. 'Tell us where that car is, or you'll be one sorry man.'

The fingers tightened on his scalp; tears started from his eyes and tumbled down his cheeks. His arm went numb and he thought he was going to faint. 'I don't know where it is,' McKeever choked, 'honest to God ...'

His face was shoved back against the cold brick. There was a babble of rough country voices, shouting and cursing, then one voice stood out above the rest.

'Leave him alone, I'll deal with this.'

The hands released him.

A portly man in a dark overcoat lit a cigarette and reached up to peel a flake of tobacco from his lip.

'What's your name?' Megarry asked.

'Jim McKeever.'

The police chief nodded. 'You're in trouble, Jim. You've been a foolish boy, a very foolish boy.' He spoke in a soft voice, but the gravity in his tone struck fear into McKeever's heart.

'I was only minding it.'

'Minding it is serious, Jim. You're an accessory. You'll go down, you'll go down for a long time.'

McKeever felt the sweat break along his scalp. 'But I didn't do anything.'

'You don't have to do anything. You're an accomplice, that's enough. Where is it now?'

'It's gone. The cripple took it.'

Megarry had a photograph in his hand. He shoved it into McKeever's face. 'Is that him? Is that the guy who took it?'

McKeever squinted. 'Yes.'

'When?'

'Tuesday afternoon.'

'Did he say where he was going?'

'Out for a drive.'

'So he was meant to bring it back?'

McKeever felt his head spin – all these questions, he could hardly think.

'Yes. They weren't supposed to take it until Thursday.'

The policeman tapped ash from the end of his cigarette. 'Say that again.'

'Thursday, today.' McKeever looked into the policeman's eyes as the realisation dawned on him. 'The car wasn't supposed to be moved until today.'

Megarry dropped the cigarette and crushed it.

17

Raymond Boyd walked slowly along the corridor, past the crowded common room, where there was already a bustle around the coffee urn and hands were reaching politely for biscuits. He didn't feel like coffee. He didn't feel like the small change of chit-chat, the gossip and complaints that passed for conversation during the afternoon break.

He walked past the stern bust of the founder, the plaque to the school benefactors and the glass case with the trophies. Every now and then he stopped to peer through the windows, down across the green sward of the lawn, as if expecting someone. When he came to the door that led out to the playing fields he stopped again and checked his watch; he had time to spare. Stepping out into the cold afternoon sun, he decided to smoke a cigarette and stroll along the path beneath the gaunt branches of the sycamore trees. It would give him a chance to think.

On the bottom field he could see the flash of red jerseys, hear the clack of hockey sticks and the shouts of encouragement from the small band of supporters huddled for warmth behind the goal. The sounds were comforting, in the way of all regular things. In the last few days, he had begun to draw succour from the small routines of the school, as though they provided a refuge from the brutal reality of life outside. He had grown used to them; he would miss them when he left.

As he walked, his mind kept returning to the phone call he'd received yesterday. He could still hear Mr Cronin's anxious voice as it echoed down the line. 'Something has come up. I need you to do me a favour.'

'What sort of favour?'

'Nothing much. It's quite simple, really.'

Boyd knew that Mr Cronin's request would concern Caroline; he had known since that night in the Pike Club when he had foolishly talked about her. In the days and weeks since then, Mr Cronin had pumped him for information about her father, her mother, their household, their routine, gathering in all the debts and favours he had paid out to Boyd and his family over the years.

'What time does school finish tomorrow?' Mr Cronin asked.

'Early, it's a half-day.'

'Good. Now here's what I want you to do. You won't be involved, it's totally safe. Now listen carefully.'

Boyd followed the path down past a small rose garden, where a few flowers struggled to bloom in the dying winter sun. He could still hear Mr Cronin's voice whispering – all night he had remembered it. It had wakened him from his sleep.

He felt his feet sink into the rich carpet of leaves strewing the path. The air was still. He heard the chirp, chirp of a songbird and the answering call from across the fields. He dropped his cigarette and crushed it with his foot, checking his watch. Any moment now. Then he saw her, hurrying along the path to meet him, long legs striding, blonde hair flying, her face radiant.

He started towards her, and his heart sank with every step he took.

As soon as he got back to the car, Megarry rang Drysdale on the mobile phone.

'I need help, Jack. The kidnap attempt. I think they're going for it today.' He tried to speak slowly and calmly.

'Today?' Drysdale gave a low whistle.

193

'Yes, today. I need roadblocks. All traffic heading south out of the city.'

'How soon?'

'Immediately. I want them up now.'

Drysdale began to protest. 'That's a tall order, Cecil. You're talking twenty or thirty streets. Maybe a hundred men. I can't just pull them out of a hat.'

'But this is urgent, for Christ's sake. How long will it take?'

'I don't know – twenty minutes, half an hour?'

'Forget it,' Megarry said, 'I can't wait that long. Put road-blocks on Shaftesbury Square and Lisburn Road. We're looking for a Toyota Sprinter, turquoise colour. I have the registration. Have you got a pen?'

He waited while Drysdale wrote it down.

'Detain the occupants, and tell your people to take no chances. These guys are dangerous and almost certainly armed.'

'Anything else?'

'Mountpleasant School. Upper Lisburn Road. Do you know it?'

'We'll find it.'

'Get a couple of cars up there. Tell them to block the entrance. Nothing's to get in or out until I arrive. I'll be there in ten minutes.'

Colonel Flatman looked up from his papers when the phone rang in the adjoining office. A red light came on the console to indicate that his assistant had taken the call. He put down his pen, stretched his hands behind his back and took a deep breath so that his lungs filled with air.

He was aware that he got little exercise. The tight security situation didn't allow it. When he was at home in Epsom, he used to swim regularly and jog when the weather was good, but all that had come to a stop when they sent him to Northern Ireland. It was another downside to this posting. To compensate, Flatman walked around the building as much as he could, rarely took the lift and had recently started stretching and breathing exercises which he could do at his desk.

194

He had also started work on a new project: to disseminate information about a number of politicians regarded as unfriendly. The information was not particularly appealing – it had to do with their private lives, their sexual predilections, their drinking habits and their debts. He had conducted a similar study six months before, aimed at a number of paramilitary figures, and it had been a resounding success. Damaging information was gathered from his network of informers and dispersed through a handful of reliable journalists. It wasn't necessary for the information actually to find its way into newspaper articles, word of mouth was enough. But it was vital that the information be correct.

Colonel Flatman didn't particularly enjoy the work. There was a certain grubbiness involved, but he was pleased with the progress he had made. One of the men he had targeted had a serious alcohol problem, another was a wife-beater. A third was supposed to be interested in under-age boys, but this was not confirmed.

He let the air escape from his lips in a slow release and filled his lungs again. Outside the window was a smooth expanse of countryside, fields lying open with hardly a tree or a hill to catch the eye. He liked this view, found it restful. In the summer, when the weather was fine, he could sometimes see the spires and chimneys of Belfast shimmering in the distance. But not today: today the sky was dull and overcast and rain seemed likely.

Through the frosted glass that separated the two offices, Colonel Flatman saw his assistant's head nodding vigorously into the phone. The call was taking a long time, longer than it should reasonably take to write down a simple message. He turned back to the papers on his desk but looked up once more when the door opened and his assistant's eager face peered at him from the doorway. He approached the desk and spoke in a soft voice.

'It's Superintendent Megarry, sir. I tried to tell him that you were engaged, but he insisted on speaking to you. He says it's a matter of the utmost importance.'

Colonel Flatman waved his hand, 'It's all right, Broadbent, I'll talk to him.' He leaned forward to lift the phone.

'Superintendent,' he began in a confident tone, 'good to hear from you. What can I do?'

Charlemont Street was quiet as a tomb when Morgan called. Nothing stirred along the solid phalanx of redbrick Victorian houses, not even a leaf on the branches of the elm trees along the damp, grey pavements.

He approached Bates's house cautiously, stopping to make sure that no unseen eyes were watching from behind the prim lace curtains, no loiterer had been missed, no spy monitoring his movements.

Since his earlier meeting with Mr Cronin, his nerves had been on edge. The police were looking for him; that could mean only one thing. It had to do with the car. He wondered if Mr Cronin had told him all he knew, whether he suspected him and Queenie. But he hadn't said, and in the end seemed to have regained his composure. He had become the old Cronin, cracking jokes to put them at ease, telling them over and over that nothing could go wrong and that the whole operation would be just like taking candy from a baby.

He let his eye scan the street; it was just as before. The only thing that moved was a plump tabby cat that jumped down from a window ledge and rubbed itself against his leg. The garage was beside the house, its paintwork peeled and cracking. Bates was at work so there was no need to ring the bell. The thing to do was to act nonchalantly, get the car out and away as quickly as possible and hope that no busybody would see anything out of the ordinary. As he fumbled for the key, he thought about the strange way everything had turned out – it had all been done in a rush, Mr Cronin with his pointer and map giving them new instructions. All the previous planning had been cast aside, all the work they had put in, night after night in the cold room above the Pike Club. Mr Cronin had said something that seemed important: a revolutionary must learn to adapt, to seize the vital moment, to use the element of surprise. Nothing was permanent; nothing was fixed. Even things that seemed sacrosanct were subject to change.

Morgan quickly inserted the key and pulled open the garage door. The car was as he had left it, and he felt a thrill of pleasure. He put on his gloves, got into the driver's seat and checked the controls. The petrol tank was three-quarters full. He turned on the lights, tried the indicators, then fired the engine. There was a smooth hum as the motor caught.

He reversed carefully into the street and parked along the kerb, got out and locked the garage doors again. The car was now pointing towards the Lisburn Road. He felt in his pocket for the little map Mr Cronin had drawn: Cardiff Drive. It was marked with an arrow, and an X for the corner where he was to pick up Queenie.

He checked his watch – plenty of time. He put his foot down gently on the accelerator and listened to the clean surge of the engine. The car was like a work of art: everything so new, so smooth, so fast and efficient. It would pain him when he had to set fire to it and reduce it to a mass of meaningless steel.

Morgan drove carefully, turning over in his head what Mr Cronin had said. Mr Cronin had impressed on him the need to relax, to behave normally, to do nothing that might attract attention. He wished now that he had acted like that when he had heard the bomb, when he'd been stopped by the police.

The butt of a small automatic pistol nestled at the base of his spine, just where the pain had been. And there was a strange thing, the pain had gone.

He slowed down when he saw the sign for the Antrim Arms. The trestle tables and benches looked sad and deserted. On one table a couple of empty beer glasses rested forlornly in a pool of water where the rain had gathered.

Queenie was waiting at the entrance to the car-park, wearing her nurse's uniform, starched blouse and skirt of blue and white and a dark cape to keep out the cold. She had put on a blonde wig, as Mr Cronin had instructed. He opened the door and she got in beside him. She had never seen him drive before. Until now, it had all been talk, empty theory. Now he had a

197

chance to show her what he could do. He was the driver, the key person on the operation.

She put her hand on his wrist and he saw that she was trembling. 'Are you cold?' he asked. 'I can turn on the heater.'

She shook her head. 'No. Just a wee bit afraid.'

Nelson drove on to the pavement and parked the car across the school gates so that the entrance was effectively blocked. He switched off the engine and sat surveying the scene before him. Then he turned quickly to Megarry and gave a weak smile. 'I think we've made it.'

'Yes,' Megarry said, and opened the door.

Mountpleasant School was peaceful in the afternoon sun. Across a rolling lawn, he could see a redbrick building and the sun glinting off the cars parked along the gravel drive. It seemed to Megarry that all was as it should be, that inside those walls rows of youthful faces were bent over their books, oblivious of the drama outside. As he stepped on to the pavement he became aware of voices singing, a chorus swelling from an open window. It was a hymn of thanksgiving, a tune he remembered from long ago. He looked along the deserted drive and back to the road where the traffic was moving at its usual pace and suddenly it seemed that the hymn was appropriate; he felt a wave of relief wash over him.

All the way across town, as they had raced along back streets and through traffic lights, Megarry had sat tight-lipped; beside him, Nelson's mouth had moved in silent prayer. In the end this irritated Megarry and he had snapped, 'Why involve God in this? We're either late or we're not. Why should God care?' Immediately regretting his outburst, he had patted the younger man's shoulder and urged him to greater efforts.

The singing stopped. In its place, Megarry heard the sound of a game being played, the smack of a ball, the cries of support. They were in time, of that he had no doubt.

'What do we do now?' Nelson asked.

'We wait. Or rather, you wait. I'm going to take the girl out. Nice and easy. No fuss or panic. You stay here and keep an eye on the situation, I won't be long.'

He started towards the drive but, as he did so, he heard the faint squealing of an alarm. A squad car came speeding through the traffic, followed closely by another, their lights flashing and sirens wailing. They pulled in beside the gates; a grey-haired sergeant got out and walked towards him.

'Superintendent Megarry?'

'That's me.'

The man saluted, 'I was told ...'

'I know what you were told, sergeant, but I think we've got matters under control. You can help by monitoring the traffic. Don't let anybody stop and make sure that no one gets in or out of the school until I give clearance.'

'Yes, sir.'

'And sergeant,' Megarry pointed towards the squad cars with their racing lights, 'knock off the sirens. Next thing we know, we'll have a crowd of gaping sightseers.'

Another car pulled in, a sleek black Mercedes.

Nelson recognised it at once. 'That's Flatman's car.'

'I know,' Megarry said. 'I called him.'

The sergeant was already trying to move the Mercedes along.

Megarry went forward to intervene. 'It's all right, I'll vouch for this man.'

Flatman got out of the car and walked towards them. He was wearing the same fawn overcoat that Nelson remembered. His face was pale and drawn; Megarry could see his hands shaking.

'She's safe,' Megarry began, 'you can relax.'

Flatman's expression didn't change. 'Where is she?'

'Inside the school. I've got roadblocks at Shaftesbury Square and the Lisburn Road. We know who we're looking for. There's no way they can touch her.'

'What about the back entrance?'

'There's no back entrance. I've checked.'

'There's a gate,' Flatman said. 'It's rarely used. It leads into the grounds. Maybe you should ...'

Megarry felt the blood drain from his face.

* * *

Caroline came hurrying towards Boyd, her shoes making a squishing sound on the wet leaves.

He had suggested the meeting so that they could go over a project she was working on, an essay on *Macbeth*. When he had mentioned it, her face lit up with pleasure. She enjoyed these encounters, quoting poetry, making observations, showing off her knowledge of literature in a childish way. But it was also because they could be together, and this made him uneasy. When she reached him she opened her satchel and took out a little parcel, tied with a blue ribbon. She pressed it awkwardly into his hand.

'What is it?' he asked, confused.

'It's a present. To show my appreciation.'

It felt like a bottle of some kind. He raised it to his nose and sniffed. 'Aftershave?'

'Yes. You use it, don't you? I know you do, I've smelt it.'

'But there's no need, Caroline. You shouldn't have done this.'

He felt a wave of guilt. The child was so open, so honest. She trusted him and he was about to betray her.

'There is, you've been kind to me. I wanted to thank you.'

She fell in beside him, swinging along. Boyd put the bottle carefully in an inside pocket.

'I thought we'd walk in the woods, down towards the back of the school. It's peaceful there, and the woods have a special atmosphere at this time of year; the leaves gone and the branches so stark and bare.'

A small smile puckered the corners of her mouth.

'You have a poet's soul,' she said. 'You like nature, don't you?'

'Of course. Where I grew up it was all concrete and bleak mill chimneys. We had to go for miles to see trees and fields.'

'Back in Epsom, there was plenty of open space and the downs. I have a pony, and every day I went cantering on the downs.'

They were crossing a small path which led to the back gate of the school. He had come here in his first weeks to sit and read or to mark homework. He thought of those days now, as he led her, innocent and willing, towards her fate.

'Tell me about where you grew up,' she said.

'There's not much to tell. It was a tiny house, in a street with

200

forty or fifty similar houses, and another street just the same and another and another.'

'What did you do when you wanted to relax?'

'Oh, we had plenty of amusements. We played football or handball.'

'In the street?'

'Yes, there was nowhere else. But we had to watch out for the police. It wasn't allowed, you know.'

'Was it difficult?'

'I don't think we looked at it like that. We didn't know anything else, so we had nothing to compare it with. I suppose we were content in our way.' He found it difficult to keep up this small talk, especially since she'd given him the present. He hadn't expected that; it underlined his treachery and filled him with a sense of worthlessness. He looked nervously at his watch and decided to smoke another cigarette. He cursed Mr Cronin, cursed the day he had mentioned her name, the time when he had agreed to pass information about her father.

'We're supposed to be discussing Macbeth,' Boyd said, deciding to change the subject. 'Tell me what you like about the play.'

He saw her shake her head. 'I don't.'

'Why not?'

'Too much blood.'

'But that's the whole point, Caroline. In all Shakespeare's tragedies there's a great deal of blood spilt. Audiences expected it; they still do.'

'We're more civilised now. In those days they had bear-baiting and cock fights. They burnt people at the stake if they didn't agree with them, or they hanged them from a gibbet and cut their tongues out.'

'Maybe,' Boyd heard himself say, 'but Shakespeare's plays have survived because, like all great literature, they tell us something about ourselves, something about the human condition. Maybe we haven't changed all that much in four hundred years.'

She smiled at him. Stop it, he thought, don't make it so hard for me.

They reached the gate. There was a wooden seat, damp from the earlier rain. Boyd took out his handkerchief and wiped it dry and they both sat down. He stretched his legs and started again. 'Shakespeare's tragedies deal with a single individual and how he is brought low by a fatal flaw. Each of his tragic heroes has this characteristic – Othello, Lear, Hamlet. What do you think is Macbeth's fatal flaw?'

'I don't know.'

'Think, Caroline. What drives him on?'

'He wants to be king.'

'Of course. Macbeth's fatal flaw is ambition.'

He thought he heard a car drive along the road outside and come to a halt.

'Macbeth wants to be king. The witches tell him he will be king, but he isn't content to wait for it, he decides to *make* it happen.'

'And what about Lady Macbeth?'

'At the beginning she's more ambitious than her husband. She encourages him, but then she ...'

Caroline wasn't listening. He looked up and saw a woman in a nurse's uniform come through the gate and hurry towards them, out of breath, the light through the trees making patterns on her dark glasses.

'Caroline Flatman?' the woman asked.

She stopped when she got to them, and bent urgently to talk to Caroline. Boyd saw the blonde hair under her nurse's cap.

'Yes.'

'I've got bad news, I'm afraid. There's been an accident. You'll have to come with us to the hospital, I've a car waiting.'

'What sort of accident?'

'Your mother's been injured.'

Caroline's face filled with horror. She's going to cry, he thought, and felt revulsion rise like a sickness. But the nurse had raised her from the seat and had her arm around her shoulder. She was talking softly, consoling her. 'There's nothing to worry about, your mother's going to be all right, but she's been asking for you.'

Caroline turned quickly towards him, but before she could

speak, he laid a hand on her shoulder. 'You must go, I think it's the best thing.'

The nurse led her towards the gate and the road outside, walking slowly, speaking soft comforting words. Caroline turned and looked back at him, but he lowered his eyes. When he looked up, they had gone. A car engine started up.

Boyd saw that she had left her satchel on the seat, and he considered taking it, but changed his mind. He turned on his heel and started back through the woods towards the school, tears wetting his cheeks.

18

At the front gate, the sirens on the police cars fell silent. Out of the corner of his eye, Megarry saw Nelson shifting uneasily as he waited.

'I didn't realise,' Megarry said, 'I was told there was no other entrance.'

The words stuttered in his throat and sounded lame.

Flatman turned and was running towards his car. Megarry started to follow, trying to restrain him. 'We still have time, school hasn't come out yet.'

He got into the passenger seat beside Flatman and rolled down the window. He shouted to Nelson, 'Get the sergeant up to the school. You follow us.'

Flatman was struggling with the steering wheel. The car suddenly reversed, straightened up, and bucked forward again. The tyres screeched on the road. Behind them, the school gates disappeared in a blur of shapes. Megarry felt for his shoulder holster.

They took the first turning on the right, a quiet suburban avenue lined with trees. Flatman spoke, breaking the tension, 'How did you learn about this?'

'It's the case I've been working on. It started with the bank raid.'

'Why didn't you tell me sooner?'

'Your cover.'

Flatman didn't respond. He said, 'Where did you get my number?'

'You gave it to me yourself. You told me to ring you from time to time, don't you remember? After the last security meeting, you gave me your card?'

He saw again Flatman standing in the crowded hallway, nervously shifting his overcoat from hand to hand as he attemped to apologise.

Megarry had known for sure that Fleming was Flatman the moment he saw Nelson's photograph.

He glanced towards him. Flatman's eyes, normally vapid, were full of fear. He's just a frightened parent, Megarry thought, like anyone would be, scared his daughter will be harmed.

'It was you who asked for me to be put on this case in the first place. Isn't that so?'

Flatman's eyes flickered, but he didn't speak.

'When the bank informed you that your private papers had been taken in the raid, you were alarmed. And round about the same time, you heard a kidnap was being planned – the Commander mentioned it. You talked to him and got the Security Committee to recommend me. Is that what happened?'

'Yes.'

'But you must have known it would lead me to you.'

'No,' Flatman said, 'I thought it would be a simple matter of getting the papers back.'

'Why didn't you tell me?' But he knew what the answer would be.

'I couldn't ... the nature of my work.' Flatman hesitated and then added, 'I thought it would be me. I thought if anyone was in danger, it was me. I never dreamt they'd pick Caroline.'

They turned again, another street like the last, but the place was deserted. There was a little gate in the wall, but it was shut and no one was in sight.

'Is this it?' Megarry asked.

Flatman nodded. Megarry wondered if they had made a

mistake, got the wrong day and she was safe, still inside the school. Then near the bottom of the road, he saw the glint of a car roof as it turned into a side street. Flatman saw it too.

They shot forward again. At the end of the street was a junction. They turned left and saw the car clearly – a turquoise Sprinter on the main road, travelling fast away from town. In the back seat, they could make out a blonde head and a woman with a cap, a nurse's cap.

The sight enraged Flatman. He stamped his foot down and the car accelerated, but the Sprinter kept out in front. They began to overtake traffic; cars and lorries rushing past in a splash of colours. Megarry glanced at the gauge; the arrow hovered at ninety mph.

'They've spotted us,' he said, 'they know we're following.'

'But it's only a Sprinter, I can catch it.'

'Don't be so sure, they've probably souped up the engine. Let me phone. I'll get them intercepted.'

But Flatman was shaking his head. 'They'll get away.'

Megarry caught the fear in his voice. He's irrational, he thought, he can't think clearly. Flatman pumped his foot on the accelerator, willing the car forward.

He looked back but there was no sign of Nelson. The road was narrowing and they were leaving the city behind; soon they would be in open countryside. This would suit the smaller car.

Megarry made a decision. He reached into his holster and took out the pistol, broke it open and checked the chamber.

'What are you doing?'

'I'm going to shoot out the tyres.'

'No. It's too dangerous. What about my child?'

'It's not as dangerous as this crazy chase. We're going to crash if you don't slow down.'

'But they'll escape.'

'They'll escape anyway. They have a better engine and the driver knows how to handle the car.'

He rolled down the window. A rush of wind rattled against the roof like a drumbeat. He leaned out, straightened his arm and sighted along the barrel of the gun.

The first shot hit the mudguard and bits of plastic spun away in a puff of dust. He steadied his arm and took aim again.

All at once the Sprinter began to weave away from its lane, out into the middle of the road, as the driver realised what was happening. The second shot hit the tarmac and kicked up a cloud of gravel.

'Damn it,' Megarry said angrily. 'Stay still, can't you?'

He squeezed the trigger once more. There was a popping sound and the right back tyre began to explode, crumbling like a broken eggshell. An acrid smell of burning rubber rose as the car bounced on its three good wheels.

Megarry shouted to Flatman, 'Slow down. We'll run into the back of it.'

The Sprinter was losing direction; the driver was struggling desperately with the wheel. In the back seat the young woman in a nurse's uniform was holding Caroline. They seemed to cling to each other as the car bucked and reared.

Flatman was yelling. He pulled into the side and flung the door open wide. The Sprinter was now completely out of control – it hit a tree, then bounced away and struck a hedge. As Megarry watched in horror, it smashed into a fence, splitting the wood before tumbling into a field.

Flatman scrambled out and began running up the road. There was a screech of brakes and Nelson's Ford Escort pulled in behind. Any moment now, there would be the sirens and police cars. Megarry followed Flatman, struggling to catch his breath as he ran.

The Sprinter was lying on its roof, its wheels spinning wildly in the air. The driver's door was hanging open and a man had struggled free. He had the young woman in nurse's uniform by the arm. She seemed to be injured, and he was trying to pull her clear.

Megarry heard Nelson call out, 'Halt or I'll fire.'

He turned and ran towards Nelson, trying desperately to strike the gun from his hand. 'No!' he shouted, 'for God's sake, no.'

But he was too late.

There was a crack and the woman faltered. Her nurse's overall was splashed with blood.

My God, Megarry thought, it's happening again – the flash, the smell of cordite, the blood, the pointless taking of human life.

The man turned and Megarry saw his face. It was the face in the photograph and was filled with utter horror.

Megarry struck out and knocked the gun from Nelson's hand. He cleared the ditch and jumped into the field. Flatman was bending into the wreckage and lifting his daughter, scooping her up in his arms like a doll.

Megarry shouted to him across the quiet fields, 'Get away from the car.'

Flatman began to struggle with his burden towards the road. Megarry reached the nurse and took her arm. Her skin felt cold but she was breathing, low and muffled like a sleeping child. He began to pull her free, dragging her through the damp grass.

Then there was a roar and the car exploded, lighting up the field in a shower of sparks. He crouched and covered his face.

When he looked up, the wreckage was on fire, and Nelson was bending over him.

'I'm okay,' Megarry said, dazed. He sat for a moment and then struggled to his feet. His legs were sore from when he'd jumped into the field. His wrist was cut and smeared with dirt.

The young woman lay beside him on the grass. She was moaning and her overall was soaked in blood. It seemed to be everywhere: on her arms and face, on his hands where he had lifted her. Flatman had gone, taken the child with him. There was someone missing.

'The driver? where's the driver?'

He looked across the field and saw a pitiful figure hobbling through the grass, dragging his foot.

'Get an ambulance,' Megarry said.

He began to run. The grass was damp and his feet slipped in the soft heather. The figure had reached the top of the field where there was a hedge of brambles and a gap into another field. The man stopped, looked back, then disappeared.

Megarry hurried forward, his breath coming in laboured

208

gasps. He began to sweat until it ran down his face like drops of rain. He called out, his voice echoing, 'Give yourself up. You've no chance. We have more men coming.'

There was no response. Everything was silent. He took out a handkerchief and wiped his face. He heard a sound, but it was only a bird, a woodpigeon that flew up in a bustle of blue feathers.

When he came to the top of the field, there was another field and then another, stretching in a patchwork to the smoke of chimneys on the fringes of the town. The land lay empty before him; the driver had gone. Megarry could see a belt of gorse and beyond it a farm labourer's cottage, abandoned to the elements, slates missing and the windows smashed. He started towards it, huffing and puffing, his shoes and trousers damp from the grass.

He called out again, 'Come out. Give yourself up.'

The words echoed back, mocking him.

When he came to the door of the cottage he stopped and listened, but heard no sound. He took out his pistol, then leaned against the door and eased it with his shoulder. It opened with a creaking sound and he smelt the pungent odour of damp and decay.

The room was dark and appeared to be empty with a thick layer of dust on the floor and windows. In the corner was a broken sofa and a dripping tap. He advanced slowly into the room, the pistol tight in his fist. For a moment he thought that he was wrong, that the driver was somewhere else, then he heard a sound. He turned quickly, but too late; a blow crashed against his arm and the gun spun from his hand.

'Don't move,' a voice said.

A small figure scrambled across the floor and turned. The face looked frightened and his hand trembled as it held the gun.

'Why did you shoot?'

Megarry heard his words echo in the tiny room. 'It was a mistake.'

'Is she hurt? I saw the blood. Is she wounded?'

'She'll be all right. We're getting an ambulance.'

'And the kid, what about her?'

'She's okay. They're both okay. They're being looked after now.'

He thought he heard a sob.

'Give yourself up,' Megarry said, 'this is no use.' He was amazed how calm he was. His arm throbbed with pain from the blow, and he tried to touch it, but the other man waved the gun.

'Don't.' There was a pause, then Morgan said, 'Who are you?'

Megarry started to lie, then changed his mind. This has haunted me all my adult life, he thought, now I have a chance to exorcise it.

'Megarry.'

He waited for recognition but none came.

'I knew your father.'

The man choked, a small muffled cry. 'Not Cecil Megarry?'

'Yes.'

'You're a cop?'

'Yes. Special Branch.'

Morgan's voice shook. 'You helped to kill him.'

'I gave evidence. You know he shot a man?'

'In self-defence.'

'No,' Megarry said, 'that's not how it happened.' He found himself rushing on, defending himself. 'There was a raid on a house in the Lower Falls. Your father was the look-out. We broke down the door. He was sitting on the stairs, and as we came through the hall, he opened fire.'

He heard again the sound of sobbing.

'His job was to hold us back while the other men in the house escaped. That's what he did, but he killed a cop in doing it. I gave evidence and he was hanged.'

His eyes had grown accustomed to the dim light. He saw Morgan shift and raise the gun. There were tears on his cheeks.

'It ruined our lives. My mother was left with two small children. No means of support ...'

Megarry was about to say: It ruined my life too. His friends killed my father for revenge, blew up his car when he was going to a bowling match. But he heard the soft click as the pistol was cocked.

'I should shoot you,' Morgan said, 'for all you've done to us.'

'It would do no good. Solve nothing.'

'It would even the score.'

'No. It would open up another round, another score. It has to stop … with us. Here. Now.'

He held out his hand. 'Give me the guns.'

But Morgan recoiled, gathering himself into the corner of the room between the settee and the chimney breast.

'I'll see you are well looked after. I'll speak for you. I'll tell them how this happened.'

'You don't know how it happened.'

'I know enough.'

He held out his hand again. 'Don't make things worse. They'll be here at any moment. Give me the guns.'

Morgan raised the pistol again and started to take aim.

'Don't be foolish,' Megarry said. For the first time, he felt fear. 'I'll speak for you. I'll speak for your friend. You thought you were doing right. I understand that. I'll tell them you were just caught up …'

Morgan's sobs filled the room, a great convulsive spasm that reverberated around the walls.

'Drop the guns,' Megarry said, his voice soft and coaxing. 'Drop the guns, Sean.'

Morgan bent forward and Megarry thought he was going to fire, but there was a clattering sound as metal struck the concrete floor. Then Morgan was weeping again, spilling a lifetime's pain.

Megarry moved quickly and put his arm around his shoulder. 'It's all right, Sean. It's all over now. Everything will be all right.'

19

'Flatman, Fleming ... not very original, is it? What was his bloody name, anyway?'

Drysdale cocked a quizzical eye at Megarry over the rim of his glass.

'Flatman. Fleming was just an alias. And you must remember that he never expected to be found out, so in a way it didn't matter.'

'But why did he need an alias, for God's sake?'

'Because of the nature of his work – it was all very hush-hush. They were paranoid about security. They wanted to wipe out all trace of his previous military record. So they gave him this false identity, believing he would never be uncovered. They dressed him up in civilian clothes and gave him a cover job working at the Ministry of Defence. To outward appearances, he was just another civil servant.'

'And how *was* he found out?'

'Through the kid.'

'That's one of the silliest things I ever heard,' Drysdale said. 'What did he want to bring his family here for?'

Megarry shrugged. 'Who knows? Maybe he just liked to have them near him.'

'But the risk ...'

'I know. And the constant security. They had no social life, couldn't move anywhere without a guard. It wasn't much of an existence. It seems that his wife complained a lot, but it was the girl who proved the weak link in the end.'

Megarry took a long drink of Bushmills. His wrist was bandaged where he had scraped it after the car chase and his hand hurt when he raised the glass.

'She went to Mountpleasant School for Girls. Upper Lisburn Road. They had a temporary teacher on the staff ... a guy by the name of Raymond Boyd. He got friendly with her and she told him all about her father. We have him in custody right now. It seems he was a reluctant player in the whole business. He's filled with remorse and he's admitted everything.'

Drysdale nodded.

'He has implicated a man called James Cronin. He's an older guy. He seems to have set up the whole thing. But he's a tough nut. He's refusing to speak. Won't say anything. Won't sign anything.'

'Why kidnap the girl?' Drysdale asked.

'That wasn't their first intention. They were planning to kidnap Flatman, but when they saw the level of security, they decided to go for the girl instead. She would have been just as useful to them in the end.'

Drysdale examined his empty glass.

'Refill?'

Megarry felt an enormous tiredness, but it was tinged with satisfaction. It seemed to him as he sat here in Drysdale's office that a chapter was closing in his life. He had laid to rest some ghosts that had haunted him for years and he was free again. He would go away somewhere with Kathleen and have time to think.

'A bird never flew on one wing,' Drysdale said as he collected the glasses and walked to the cabinet where a phalanx of bottles were lined up like soldiers.

'What exactly was Flatman doing? Did you find out?'

'He was spying,' Megarry said. 'And putting out black propaganda on people he didn't like, paramilitaries and politicians. It's called Psy-Ops, in military jargon. Psychological Operations.'

Drysdale raised an eyebrow. 'Oh, who for?'

'MI5.'

'And who was he spying on?'

'You ... me. His own colleagues. The paramilitaries. He headed up an outfit called Fourteenth Intelligence. Ever hear of them?'

'I can't keep up with these people, Cecil. You know what the rivalry is like, the right hand watching the left hand ... the deceit, the duplicity. Nothing is ever as it seems.'

Megarry's mouth curled in a smile. 'You're telling me? I could write a book about it. Why do you think I got so fed up? I'm an Ulsterman, Jack, an honest Ulsterman. I appreciate plain speaking.' He held up a finger. 'And plain dealing.'

'What else did Flatman do?'

'He ran a few informers. Small time. I doubt if they were any use. But mostly he spied. He sent reports to the Commander of Land Forces from time to time, but he was largely independent. I think they were all slightly afraid of him, to tell you the truth. They never knew what he might say about them, or what he might know.'

Drysdale sighed, 'So he's going back?'

'He's no use here any more, now that his cover's blown.'

'And what will happen to him?'

'They'll probably send him to some military college for a while. Maybe they'll give him a new identity, call him Mr Roundman or something.' He smiled at his own feeble joke, but Drysdale seemed to have missed it. 'Anyway, he'll pop up again in some embassy or somewhere. You know, I actually feel sorry for him.'

He lifted a carafe and poured some water into his glass. The ice cracked. 'I think he was unhappy and was probably a weak man, which would account for all his bluster.'

Drysdale sniffed. 'What about the others? This guy Morgan? He was a cripple, wasn't he?'

'Morgan's in custody. He and the young woman, Grainne Bradley. She was injured but she'll pull through.'

'I hope the bastards go down,' Drysdale said with sudden venom.

Megarry sighed wearily, 'They aren't bad people, Jack. They thought they were doing something right. Maybe even noble. You have to understand what motivated them.'

'*What?*' Drysdale put down his glass and stared across the table.

'People don't get involved in something like this just for the hell of it. Think of the risk. And what did they stand to gain? There was nothing in it for them.'

'Sometimes you surprise me.'

'There was something in Morgan's background. His father was hanged, you know. Maybe he felt he was getting revenge.'

The door from the secretary's office opened and the young blonde woman came out with some papers. She gave Megarry a little nod of recognition.

He finished the whiskey and stood up. 'I'd better be going, Jack.'

Drysdale signed the papers, then took Megarry's arm. 'There's no rush. Have one more.'

'I have to go.'

'But what are you going to do? In your career, I mean. Everyone's delighted at the way this thing has panned out. You're flavour of the month, Cecil.'

'For how long?'

'Don't be cynical, they mean it.'

Megarry managed a tired smile and lifted his overcoat from the rack. 'I'm taking Kathleen for a holiday.'

He looked at the window, the rain beating a tattoo against the pane. 'Somewhere warm and sunny, Maybe Italy.'

'And when you come back?'

'I don't know.'

'You know they won't let you go?'

'But it won't be the same,' Megarry said, 'I've laid some things to rest. The motivation might not be there any more.'

Drysdale followed him out and stood watching over the rail as Megarry bounced down the stairs. At the bottom, Megarry stopped, cupped his hands and shouted something. Drysdale craned his ear to hear.

'I'll send you a postcard' was what he said.